DATE DUE	

THE CHICAGO PUBLIC LIBRARY

AVALON BRANCH
8148 S. STONY ISLAND AVENUE
CHICAGO, IL 60617

GEORGE WASHINGTON

Karen Price Hossell, *Book Editor*

Daniel Leone, *President*
Bonnie Szumski, *Publisher*
Scott Barbour, *Managing Editor*
David M. Haugen, *Series Editor*

San Diego • Detroit • New York • San Francisco • Cleveland
New Haven, Conn. • Waterville, Maine • London • Munich

© 2003 by Greenhaven Press. Greenhaven Press is an imprint of The Gale Group, Inc., a division of Thomson Learning, Inc.

Greenhaven® and Thomson Learning™ are trademarks used herein under license.

For more information, contact
Greenhaven Press
27500 Drake Rd.
Farmington Hills, MI 48331-3535
Or you can visit our Internet site at http://www.gale.com

ALL RIGHTS RESERVED.
No part of this work covered by the copyright hereon may be reproduced or used in any form or by any means—graphic, electronic, or mechanical, including photocopying, recording, taping, Web distribution or information storage retrieval systems—without the written permission of the publisher.

Every effort has been made to trace the owners of copyrighted material.

Cover credit: © The Corcoran Gallery of Art/CORBIS
Library of Congress, 17, 45, 55, 146, 185

LIBRARY OF CONGRESS CATALOGING-IN-PUBLICATION DATA

George Washington / Karen Price Hossell, book editor.
  p. cm. — (People who made history)
  Includes bibliographical references and index.
  ISBN 0-7377-1709-2 (lib. bdg. : alk. paper) —
  ISBN 0-7377-1710-6 (pbk. : alk. paper)
    1. Washington, George, 1732–1799. 2. Presidents—United States—Biography. 3. Generals—United States—Biography. 4. United States. Continental Army—Biography. 5. United States—History—Revolution, 1775–1783. 6. United States—Politics and government—1789–1797. I. Price Hossell, Karen, 1957– . II. Series.
  E312 .G355 2003
  973.4'1'092—dc21   2002192507

Printed in the United States of America

Contents

Foreword 6
Introduction: Private Man and Public Servant 8

Chapter 1: The Making of a Leader

1. **Washington's Ambition** *by Paul K. Longmore* 24
   From an early age, George Washington deliberately cultivated a reputation based on honor. His early role models were members of Virginia's landed gentry. Young Washington also studied a popular book of conduct to develop a code of behavior and improve his social grace.

2. **Washington the Surveyor** *by Willard Sterne Randall* 33
   Washington came of age at a time when the wilderness of western Virginia was being mapped. With the help of his neighbor, Washington trained as a surveyor and traveled around the frontier measuring distances and boundaries.

3. **Washington's Early Military Career** *by A.J. Langguth* 41
   At the age of twenty-one, Washington embarked on what was to be a long and eventful military career. But while his future included guiding the nation's first official army to victory, his early endeavors were less auspicious. Washington's first military adventures ended in failure.

Chapter 2: Farmer and Slave Owner

1. **Life at Mount Vernon**
   by Robert F. Dalzell Jr. and Lee Baldwin Dalzell 50
   Mount Vernon was Washington's home, a thriving plantation that served as an anchor in his busy life. But while Washington took refuge there, his privacy was continually interrupted by visitors. This required him to engage in a balancing act between his private world and his public one.

2. **The Squire of Mount Vernon** *by Ralph K. Andrist* 59
   Throughout his life, George Washington kept a private diary. While its entries are rarely detailed, they do provide a window into the activities and duties that consumed much of his time at Mount Vernon.

3. **Master and Employer** *by Paul Leicester Ford* 68
   While he claimed to be repelled by slavery, Washington kept his plantations running by utilizing the services of

more than three hundred slaves. Their welfare seemed to be a continual concern to him, as did their productivity.

Chapter 3: Military Leader

1. Appointment as Commander
by Douglas Southall Freeman — 80

Washington's military experience, as well as his carefully guarded reputation, made him a prime candidate to lead the Continental army in the American Revolution. Washington, however, was reluctant to take on the responsibility, fearing failure would result in irreparable damage to his reputation. Nonetheless, his quest for honor and his ambition to achieve notoriety dictated that he accept the position.

2. Assessing Washington's Strategy and Leadership
by John E. Ferling — 88

During the Revolutionary War, George Washington adopted a primarily defensive strategy to keep the undermanned Continental army from disintegrating. However, when opportunities availed themselves, Washington seized the initiative and achieved several bold victories.

3. Washington the Spymaster *by Thomas Fleming* — 98

In his quest to draw out the Revolutionary War and therefore exhaust British resources, Washington used espionage to his advantage.

4. General Washington and the Progress of the Revolutionary War *by Mackubin Owens* — 111

Some historians claim that Washington was only a mediocre military leader. But an examination of his tactics reveals that, far from being second-rate, Washington was a great strategist who justified the principles of the Revolution on the battlefield.

Chapter 4: President

1. The Washington Administration
by Forrest McDonald — 128

As the first holder of the executive office of the United States, Washington and his advisers faced several problems unique to their administration. Included in these were establishing inauguration procedures; interpreting the powers relegated to the office by the Constitution; initiating communication between the president, his advisers, and the legislature; and determining foreign policy.

2. Establishing Precedents for the Executive Office
by David E. Maas — 141

As the first president, Washington set many precedents. He knew that his actions and the protocols he set were vital to the office, and he conducted himself with an eye toward posterity.

3. **Washington's Role in the Controversy over Slavery**
   by Dorothy Twohig   151
   Some historians criticize Washington as president for not attempting to end the practice of slavery. One reason Washington avoided tackling the issue was because he knew it would create factions within the country. His primary goal as president was keeping the republic intact, and divisions were the very thing that could undo the achievements of the Revolution.

4. **Understanding Washington's Retirement**
   by Bruce G. Peabody   162
   When Washington resigned from the presidency in 1796 after serving two terms, he was indicating to the people of the United States that the executive office was nothing like a monarchy, and that it could survive without him. His decision was also based on personal motives; chief among them was his desire to return to a more private and peaceful life.

Chapter 5: The Importance of George Washington

1. **The Enlightened American Hero**
   by Gordon S. Wood   169
   Washington was the greatest president America has ever had, an unlikely hero whose character was greatly influenced by the eighteenth-century Enlightenment. He gave dignity to the presidency and established a standard that is acknowledged to this day.

2. **Above All, the Man Had Character** *by Hugh Sidey*   182
   Even during his lifetime, Washington was considered a great hero. He was highly respected, even venerated, but he did have flaws. Today, Americans should resume the tradition of searching for leaders of great character and supporting them, even while recognizing their human frailties.

Appendix of Documents	189
Discussion Questions	207
Chronology	210
For Further Research	216
Index	219

FOREWORD

In the vast and colorful pageant of human history, a handful of individuals stand out. They are the men and women who have come variously to be called "great," "leading," "brilliant," "pivotal," or "infamous" because they and their deeds forever changed their own society or the world as a whole. Some were political or military leaders—kings, queens, presidents, generals, and the like—whose policies, conquests, or innovations reshaped the maps and futures of countries and entire continents. Among those falling into this category were the formidable Roman statesman/general Julius Caesar, who extended Rome's power into Gaul (what is now France); Caesar's lover and ally, the notorious Egyptian queen Cleopatra, who challenged the strongest male rulers of her day; and England's stalwart Queen Elizabeth I, whose defeat of the mighty Spanish Armada saved England from subjugation.

Some of history's other movers and shakers were scientists or other thinkers whose ideas and discoveries altered the way people conduct their everyday lives or view themselves and their place in nature. The electric light and other remarkable inventions of Thomas Edison, for example, revolutionized almost every aspect of home-life and the workplace; and the theories of naturalist Charles Darwin lit the way for biologists and other scientists in their ongoing efforts to understand the origins of living things, including human beings.

Still other people who made history were religious leaders and social reformers. The struggles of the Arabic prophet Muhammad more than a thousand years ago led to the establishment of one of the world's great religions—Islam; and the efforts and personal sacrifices of an American reverend named Martin Luther King Jr. brought about major improvements in race relations and the justice system in the United States.

Each anthology in the People Who Made History series begins with an introductory essay that provides a general overview of the individual's life, times, and contributions. The group of essays that follow are chosen for their accessibility to a young adult audience and carefully edited in consideration of the reading and comprehension levels of that audience. Some of the essays are by noted historians, professors, and other experts. Others are excerpts from contemporary writings by or about the pivotal individual in question. To aid the reader in choosing the material of immediate interest or need, an annotated table of contents summarizes the article's main themes and insights.

Each volume also contains extensive research tools, including a collection of excerpts from primary source documents pertaining to the individual under discussion. The volumes are rounded out with an extensive bibliography and a comprehensive index.

Plutarch, the renowned first-century Greek biographer and moralist, crystallized the idea behind Greenhaven's People Who Made History when he said, "To be ignorant of the lives of the most celebrated men of past ages is to continue in a state of childhood all our days." Indeed, since it is people who make history, every modern nation, organization, institution, invention, artifact, and idea is the result of the diligent efforts of one or more individuals, living or dead; and it is therefore impossible to understand how the world we live in came to be without examining the contributions of these individuals.

Introduction: Private Man and Public Servant

Writer and eminent early American physician Dr. Benjamin Rush once wrote that "Every man in a republic is public property. His time and talents—his youth—his manhood—his old age—nay, more, life all belong to his country."[1] Perhaps no man in America, before or since, has displayed this model of the republican man better than George Washington. He served his country for much of his adult life, and many considered him public property. But even though Washington was constrained by a sense of duty and honor to put his country above his own desires, the sacrifices he had to make to do so were not always done willingly. Throughout his life, Washington was torn between his desire for peace and privacy, or personal freedom, and what he believed was his obligation to serve his country.

Washington's Early Influences

Although he may not have been aware of it at the time, from an early age Washington began to cultivate himself for public life by gravitating toward models of decorum. Among the first of these models was the book *Rules of Civility and Decent Behaviour in Company and Conversation*. Written in France in 1595, the tome provides rules of how a gentleman should act to be accepted into polite society. The maxims in the book primarily cover politeness and cleanliness.

In Washington's time it was the custom for young students to practice writing by copying poems and other writings into notebooks. Washington copied lists of instructions from *Rules* into his school notebook, including such maxims as "Be not curious to know the affairs of others, neither approach those that speak in private" and "Laugh not aloud, nor at all without occasion." Because Washington seemed to follow these exhortations for polite behavior and self-control throughout his life, many historians believe that he was strongly influenced by this book. William Guthrie Sayen, for example, writes that the rules "gave George practical instruction in the self-control, composure, discretion, modesty, and knowledge of place that were essential for a young man of uncertain prospects making his way in a hierarchical world."[2]

Another strong influence on young Washington was his older half-brother Lawrence. Historian Elswyth Thane writes that George loved Lawrence "with a touch of hero-worship."[3] After his father died when he was eleven, George spent much of his youth either with his mother and siblings at the farm he would one day inherit near Fredericksburg, Virginia, or at Lawrence's plantation, Mount Vernon, on the banks of the Potomac River. Lawrence had enrolled as an American in the British army at a young age and served as an officer, and then retired to the life of a country gentleman. Lawrence's military adventures in the West Indies likely ignited George's interest in a similar career, and his later life on a Virginia plantation was another model for George to follow. When he was nineteen, Washington accompanied his brother to Barbados when he traveled there to seek a cure for the illness—probably tuberculosis—that eventually killed him in 1752. When Lawrence died, Washington was devastated.

Another powerful influence on George Washington was the Fairfax family. In fact, writer Blair Niles believes that "no one, I think, ever influenced him so greatly, not even his brother Lawrence."[4] Lawrence had married into the family when he wed Anne Fairfax, daughter of Colonel William Fairfax, who was a member of Virginia's royal governor's council. The Fairfax plantation, called Belvoir, was near Mount Vernon, and it was here that George met Colonel William Fairfax and his cousin Thomas, Lord Fairfax. They took him into their fold, giving him a glimpse into the life of the British aristocracy. It was from the Fairfaxes that George observed and learned the British social customs that were the standard for the upper crust of colonial society.

The modes of behavior Washington learned during his teen years gave him the air of a well-mannered, sophisticated gentleman. In fact, Baron Cromot Dubourg, an aide to Lieutenant General Comte de Rochambeau, commander of the French forces that helped the Americans in the Revolution, wrote of Washington in 1781 that "his manners are those of one perfectly accustomed to society, quite a rare thing certainly in America."[5] Benjamin Rush wrote of Washington in 1775 that "he has so much martial dignity in his deportment that you would distinguish him to be a general and a soldier from among ten thousand people. There is not a King in Europe that would not look like a valet de chamber [manservant] by his side."[6]

THE ART OF SELF-CONTROL

While in his youth Washington acquired many skills that served him well later in life. Perhaps the most important tool he perfected during this time was the art of self-control. He was to use this skill to his advantage throughout his life; it was perhaps his greatest ability, allowing him to veil his feelings as he sacrificed his personal freedom for public life. As Elswyth Thane writes, Washington, "except in rare instances bore his many disasters without flinching and his few triumphs without visible exultation."[7] Washington's self-discipline also allowed him to control his temper. On the rare occasions when he failed to control it, Washington's temper could be fierce. About Washington's control over his temper, Patriot Gouverneur Morris wrote, "Few men of such steady, persevering industry ever existed, and perhaps no one who so completely commanded himself. Thousands have learned to restrain their passions, though few among them had to contend with passions so violent."[8] Another testament to Washington's belief in restraint and composure is made evident by a story told by Mrs. Henrietta Liston, an acquaintance of Washington's. Near the end of his second presidential term, she told him that she could tell from his face how happy he was to be finally able to retire. Washington replied, "You are wrong. My countenance never yet betrayed my feelings."[9]

A TASTE OF ADVENTURE

Washington's early apprenticeship began to pay off in 1748 when his friendship with the Fairfax family resulted in his being invited along on a trip into the frontier to survey a vast amount of land Lord Fairfax owned. At the age of sixteen Washington accompanied the surveying party and got his first taste of true freedom away from the constraints of home and society as he rode over mountains, slept on the ground, and met Indians. It was during this trip that Washington seemed to grow from a boy to a man. Washington scholar W.W. Abbot says that the adventure "marked the passing of the farm boy and set into motion things to come."[10] Washington enjoyed surveying so much that he began to do it professionally for the next several years. With his earnings he sought out land and purchased it. By the time he was twenty, he owned more than two thousand acres in the lower Shenandoah Valley.

EARLY MILITARY CAREER

Again through the influence of the Fairfax family, Washington at age twenty was given another opportunity to further himself when he was appointed the post vacated by Lawrence's death, that of adjutant general of Virginia's colonial militia. Colonel Fairfax then persuaded Robert Dinwiddie, Virginia's governor, to give to Washington the important task of delivering a message to French troops who had made camp in what was then the frontier—the Ohio Valley region. The French, hoping to connect land they possessed in the north with other claims in the south, were moving into what Virginians considered their territory. If the French were successful in claiming land southward, the British colonies would be hemmed in between French territory to the west and the Atlantic Ocean to the east.

The message Washington was instructed to deliver informed the French that they were in British territory and demanded that they leave. The journey Washington and his aides made through the wilderness was arduous, and when he finally delivered his message, the French politely refused to withdraw. Washington had fulfilled his mission, however, and his adventures in the wilderness resulted in the publication of his journal about the trip. Dinwiddie was apparently so impressed by Washington that he increased his military responsibilities.

A year later, in 1754, Washington, now a colonel and regimental commander, led a small band of colonial troops and attacked French soldiers still encamped in the Ohio Valley. The French retaliated and overwhelmed Washington's force at Fort Necessity. These skirmishes marked the beginning of the Seven Years' War (also known as the French and Indian War). In 1755, Washington volunteered to be an aide-de-camp to British major general Edward Braddock in another expedition against the French in the Ohio Valley. During that mission, Braddock was killed; Washington, however, was lauded as a hero for his part. Through the publication of his journal and his military exploits, Washington's name was becoming known throughout the colonies.

MOUNT VERNON AND MARRIAGE

When those military adventures were over, Washington settled at Mount Vernon and the home that was to become his haven from the pressures of the outside world. Elswyth Thane points out that, although for about half his life Washington was a very public man, for the other half he enjoyed a fairly private life at his plantation, "and without these tranquil intervals he might have found it impossible to support the burden of the other half."[11] After he married Martha Custis in 1759, Washington expected to settle down as a country farmer. Soon after their wedding he wrote, "I am now I believe fixed at this seat with an agreeable consort for life and hope to find more happiness in retirement than I ever experienced amidst a wide and bustling world."[12]

Mount Vernon was more than a peaceful retreat, it was a working plantation. Washington owned farms in the surrounding region as well, with landholdings exceeding four thousand acres. Washington kept busy experimenting with various agricultural techniques and making improvements to the buildings and land at Mount Vernon. He loved farming beyond any other pursuit. In fact, W.W. Abbot writes, "It is fair to say, I believe, that whereas the Revolution and the presidency forced upon Washington a role in history—a role, I hasten to add, he embraced eagerly and played to the hilt—his career in agriculture, of his own choosing and design, had on him a stronger and more enduring hold than did either war or politics."[13]

APPOINTED COMMANDER IN CHIEF

Because Washington loved the life that he led at Mount Vernon, he was determined to ensure that this way of life continued—and that others could also pursue their dreams, independently. For this reason—and because it was expected of a man in his position—Washington became involved in politics, both in his local district and as a member of the Virginia colony's House of Burgesses.

It was Washington's involvement in the Virginia legislature that made him more aware of England's encroachment on the colonial governments. In 1765, for example, when England's Parliament imposed the Stamp Act on the colonies, Washington decried it and vowed to boycott British products. Four years later, when more taxes were imposed by Parliament, Washington wrote to his agent, Robert Cary, about items he had ordered for the farms:

> If there are any articles contained in either of the respective invoices (paper only excepted) which are taxed by Act of Parliament for the purpose of raising a revenue in America, it is my express desire and request that they may not be sent, as I have very heartily entered into an Association not to import any article which is now or hereafter shall be taxed for this purpose until the said Act or Acts are repealed. I am therefore particular in mentioning this matter as I am fully determined to adhere religiously to it.[14]

In September 1774, colonial leaders decided to hold a congress in Philadelphia to discuss the problems they were having with Parliament. Members of the Virginia House of Burgesses selected Washington to be one of their colony's delegates to the congress. At the First Continental Congress, Washington's reputation in the French and Indian War preceded him. Though he was essentially silent at most of the proceedings, he spent evenings socializing with the other delegates.

In April 1775, colonial and British forces traded shots at Lexington, Massachusetts. A Second Continental Congress was called, but this time the debate was not focused on appeasing Parliament. The representatives, feeling war had been thrust upon them, turned to building an army. Based on his reputation as a brave soldier and a leader, Washington was named to lead the Continental army. But Washington was reluctant to take on this responsibility. He wrote to his brother John Augustine soon after his appointment that "I have been called upon by the Unanimous Voice of the Colonies to take Command of the Continental Army; an Honour I neither sought after nor desired."[15]

Washington's reluctance was based in part on his realization that accepting the position meant he would leave behind his wife, Martha, and his home, Mount Vernon, for an indeterminate length of time. He did not even have a chance to say good-bye to Martha in person. Instead, he wrote to her from Philadelphia just before he began his command: "I should enjoy more real happiness in one month with you at home, than I have the most distant prospect of finding abroad, if my stay were to be seven times seven years."[16] Fortunately, Washington was able to be with Martha during part of the time he spent commanding the army; she traveled along with him for some time during the war.

Washington was also reluctant to accept the responsibility because he believed that if he failed to gain victory over the British, his reputation would be scarred. This feeling put to the test his firm belief that duty and responsibility came before personal desires. But as difficult as it was, Washington knew he had to accept the opportunity being offered. To gain independence and unity for his country, he had to put aside much of his personal freedom, putting on hold the days when he could ride around his plantation or relax on his piazza gazing out at the Potomac River. It was a sacrifice, but Washington knew that the personal price he had to pay would result in something he could not put a price on—freedom.

For the next eight years, Washington was a public man. He spent only a few days during that time at Mount Vernon. The rest of his days were spent planning military strategy and petitioning Congress for funds to buy supplies for the Army, which suffered from lack of the most basic necessities. Washington and his generals purposely dragged out the war, hoping to exhaust and deplete the British. Although they suffered several failures, ultimately the Americans were victorious.

A Private Citizen Again

After leading the Continental army to victory, Washington settled back into life at Mount Vernon, never planning to return to public life. In 1784, he wrote to his dear friend the Marquis de Lafayette,

> At length my Dear Marquis I am become a private citizen . . . & under the shadow of my own Vine & my own Figtree free from the bustle of a camp & the busy scenes of public life. . . . I am not only retired from all public employments, but I am retireing within myself; & shall be able to view the solitary walk, & tread the paths of private life with heartfelt satisfaction . . . & this my dear friend, being the order for my march, I will move gently down the stream of life, until I sleep with my Fathers.[17]

Having completed the formidable task of leading the United States to victory against the British, Washington fully expected to return to farming. To Washington, Mount Vernon not only represented peace and personal freedom but was a symbol of national freedom as well. It stood for what he and his troops had fought for: a chance to make their own way, to be lords over even the tiniest piece of land, and to be able to take advantage of the opportunity the country promised. So Washington turned from the swords of war to the plowshares of peace, managing his farms and riding his horse across the fields that he fought to make free.

Washington's relief at being free of the heavy responsibilities he had endured during the war can be seen in a letter he wrote in 1784 to Major General Henry Knox. In it, he describes how it felt to be home after eight long years of commanding the army:

> I am just beginning to experience that ease and freedom from public cares which, however desirable, takes some time to realize; for strange as it may tell, it is nevertheless true, that it was not till lately I could get the better of my usual custom of ruminating as soon as I waked in the Morning, on the business of the ensuing day; and of my surprise, after having revolved many things in my mind, to find that I was no longer a public Man, nor had anything to do with public transactions.
>
> I feel now however, as I conceive a wearied traveler must do, who after treading many a painful step with a heavy burthen on his shoulders, is eased of the latter, having reached the haven to which all the former were directed; & from his house-top is looking back & tracing with an eager Eye, the meanders by which he escaped the Quicksands & mires which lay in his way; & into which, none but the all-powerful guide, & great dispenser of human events could have prevented his falling.[18]

THE PUBLIC MOUNT VERNON

From 1784 to 1787 Washington continued at Mount Vernon, managing the various farms he owned in the area, experimenting with crops and farming techniques, and entertaining the many guests who passed through his gates. For even though Mount Vernon was a private refuge for Washington, in keeping with the dichotomy that prevailed throughout his life, it was also a public place, particularly after Washington became famous for his role in ensuring freedom for the United States. It was not uncommon in those days for people with large homes to put up strangers overnight in districts where there were few or no taverns that could do so. Mount Vernon was no exception; hundreds of guests, invited or not, visited it each year. Some of those who passed through its doors were members of the aristocracy and military and political leaders. But many who visited were ordinary citizens who thought nothing of invading Washington's privacy just to get a glimpse of the famous man and the way he lived.

Washington discovered that some of his visitors wanted more from him than a room for the evening or a meal: Some guests expected Washington to give them money. They figured that his public stature, combined with his vast landholdings, provided him with a never-ending supply of funds, and they fully expected handouts. In November 1785, for example, Washington wrote in his diary, "In the afternoon a Mr. Lee came here to sollicit Charity for his Mother who represented herself, as having nine children—a bad husband—and no support."[19] He also received many letters from people with requests. The private Washington became frustrated with the demands on the public Washington. In February 1785 he wrote to his wartime aide-de-camp, David Humphreys, that he had been delayed in writing to him because,

> What with letters (often of an unmeaning nature) from foreigners, Enquiries after Dick, Tom, and Harry, who may have been in some part, or at sometime, in the Continental service. Letters, or certificates of service for those who want to go out of their own State. Introduction; applications for copies of Papers; references of a thousand old matters with which I ought not to be troubled, more than the Great Mogul, but which must receive an answer of some kind, deprive me of my usual exercise; and without relief, may be injurious to me as I already begin to feel the weight, and oppression of it in my head, and am assured by the faculty, if I do not change my course, I shall certainly sink under it.[20]

THE PRIVATE MOUNT VERNON

Even with all these visitors, Washington managed to maintain some privacy at his home. He was known to ride away in the morning, alone, and not return until the late afternoon. Some visitors commented on how they saw him only from a distance, or for a few minutes before he excused himself.

Washington also maintained his privacy by incorporating a private wing in his home. His private study, which few visitors ever saw, was on the first floor of the wing, and his and Martha's bedroom occupied the second floor. Through a private stairwell the couple was able to pass from one room to the other and meet privately.

It was at Mount Vernon, as Thane writes, that Washington "strove to preserve some such peaceful pattern of life against the encroachments of relentless destiny."[21] For Washington was destined for greater things than farming. Americans admired the successes of his public life and his leadership qualities. They desperately needed someone to guide their new nation, and for many, Washington was the only person to assume such a duty.

THE CONSTITUTIONAL CONVENTION

In 1787 Washington's respite from public life ended when he was asked to attend a convention in Philadelphia to revise the Articles of Confederation, the document written in 1776 that outlined the first government of the United States. The confederation government was weak, primarily because it gave Congress so little power.

Washington claimed to be reluctant to attend the convention. Though he had become a Federalist, emphatically believing that the U.S. government should be stronger and more centralized, he said that he feared that if the convention failed, it would damage his reputation. He may have been concerned about his reputation beyond the convention as well. During the first week of the proceedings, hints were dropped that Washington was the man delegates expected to be the nation's first president. Pierce Butler, a delegate from South Carolina, wrote that during the convention, "many

Washington's presence at the 1787 Constitutional Convention instilled confidence in the American public's perception of the government.

members cast their eyes toward George Washington as President and shaped their ideas of the powers to be given to a President, by their opinions of his virtue."[22]

Whatever his reasons for hesitating to attend, Washington journeyed to Philadelphia for the convention. The unity of the confederacy was threatened, and a new government had to be formed. He wrote to Lafayette on June 6, 1787, that

> the pressure of the public voice was so loud, I could not resist the call to a convention of the States which is to determine whether we are to have a Government of respectability under which life, liberty, and property will be secured to us, or are to submit to one which may be the result of chance or the moment, springing perhaps from anarchy and confusion, and dictated perhaps by some aspiring demagogue who will not consult the interest of his country so much as his own ambitious views.[23]

At the convention Washington was appointed to preside over the proceedings as president. He made sure the delegates followed the rules of parliamentary procedure, but he rarely spoke. Nonetheless, his very presence lent dignity to the convention and instilled a confidence in the American public that no other man could. Washington had led the country to victory over England. Now he would help lead some of the best minds in the land as they worked out how best to govern the young nation.

PRESIDENT WASHINGTON

The delegates at the Constitutional Convention soon decided to throw out the Articles of Confederation and write a new constitution. When the convention was over and the U.S. Constitution was being considered for ratification in the states, Washington had some inkling of what was to happen next. There were rumors that the American public would accept no other man as its chief executive; indeed, even as early as 1780 an American named Ezekiel Cornell expressed the feelings of many Americans about Washington's ability to hold the United States together when he wrote that "the necessity of appointing General Washington sole dictator is again talked of as the only means under God by which we can be saved from destruction."[24] There was even talk among some of making Washington king.

Knowing that ideas such as these were swirling around the country, in 1788 Washington wrote to fellow Federalist and convention delegate Alexander Hamilton:

I have always felt a kind of gloom upon my mind, as often as I have been taught to expect, I might, and perhaps, must ere long be called to make a decision [about whether he would accept the position of President].You will, I am well assured, believe the assertion . . . that if I should receive the appointment and if I should be prevailed upon to accept it; the acceptance would be attended with more diffidence and reluctance than ever I experienced before in my life.[25]

In early 1789, the eleven states that had ratified the Constitution (Rhode Island and North Carolina had not) sent members of their electoral colleges to their state capitals to vote for president. As expected, Washington was chosen, although he did not receive official notice until April 14, 1789. In keeping with his show of reluctance to leave the peace of his home for public service, Washington said in a speech at Alexandria, Virginia, on April 16, 1789, "My love of retirement is so great, that no earthly consideration, short of a conviction of duty, could have prevailed me to depart from my resolution 'never more to take any share in transactions of a public nature.'"[26]

Washington's sense of responsibility and his desire that the nation remain unified were strong. He knew that his sense of duty would force him to set his personal feelings and personal freedom aside once again to serve his country. Washington was highly concerned with the fate of the United States. Factions, particularly among regions such as the North and South, were forming, and some states were complaining that the federal government had too much power. Washington and other Federalists sensed that the factions would divide regions, even states, and that the union upon which the strength and success of the United States depended could weaken or even dissolve.

After becoming the nation's first president, Washington lived at first in New York City, which was the temporary federal capital. In 1790, the capital was moved to Philadelphia. The many letters that traveled back and forth between his manager at Mount Vernon and the president's office, however, show that even as the public man was fulfilling his duties, the heart of the private man was more than one hundred miles south in Mount Vernon.

Washington served two terms as president, although he wished to retire after his first term. In fact, when he agreed to a second term, he told a friend that in doing so, "I relinquish those personal enjoyments to which I am particularly attached."[27]

Washington knew that his presidency would set precedents and acted with that knowledge. He set a foreign policy of neutrality and worked to open the west to settlers. Implementing the policies of Alexander Hamilton, his secretary of the treasury, he achieved financial stability for the United States.

Washington finally retired again to Mount Vernon in 1797. Once settled, Washington, in a demonstration of what Mount Vernon meant to him as well as to announce the kind of life he now wished to lead, ordered a weather vane for the top of his home that was fashioned into a dove with an olive branch in its mouth, the universal symbol of peace.

IN COMMAND AGAIN

As much as he loved his peaceful private life, when he was asked whether he would lead the army again in what seemed to be an imminent war with France, Washington accepted. When he did so, he wrote to his friend and colleague Major General Henry Knox in July 1798 that,

> Little did I imagine when I retired from the theater of public life, that it was probable, or even possible, that any event would arise in my days, that could induce to entertain, for a moment, an idea of relinquishing the tranquil walks, and refreshing shades, with which I am surrounded. But it is in vain, I perceive, to look for ease & happiness in a world of troubles.
>
> The call of my Country, and the urgency of my friends to comply with it, have produced a letter from me to the President of the United States . . . that I will accept the Commission with which the Secretary of War came charged.[28]

Once again Washington reveals the conflict between his personal desires and his call to duty. He left for Philadelphia in November, spending a month there planning the organization of a provisional army. War was averted when Washington advised President Adams that a former diplomat told him that France wanted to avoid war. Adams then sent another envoy to France to negotiate an end to the conflict.

On December 14, 1799, George Washington died. Much praise was lavished upon him at his death. Nineteenth-century historian Henry T. Tuckerman provided an apt description of the forces that drove Washington throughout his life when he wrote, "He gained the influence so essential to success—the ability to control others—by virtue of sublime self-government. It was, in the last analysis, because personal interest, selfish ambition, safety, comfort—all that human instincts endear—were cheerfully sacrificed."[29] While it may not be completely accurate to say that Washington made these sacrifices cheerfully, he did make them. Although he highly valued his private life and personal freedom, he unfailingly answered the call of duty when his country's future was at stake.

NOTES

1. Quoted in Steven M. Gillon and Cathy D. Matson, *The American Experiment: A History of the United States.* New York: Houghton Mifflin, 2002, p. 225.
2. William Guthrie Sayen, "George Washington's 'Unmannerly' Behavior," *Virginia Magazine of History and Biography,* Winter 1999, p. 4.
3. Elswyth Thane, *Potomac Squire.* New York: Duell, Sloan, and Pearce, 1963, p. 28.
4. Blair Niles, *Martha's Husband: An Informal Portrait of George Washington.* New York: McGraw-Hill, 1951, p. 1.
5. Quoted in Morton Borden, ed., *Great Lives Observed: George Washington.* Englewood Cliffs, NJ: Prentice-Hall, 1969, p. 84.
6. Quoted in Borden, *Great Lives,* p. 72.
7. Thane, *Potomac Squire,* p. 4.
8. Quoted in Forrest McDonald, "Presidential Character: The Example of George Washington," *Perspectives on Political Science,* Summer 1997, p. 5.
9. Quoted in McDonald, "Presidential Character," p. 6.
10. W.W. Abbot,"The Young George Washington and His Papers," *The Papers of George Washington.* www.virginia.edu/gwpapers, p. 6.
11. Thane, *Potomac Squire,* p. 1.
12. Quoted in Thane, *Potomac Squire,* p. 52.
13. W.W. Abbot, "George Washington in Retirement," *The Papers of George Washington.* www.virginia.edu/gwpapers, p. 2.
14. Quoted in Borden, *Great Lives,* p. 19.
15. Quoted in Saul K. Padover, ed., *The Washington Papers: Basic Selections from the Public and Private Writings of George Washington.* New York: Harper & Brothers, 1955, p. 165.
16. Quoted in Thomas J. Fleming, ed., *Affectionately Yours, George Washington: A Self-Portrait in Letters of Friendship.* New York: W.W. Norton, 1967, p. 56.
17. Quoted in Fleming, *Affectionately Yours,* p. 54.
18. Quoted in W.W. Abbot and Dorothy Twohig, eds., *The Papers of George Washington: Confederate Series 1, January–July 1784.*

Charlottesville: University of Virginia Press, 1992, p. 137.
19. Quoted in Ralph K. Andrist, *The Founding Fathers: George Washington: A Biography in His Own Words*. New York: Newsweek, 1972, p. 251.
20. Quoted in Andrist, *Founding Fathers*, p. 259.
21. Thane, *Potomac Squire*, p. 41.
22. Quoted in John E. Ferling, *The First of Men: A Life of George Washington*. Knoxville: University of Tennessee Press, 1988, pp. 363–64.
23. Quoted in Borden, *Great Lives*, p. 44.
24. Quoted in Borden, *Great Lives*, p. 82.
25. Quoted in Fleming, *Affectionately Yours*, p. 214.
26. Quoted in "Today in History: December 14," Library of Congress. http://memory.loc.gov.
27. Quoted in Niles, *Martha's Husband*, p. 235.
28. Quoted in Andrist, *Founding Fathers*, p. 395.
29. Quoted in Borden, *Great Lives*, p. 121.

CHAPTER 1

THE MAKING OF A LEADER

 GEORGE WASHINGTON

Washington's Ambition

Paul K. Longmore

> Throughout his life, George Washington saw himself as an actor on stage. As a member of Virginia's gentry—the colony's ruling class—Washington realized what would be expected of him, and from an early age he cultivated the characteristics that he believed were necessary to play the role of country gentleman. As he developed these traits, he paid close attention to and copied his most important early influences, including his half-brother, Lawrence Washington, and the male members of the Fairfax family, who were his neighbors and members of British nobility. Young Washington also studied the "Rules of Civility and Decent Behaviour in Company and Conversation" from a school primer and meticulously copied its tenets in his notebooks. In this article, historian Paul K. Longmore shows that the kind of man George Washington became was the result of these early ambitions and efforts.

Throughout his life, the ambition for distinction spun inside George Washington like a dynamo, generating the astounding energy with which he produced his greatest historical achievement, himself. Even before the Revolution, that hunger for recognition prodded him to great exertions. In his twenties, he ceaselessly promoted his "interest," presenting himself to the attention of influential and powerful men. . . . Indefatigably, he sought honor from his country and the good opinion of leading men in Virginia and the British military establishment. . . .

CULTIVATING A REPUTATION

Washington's striving for recognition might also readily be explained in terms of Anglo-Virginian gentry values. That competitive culture fanned his ambitious energies, while its ethos of honor instructed him to seek public validation of his

Paul K. Longmore, *The Invention of George Washington*. Los Angeles: University of California Press, 1988. Copyright © 1988 by The Regents of the University of California. Reproduced by permission of the author.

social merit and character. . . . The individual must lay the claim of his "self-assessment before the public." The public, the community, would then appraise that claim by examining his behavior. In that sense, a gentleman's honor meant his public reputation. The most important component would be his reputation among other honorable gentlemen. To hold securely one's own sense of honor, one's self-assessment must concur with the community's assessment. Personal identity was, then, inseparable from public reputation.

George Washington lived by the ethos of honor. That ethos taught him to seek the approbation of his society and especially "the esteem of the truly valuable part of mankind," gentlemen of the first rank. He strove, therefore, not only to act honorably, but to cultivate a reputation for doing so. An inner conviction might try to reassure him that he had conducted himself as a virtuous and honorable gentleman, but always nagging was the internalized cultural need for public validation. Throughout his life he would grow uneasy when his hard-won reputation was questioned or put into jeopardy. And so he quested after honor, first from Virginia and then from all America. . . .

LEARNING THE SOCIAL GRACES

When George was a boy, his father frequently left the family, energetically pursuing his business ventures, repeatedly voyaging to London. In 1735, Augustine Washington settled his second family at Hunting Creek, a plantation on the Potomac that would later be renamed Mount Vernon. In about 1740, he moved them to the new town of Fredericksburg [Virginia]. When Augustine died in 1743, eleven-year-old George was sent back to Mount Vernon to live with his half-brother Lawrence, who became largely responsible for the lad's upbringing.

That same year, Lawrence married Anne Fairfax, forming a connection with the powerful Fairfax clan that proved important for himself and a key aid to the early career of young George. Anne's father, Colonel William Fairfax, sat on the Council of the colony and served as agent for the vast Fairfax land grant. Belvoir, the Fairfax family seat, was within sight of Mount Vernon. George often visited there. Lawrence Washington and William Fairfax became, in effect, his teachers and models in business, social intercourse, and public responsibility.

Probably George's father had hired a tutor to instruct him privately, intending to send him to school in England later, as he had the sons of his first marriage. The elder Washington's death put an end to that plan. Instead, when the boy went to live at Mount Vernon, he apparently attended a school in the neighborhood for a time.

His studies included mathematics, covering arithmetic, geometry, trigonometry, and surveying. He learned to calculate the cubic volumes of timber and stone and liquids. One of his school exercise books contains "forms of Writings and Rules of Civility." The first section of this bound volume provides specimens of frequently used legal forms, including a bill of exchange, a tobacco receipt, a bail bond, a servant's indenture, a short will, a land conveyance, a land lease, and a Virginia land patent. The latter part of the book is the famous "Rules . . . of Civility & Decent Behaviour in Company and Conversation," a selection of 110 maxims from the English translation of a sixteenth-century French handbook of gentlemanly deportment. Probably one of his teachers required him to copy it over as practice in penmanship and instruction in social etiquette.

Most of the "rules" prescribe considerate behavior in the presence of others: Rule 1, "Every Action done in Company, ought to be with Some Sign of Respect, to those that are Present." Rule 100, "Cleanse not your teeth with the Table Cloth Napkin Fork or Knife but if Others do it let it be done wt. a Pick Tooth[.]" Rule 18, "[C]ome not near the Books or Writings of Another as to read them unless desired or give your opinion of them unask'd also look not nigh when another is writing a Letter." Rule 21, "Reproach none for the infirmaties of Nature, nor Delight to Put them that have in mind thereof."

Many rules establish proper conduct suited to the social rank of the other person: Rule 28, "If any one comes to Speak to you while you are Sitting Stand up tho he be your inferiour, and when you Present Seat let it be to every one according to his Degree[.]" Rule 40, "Strive not with your Superiers in argument but always, Submit your Judgment to others with Modesty[.]" Rule 52, "[K]eep to the Fashion of your equals. . . ."

Although most of these maxims prescribe decorous and deferential manners, a few command the student to cultivate moral integrity and good repute: Rule 48, "Wherein . . . you reprove Another be unblamable yourself; for example is more prevalent than Precept[.]" Rule 56, "Associate yourself with men of good Quality if you Esteem your own Reputation; for t's better to be alone than in bad Company[.]" Rule 109, "Let your Recreation be Manfull not Sinfull." Rule 110, "Labour to keep alive in your Breast that Little Spark of Celestial fire Called Conscience."

As he copied over this code of manners and morals, the Virginian youth inscribed it in his memory. It established the foundation that would guide his conduct. Half a century and more later, he reiterated to his nephews and to his stepgrandson the substance of the ethical dicta. In adulthood, he also acquired a copy of Lord Chesterfield's widely popular *Letters to His Son*. These essays taught him more of the art of elegant self-presentation. . . .

IMPROVING HIMSELF

Near the end of his formal schooling, young Washington studied geography and astronomy, gaining an elementary knowledge of the continents, the globe, and the heavenly constellations. This whetted a lifelong appetite for books on geography and travel and spawned a kind of hobby of collecting a wide variety of maps, an interest unsurprising in a land speculator and soldier.

To what extent his academic training included instruction in composition and grammar the scanty records fail to show. Apparently George himself thought it insufficient, because within a year or two of leaving school he acquired the third edition of James Greenwood's *The Royal English Grammar*. This manual claimed to contain "what is necessary to the Knowledge of the English tongue . . . , Shewing the Use of the Parts of Speech, and joining Words together in a Sentence."

Washington's collected correspondence reveals that he worked throughout his career to improve his writing. He progressively polished his grammar and corrected his spelling. He even altered his penmanship, on the eve of the Revolution replacing his rather ornate early style with a simpler, clearer hand. Most important, he straightened out his sometimes convoluted syntax, rid himself of a tendency to use florid phrasing, and developed into a writer of usually direct, forcible prose.

This composed George's formal education. Unlike many sons of the Virginia gentry, he missed the opportunity to complete his preparation at the College of William and Mary.

He supplemented his schooling with excursions into literature, history, and geography. At the age of sixteen, he was reading *The Spectator* and an unspecified history of England. In the next few years, he acquired Sir Richard Steele's *The Guardian*, Henry Fielding's *Tom Jones*, Tobias Smollett's *The Adventures of Peregrine Pickle*, Daniel Defoe's *A Tour through the Whole Island of Great Britain*, and *A Compleat History of the Piratical State of Barbary*. Doubtless at the insistence of Lawrence Washington and William Fairfax, the eager youth became acquainted with Roman classicism by reading Sir Roger L'Estrange's popular version of Stoic philosophy, *Seneca's Morals*, as well as Julius Caesar's *Commentaries* in translation and perhaps the writings of other Roman generals.

Despite its limitations, George's schooling supplied practical preparation for a young man intent on rising in Virginia's ruling class. It imparted the legal and business knowledge and the surveying skills necessary to a would-be planter and land speculator. It inculcated the social graces and the sense of social roles essential to a gentleman. The supplemental tutelage of Lawrence Washington and William Fairfax held up for his emulation models of Roman patriotism and virtue, thereby instructing him in the public responsibilities of the landed gentry and in the nobility of character proper to a man of his station. Such an education aimed, not at training in scholarship, but at preparation for practical leadership, at the continued dominion of the sons of Virginia's propertied elite.

Learning to Be a Gentleman

The stress on gentlemanly breeding, the acute attention to social rank and to one's own place within that ranking, and the earnest cultivation of personal and public virtue were the ethical and behavioral concerns of an honor-based culture. Washington sought to adhere to these standards because his culture upheld them as ideals of behavior. From his youth, his preceptors and reading had propounded to him the code by which he would win or lose good repute.

If education and etiquette were badges of gentility, so too was dress. The code of honor held that a man's appearance reflected not only his social standing, but his inner worth as well. George early began to take great care in the selection of his clothes. In 1748 at the age of sixteen, he wrote a memorandum to himself to have a coat made according to his specifications. It totaled 152 words. That same year, listing items he would need for a visit to Fairfax County, he included nine shirts, six linen waistcoats, a cloth waistcoat, and other wearing apparel.

The "Unmannerly" Washington

While Washington spent many youthful hours studying the book Rules of Civility and Decent Behaviour in Company and Conversation, *he sometimes failed to follow its edicts. As a young man, he was known for his brash behavior and quick temper. In this excerpt, University of Connecticut lecturer William Guthrie Sayen points out that many of Washington's contemporaries and some of his biographers found the young Washington to be unlikable.*

During the French and Indian War . . . Washington repeatedly violated the very rules that had assisted him in his social, economic, and military ascent. Lieutenant Governor Robert Dinwiddie, the man who had promoted him to the highest military office in Virginia, finally lost patience with his protege's habitual carping and charged him with being "unmannerly"—a baser crime then than now. Even admiring biographers cannot overlook Washington's arrogance and ingratitude during his first military career. Marcus Cunliffe, author of a classic interpretation of Washington, concluded, "There is something unlikable about the George Washington of 1753–1758. He seems a trifle raw and strident, too much on his dignity, too ready to complain, too nakedly concerned with promotion."

William Guthrie Sayen, "George Washington's 'Unmannerly' Behavior," *Virginia Magazine of History and Biography*, vol. 107, Winter 1999.

Correspondence between outward appearance and inward reality was not inevitable, though. An individual might display the veneer of a gentleman while lacking the character of one. To some Virginians, it seemed that too many gentrymen were cultivating externals and ignoring essentials. They were merely keeping up appearances. These critics called for restoration of genuine honor and virtue. One of them, Landon Carter, who was also one of George's mentors, advised him "always . . . [to] regard the inward Man. . . ." Thus the young Virginian was taught to put on the character and not just the clothes of a gentleman.

Eighteenth-century Virginia was a provincial culture attempting to emulate English metropolitan culture. This was another reason for the gentry's attention to proper etiquette, fashion, and self-presentation. Washington copied the "Rules of Civility" and read *The Spectator* and, later, Lord Chesterfield and the *Country Magazine* because he too based his deportment and style of life on the model of the English country gentleman. He would plan Mount Vernon's architecture and landscaping in imitation of English estates. For instance, he would never give up trying to grow "live fences," hedgerows, even though the heat and frequent droughts of Chesapeake summers always thwarted him.

During the era of George's youth and early adulthood, Americans, especially members of the colonial elite, manifested divided feelings about English civilization. They measured themselves and their societies against its standards and found both wanting. Yet increasingly they resented metropolitan disdain of their provincialism, and more and more they thought the New World morally superior to the Old. All of this, the imitation, the sense of inferiority, the resentment, and finally the assertion of superiority based on native standards marked the social and cultural maturation of colonial America. Still dependent, it was seeking, in both that imitation and that rejection, to fashion an independent identity.

As a gentleman and a soldier, Washington would work tirelessly to match English standards. To his bitter distress, imperial leaders would refuse to acknowledge fully his attainment of them. He would never entirely let go of English ideals, but he *would* labor to redefine his identity in American terms. Ultimately, he would conduct that redefinition publicly in collaboration with his countrymen. They, in turn, would make him the exemplar of the new nation's values.

The colonial Virginia of George's early years was a highly competitive society. Mundane activities became means to win personal and social distinction. His biographers have reported his reputation in his own day as an excellent horseman and an eager and energetic dancer. What they have failed to recognize is the contemporary cultural and social significance of that reputation.

A Dancer and a Horseman

Horses were a means of personal display. Virginians talked of them endlessly, talked of horse breeding and horse racing and horsemanship. Virtually everyone rode and virtually everyone, even the poorest, kept horses. Horses, said an English traveler, were the Virginians' "pleasure and pride." They became extensions of their owners, "adjunct[s] to virile self-presentation. . . ." In horsemanship as in all else, gentlemen tried to distinguish themselves from lesser folk. They fashioned a style of riding commonly called "a Planter's Pace, . . . a good sharp hand-Gallop." This manner of passage through the social and physical landscape impressed and even awed social inferiors, as it was meant to do. In a society that gave such attention to equines and equestrianism, George Washington became known as a superb horseman.

Dancing was another primary mode of self-assertion and competition. The gentry employed dancing masters to instruct themselves and their young people in the fashionable dances current in Britain and Europe. By this means, they further marked the difference between themselves and the lower orders. Equally popular with all ranks of Virginians were vigorous and highly competitive jigs. Solo dancers contended for the approval of the audience as the onlookers repeatedly eliminated competitors until it was determined who was the "best of the ball." At other times, these individual performers would vie with the fiddler in contests of endurance. Even at play, Virginians expressed the fundamental character of their culture. It is unsurprising, then, to find that George Washington studied formal dancing as a teenager and enjoyed attending balls through much of his life. Most important, this young man, eager for public recognition, acquired a name as an energetic and skillful dancer.

It was undoubtedly George's skill as a dancer and horseman that, when added to his natural strength and prowess, made him lithe in all his movements. His physical grace was an important part of the personal presence that from early on so vividly impressed those who met him. Once again, the ethos of honor took external appearance as a sign of inner merit.

The social life of colonial Virginians provided many occasions for dramatic self-presentation. Horse races and even ordinary horseback riding, dances and other social gatherings, court days and election days and public meetings, all served as stages on which individuals, and especially gentrymen, might act out their claims to public honor and have them validated by the community. As his career advanced,

Washington became an increasingly skillful public actor. An enthusiastic patron of the theater throughout his life, he may have learned something of the relationship between a performer and his audience by watching professional actors practice their art. . . .

In all he did, young Washington shaped himself to the pattern prescribed by his culture. From early on, he labored to win the position and fortune that not only would establish him as an independent, virtuous, and honorable gentleman, but would rank him with the great Virginia planters. Yet gentlemanly deportment and attire, skill as a horseman and dancer, wealth in land and slaves, leadership in local politics and the local militia could never give him the eminence he wanted. Virginia boasted many rich gentlemen colonels. He must find a means to greater glory. He turned his ambitious energies to arms. Soon he would have his own war to fight in quest of military renown.

Washington the Surveyor

Willard Sterne Randall

In his teens, George Washington became interested in the profession of surveying, the determination of boundaries and the contours of the earth's terrain. The tools he used in surveying included posts joined by a chain, which were used to mark straight lines, and a theodolite, which the surveyor looked through to find horizontal and vertical angles. He was soon able to make a living using this skill.

By the middle of the 1700s, more colonists were moving into the frontier, which, in most cases, began at America's easternmost mountain ranges, such as the Allegheny Mountains in Pennsylvania and the Appalachian Mountains farther south. These frontier settlers usually built homes on land they claimed but did not legally own. One huge tract in the western part of what was then Virginia had been granted to Lord Fairfax. The Fairfax estate, Belvoir, was very near one of the Washington estates, Mount Vernon. Because of their proximity and Lawrence Washington's marriage to Anne Fairfax, George became well acquainted with the Fairfax family.

In 1748, Lord Fairfax decided to have his frontier tract surveyed and hired George to assist in the job. This selection by historian Willard Sterne Randall describes how the surveying team met up with Native Americans and unfriendly German settlers who realized that their landlord was finally claiming the land on which they had settled. Randall, a well-known biographer, has also written books on Revolutionary figures, such as Thomas Jefferson, Alexander Hamilton, and Benedict Arnold.

Willard Sterne Randall, *George Washington: A Life*. New York: Henry Holt and Company, 1997. Copyright © 1997 by Willard Sterne Randall. Reproduced by permission of Henry Holt and Company, LLC.

33

[In 1748], Virginians won the agreement of [the Native Americans who lived in the frontier] to allow them to hunt and trap and map the lands unmolested. It was now safe for Lord Fairfax to send an expedition into his five million acres, a wilderness empire he intended to map, plot, sell, and lease.

In the two years following the first mapping expedition, a fever of excitement had raged in the Virginia Tidewater as a new speculative land rush loomed. For years, the Northern Neck and the Shenandoah had been off-limits to settlers. With a cloud of dispute over the land titles, no one dared settle there. Now, in the drawing rooms at Mount Vernon and Belvoir, rich, fertile, vacant land only a few days' ride to the west dominated the conversation. Lord Fairfax and his cousin, Colonel Fairfax, laid plans for opening up the vast new Virginia frontier.

Lord Fairfax, too, had grown fond of the tall, elegantly mannered George Washington and was inclined to do the lad a favor. His best surveyor, James Genn, a member of the 1746 mapping team and a prominent surveyor of [Maryland's] Prince William County, needed a strong young assistant to manhandle the supplies, care for the horses, clear the underbrush, haul the chains, carry the theodolite, and hold steady the rod for his sightings.

BECOMING A SURVEYOR

Young Washington's studies of surveying had progressed steadily, evolving alongside his mastery of trigonometry, exhibited by his third and final "miscellaneous" notebook. His struggles with the highest level of mathematics available in Virginia in 1747 show not only a tenacity that would serve him well in working out problems far from books and libraries, but a basic understanding of principles that would make him a master of selecting land for cultivation and, later, for fortifications and battlefields. His close reasoning, patience, and sharp eye for detail equipped him well. The surveying problems he puzzled over match exactly several that appeared in William Leybourn's *Compleat Surveyor*, the second edition, printed in London in 1657, at the time John Washington [George's grandfather] first sailed for Virginia. (George was probably using his grandfather's book and tools.) Leybourn's was probably the most practical and influential field guide to surveying. Its plain style was ideal for a bright young boy essentially teaching himself to survey.

Washington struggled with the problem of "how to take an inaccessible distance at two stations," basic for figuring out not only wooded terrain in the Shenandoah but for artillery fire. He puzzled over "how to measure a field in which bog or marsh interferes with chaining," important in mapping and plotting much of the swampy Virginia wilderness Washington was to survey. It was quite a feat for a fifteen-year-old boy to learn "to measure" any piece of ground, be it ever so irregular, and to "cast up the content thereof in acres, rods and perches and likewise to examine ye truth of ye survey." Now the abstract exercises were to become concrete.

As a young man George Washington often helped fence the fields he surveyed and by age sixteen he had developed powerful arms and tough hands. He also possessed what mattered most on a frontier expedition: endurance. A day's ride west of Mount Vernon and the Tidewater estuaries, the land of the backcountry began to rise. Two days out came the foothills of the Blue Ridge Mountains, the limit of white settlement. Forest clearings came farther apart; the houses were smaller. Few settlers had ventured into the Shenandoah Valley. No white man lived legally beyond the valley's western wall, the solid barrier of the Allegheny Mountains. Virginia claimed this land "from sea to sea" under its seventeenth-century charter, but, in fact, Indian hunting parties had kept the forests primeval.

An Expedition to the Frontier

On March 11, 1748, only a few weeks past his sixteenth birthday, George Washington set out on horseback from Belvoir with his twenty-three-year-old friend George William Fairfax. An embarrassed George had to stop to get his mother's reluctant permission to make the western trip. After George pointed out he would be paid as one of James Genn's chainmen, she gave her approval. That first day out, the Dumfries Road was hardpacked after the cold winter. It was necessary to complete the mission before spring: the theodolite could not be sighted through foliage. The two riders were exuberant. They rode forty miles, not stopping until they reached George Neville's plantation, which doubled as an unlicensed tavern for travelers. The next morning, surveyor Genn and his team of chainmen and hunters joined them and "we travelled over the Blue Ridge to Captain Ashby's on the Shenandoah River. . . . Nothing remarkable happened," Washington recorded in his first diary, his earliest surviving document.

Nothing remarkable happened! At sixteen, free from parental and patriarchal control and riding into the unspoiled Shenandoah, George Washington was metamorphosing from naive boy to typical eighteenth-century gentleman: unromantic, unimpressed by nature. That would come later, officially too late for him, in the Romantic Age, when people flocked to cities and began to romanticize life in the countryside and the forest. For now, George was caught up in being part of an adult mission to perform a highly technical and practical task in a wild place. Crossing through Ashby's Gap, by the third day out the surveying party reached Lord Fairfax's "quarter," his unsurveyed lands four miles farther north on the Shenandoah near Howell's Point. There, young Washington waxed as rhapsodic as he ever got in this primitive paradise. "We went through most beautiful groves of sugar trees and spent the best part of the day in admiring the trees and richness of the land."

WASHINGTON'S OBSERVATIONS

George Washington was already knowledgeable about land, timber, terrain, crop yields, all part of the well-trained eighteenth-century surveyor's kitbag. He was able to cast a discerning eye on the commercial possibilities of the wilderness:

> Monday 14th. We sent our baggage to Capt. Hites (near Frederick Town) went ourselves down the river about 16 miles to Capt. Isaac Pennington's (the land exceeding rich & fertile all the way produces abundance of grain, hemp, tobacco, etc.) in order to lay off some lands.

The scale of expectations in the west must have dazed the young man. At Frederick Town, now Winchester, at the head of the Shenandoah Valley, Washington encountered prosperous German settler Jost Hite, born in Strasbourg, Alsace, and arriving in America thirty years earlier. Settling first on the Hudson and then in Pennsylvania and finally, in 1731, purchasing 40,000 acres in Frederick County, Virginia, this successful land speculator eventually settled families on 94,000 acres he owned. The young surveyor's luck changed the fifth day out. It rained harder and harder.

> We set out early with intent to run [lines] round the said land but being taken in a rain and it increasing very fast obliged us to return. It clearing about one o'clock & our time being too precious to lose, we a second time ventured out and worked hard till night and then returned to Pennington's.

Dragging heavy 33-foot wrought-iron chains with eight-inch links or shouldering the tripod and the circumferentor, which measured off the land, hacking brush and trees to make a clear path for the sightlines, and blazing marks on trees with an axe, young Washington was wet and cold and tired in a way he never experienced before. . . .

> We got our suppers & was lighted into a room & I not being so good a woodsman as the rest of the company stripped myself very orderly & went into the bed, as they called it, when to my surprise I found it to be nothing but a little straw matted together without sheets or anything else but only one threadbare blanket with double its weight of Vermin, such as lice, fleas, etc. I was glad to get up (as soon as the light was carried from us) & put on my clothes and lay as my companions. Had we not been very tired, I am sure we should not have slept much that night. I made a promise not to sleep so, from that time forward choosing rather to sleep in open air before a fire.

Arriving the next day at Winchester, the young gentleman-surveyor was delighted to wash—and made a note of it: "We cleaned ourselves to get rid of the game we had catched the night before." That night was more "agreeable" to George's taste. After a stroll around town, "we had a good dinner prepared for us [with] wine & rum punch in plenty and a good feather bed with clean sheets." From then on, where and how George Washington slept became noteworthy.

Blocked by flooding of the Potomac, which had been caused by the sudden runoff of snowmelt high in the Appalachians, Washington made the first of many visits to Warm Springs (now Bath, West Virginia). "We this day called to see the famed Warm Springs. We camped out in the field this night." After a three-day delay, the surveying party couldn't wait any longer for the floodwaters to recede. "We in the evening swam our horses over" to the Maryland shore. It was a dangerous passage in the fast-moving current and only a superb horseman would have stated its achievement so matter-of-factly. After leaving the horses in a pasture, they canoed "up the Maryland side all day in a continued rain." At the mouth of the South Branch of the Potomac, they followed "the worst road that ever was trod by man or beast." The rain continued, as did the flooding, and the road kept washing out.

On March 23, on their eleventh day out, the rain stopped in midafternoon and the surveying party stumbled upon a group of thirty Indians, the first Washington had ever seen close up. They were "coming from war with only one scalp." Washington wrote that "we had some liquor with us of which we gave them part, it elevating their spirits, put them in the humor of dancing." Washington was fascinated and amused by the Indians more than fearful:

> We had a war dance. Their manner of dancing is as follows: They clear a large circle and make a great fire in the middle, then seat themselves around it. The speaker makes a grand speech, telling them in what manner they are to dance. After he has finished, the best dancer jumps up as one awaked out of a sleep & runs & jumps about the ring in a most comical manner. He is followed by the rest. Then begins their musicians to play the music. [There] is a pot half [full] of water with a deerskin stretched over it as tight as it can & a gourd with some shot in it to rattle & a piece of an horse's tail tied to it to make it look fine. The one keeps rattling and the other drumming, all the while the others [are] dancing.

So unimpressed was Washington at "being with the Indians all day" the next day that he wrote "nothing remarkable was happening so shall skip it."

More interesting to him was crossing the rain-swollen river in a canoe while they "swum our horses over." As they canoed and camped ever deeper into the wilderness, Washington was scandalized to see how raw the way of life was becoming. They dined at the home of Squire Solomon Hedges, a Quaker and justice of the peace for Frederick County. "When we came to supper there was neither a cloth upon the table nor a knife to eat with but, as good luck would have it, we had knives of [our] own." Each day, they rode along the South Branch and surveyed riverfront tracts. On a typical day, Washington recorded on March 29, 1748, they "surveyed five hundred acres of land" for James Rutledge, who was buying it from Lord Fairfax, then rode to their next campsite at a place called Stumps and "on our way shot two wild turkeys."

FOUL WEATHER AND TAUNTING GERMANS

They were already short of food, having outridden their supply line. The next day, they laid out lots for four other settlers. Hunting fresh game and working hard all day, young Washington became inured to the hard outdoor life. He commented only when the weather turned foul: "Last night was a blowing and rainy night." It must have been a miserable night, but he did not complain. He only reported that "our straw catched a fire that we were laying upon & [we were] luckily preserved by one of our men's awaking." Apparently, embers from the all-night campfire inside their tent had blown into the straw in the high winds. The next night, "a much more blustering night," they tried to sleep in their tents, but "we had our tent carried quite off with the wind and [were] obliged to lie the latter part of the night without covering."

The stormy, cold, miserable conditions proved too much for the lordly young George Fairfax, who left the party and turned back at this point. After three weeks of roughing it, he headed for the comforts of the nearest inn. The remaining surveyors, old Genn and young George, struggled on, accompanied now by large numbers of German settlers "that attended us through the woods as we went, showing their antic tricks. I really think they seem to be as ignorant a set of people as the Indians. They would never speak English but, when spoken to, they speak all Dutch." Here, faced by a menacing, resentful crowd of squatters, was a young provincial Englishman buttressed by his boyish intolerance.

Their tents blowing down every night or so smoky from drenched firewood that they had to leave them, they were dogged all day, day after day, by crowds of taunting Germans. It did not dawn on the young surveyor's assistant that they were hated for coming into these woods and making surveys for a new master who was disputing their right to remain on the land.

As they left this "company" behind, they traveled downriver, only to be caught in another ferocious rainstorm. "We got under a straw [thatch-roofed] house until the worst of it was over." Thursday, April 7, was no better: "Rained successively all last night." But the hungry, bedraggled pair did feast on "a wild turkey that weighed 20 pounds" before they went out and surveyed 1,500 acres of land by one o'clock in the afternoon. Washington was happy to learn that his friend George Fairfax was at a farm nearby. "I then took my horse and went up to see him." They ate dinner together and, leading their horses, walked the two miles to the tavern where Genn was staying and back again "and slept in [Peter] Casey's house, which was the first night I had slept in a house since I came to the [South] Branch [of the Potomac]." Those had been eighteen of the worst nights of his young life, but this was as close as the young stoic came to complaining.

The amenities were not to last. By the next night, after laying off lots and riding around eight miles of impassable West Virginia ledge,

> we camped this night in the woods near a wild meadow where was a very large stack of hay. After we had pitched our tent & made a very large fire, we pulled out our knapsack in order to [refresh] ourselves. Everyone was his own cook. Our spits were forked sticks, our plate was a large chip. As for dishes, we had none.

By now, after a full month in the wilderness, Washington was ready when George Fairfax proposed that they leave Genn and head home. Their mission was finished and George had his first pay in his pocket. "We took our farewell." They traveled over forty miles on horseback "over hills and mountains reaching Winchester, Virginia, at noon the next day." Washington's terse journal entry bespoke volumes of contentment at returning to civilization: "We dined in town and then went to Captain Hite's and lodged." Sure they would be home in a few days, they set off the next morning, intending to ride due east twenty miles through Williams Gap in the Shenandoahs, but the young surveyor got lost. Exhausted, they had to ride another twenty miles before they found the gap late that night. They rode on until they reached Bull Run in Fairfax County, in all covering fifty miles on horseback in a single day. On April 13, 1748, young Washington made his final notation: "Mister Fairfax got safe home and I myself safe to my brothers."

Washington's Early Military Career

A.J. Langguth

By the 1750s, the French had begun moving into the interior of North America, and settled English colonists worried that the French would soon move east and encroach on their land. A clash between Britain and France over the rights to the American frontier seemed inevitable. In 1754, what became known as the French and Indian War began in earnest, with the French and the Native Americans they had recruited on one side and the British on the other. The war ended in 1763 with a victory for the British. But even before the war officially began, a brash young soldier named George Washington set off one of its early conflicts. In this selection, Professor and former *New York Times* journalist A.J. Langguth tells the story of some of Washington's adventures in the war.

[George Washington became the official surveyor of Virginia's Culpepper County in 1849, and] for the next four years, Washington divided his time between surveying the countryside and weeks of indulgence at Mount Vernon and Belvoir. There always seemed to be a host of pretty girls on hand, not least Mrs. [Sally] Fairfax [mistress of Belvoir, with whom Washington had become infatuated]. Washington acquired more land and was named a county surveyor. But he appeared doomed to fall in love easily and lucklessly. He wrote to one young woman in Fredericksburg three times and got no answer. As he took up his pen for a fourth attempt, he confessed to her that he was almost discouraged. Nearing his twenty-first birthday, Washington seemed to have inherited his mother's intense will and was on the way to harnessing it.

A.J. Langguth, *Patriots: The Men Who Started the American Revolution.* New York: Simon and Schuster, 1988. Copyright © 1988 by A.J. Langguth. Reproduced by permission.

A Brother's Death

Then George's prospects improved abruptly for a distressing reason. [His half-brother] Lawrence Washington's three children had died, and now he was suffering from a persistent cough that suggested tuberculosis. He sailed to the West Indies hoping that the sun would cure him. George went with him to Barbados while [Lawrence's] wife stayed behind to tend their frail fourth infant. The trip mocked their expectations. Lawrence became worse and sailed on to Bermuda alone because George had contracted smallpox, a light case that left a few scars across his nose. On his return to Virginia, George found that he had also developed pleurisy. Meanwhile, Lawrence gave up his quest and came home to die.

The foresight of Lawrence's will reflected his recent losses. During his wife's lifetime she would live on at Mount Vernon as guardian for their surviving child. If that daughter also died, Mount Vernon and the rest of the estate passed to George upon the death of Lawrence's widow. Lawrence had been one of the four majors in Virginia's militia. As his heir, George sought that commission, and the Fairfax family helped him get it. Within six months, Lawrence's infant daughter had died and his widow had remarried and moved away. George Washington began to assume responsibility for Mount Vernon. He had become a prosperous gentleman farmer, complete with a gentleman's military rank.

First Military Mission

Washington wanted his rank to be more than honorary. In 1753, at twenty-one, he volunteered for his first assignment, even though the mission seemed political rather than military. French forces had occupied a great thin curve from Canada to the Louisiana territory and were confining the British colonies to the Atlantic coast and out of the fertile Western lands. The British planned to challenge the French claims by building a fort on the Ohio River. But scouts reported that the French were constructing their own forts from the Ohio north to Lake Erie. When Virginia's acting governor, Robert Dinwiddie, drafted a letter warning France to stop its inroads into English territory, Major Washington volunteered to deliver it. The journey was arduous, nearly five hundred miles each way, and Mary Washington [George's mother] took his departure for abandonment. Years later, she continued to complain that his military service had given her no end of trouble.

Traveling by canoe and horseback along icy rivers and snowbound trails, George Washington's party took fifty-two days to reach the French camp. Washington delivered Dinwiddie's politely phrased ultimatum, and a captain named La Force composed a reply for the French that was equally civil: "As to the summons you send me to retire, I do not think myself obliged to obey it." But after several French officers had drunk quantities of wine, they assured Washington privately that they intended to take the Ohio, and by God they would do it.

When Washington returned to Williamsburg [Virginia's capital] with that response, Dinwiddie insisted that he write a full account of the episode. Washington obeyed with grave misgivings and apologies for his literary shortcomings. But Dinwiddie had the six-thousand-word account published and circulated widely, even in London. The House of Burgesses [Virginia's legislature] rewarded Washington with fifty pounds for his performance, and Virginia decided to send its militia to hold the Ohio country by reinforcing a British fort on the Monongahela River. Washington, who had just turned twenty-two, was promoted to lieutenant colonel and named second in command for the expedition.

A Second Mission

He marched west from Alexandria early in April 1754 with two companies of men. Washington was an untried soldier, but he looked imposing in the red coat and three-cornered hat of Virginia's militia officers. His youth caused him to accentuate his natural reserve. Washington thought a degree of distance was essential in a leader of men and wasn't concerned if his troops considered him aloof. Establishing his authority was especially important because he had doubts about the quality of the troops his officers had scared up. They looked to him like drifters who would be hard to control. Most of them hadn't seen any more warfare than he had, and their pay was bad—about eightpence a day. Their real incentive, which Washington understood, was the prospect of owning land. Dinwiddie had promised that the volunteers would divide the twenty thousand acres of rich frontier land that the French were contesting.

Washington brought along as his interpreter a young Dutchman who had accompanied him on the earlier mission. Jacob van Braam, who had been in America barely two years, made his living teaching French and fencing and had joined the Masonic lodge at Fredericksburg [Virginia] about the same time as Washington. Once again the march was grueling. The wagons at the outset covered eleven miles a day, but as they got farther into the wilderness Washington had to be content with little more than a mile. Rumors reached him that the French had already overrun the British garrison on the Monongahela, but Iroquois tribesmen along the route encouraged Washington to keep going. The twenty thousand warriors of the Six Nations Iroquois confederation held the balance between the French and the English, and for more than a century they had allied themselves with Britain. Washington took their advice and pressed on.

During the last week in May he reached the Great Meadows, a two-mile stretch of long grass and low bushes. As Washington rested his men there, a brave named Silverheels brought a message from his chief. Tanacharison, called the Half-King, knew where a band of French soldiers were encamped. Even though France and England were officially at peace, George Washington and the Half-King agreed to launch a surprise attack.

At 7 A.M. on May 28, forty of Washington's men and a dozen Iroquois braves caught thirty Frenchmen as they were getting dressed and making breakfast. The gunfire went on for less than fifteen minutes and killed ten of the French, including their commander, Coulon de Jumonville. As the rest tried to escape, they were blocked by the Half-King's braves with raised tomahawks. George Washington took ten prisoners and sent them under guard back to Virginia. His first taste of battle exhilarated him. He was still excited—though he tried to appear nonchalant—when he wrote about the engagement to his younger brother, John Augustine. Only one of his own men had been killed, Washington reported casually, and only two or three wounded. "I heard the bullets whistle," he added, with a bravado he would regret, "and, believe me, there is something charming in the sound."

George Washington had ordered the first shots of the French and Indian War.

A Costly Mistake

He learned belatedly from his prisoners that the French party had been only a diplomatic mission, much like the one that had taken him to Captain La Force. All the same, Washington was promoted on the spot to full colonel and made commander of the entire Virginia contingent. But he had little time to bask in his success. A large French force led by Jumonville's brother was heading toward the Great Meadows for revenge. Washington threw up hasty defenses on the plain. With an accuracy bordering on wit, he named the result "Fort Necessity."

After a month with the young colonel, the Half-King concluded that Washington was good-natured but appallingly inexperienced and unwilling to take advice. Long before the news of the French retaliation, the chief had urged him to dig in at the meadow, but Washington hadn't listened. When he was forced to act, he had pitched his fort on ground with such poor drainage that the least rain would flood his trenches. Washington also cut the trees back only sixty yards from the southeast side of his fort, which brought the trenches within musket fire. The Half-King's Iroquois warriors began to fade away.

George Washington

On July 3, during a rainstorm, the French struck. This time the battle lasted longer, about an hour, and Washington's green troops were clearly outfought. Thirty Americans were killed, including one of Washington's slaves, and another seventy were wounded. Unless he was willing to fight to the death, Washington had only one option. In the early hours of the fourth of July, 1754, he surrendered.

Jacob van Braam's translation of the French surrender document made its broad outlines sound favorable to Washington. He would be allowed to march his men out from Fort Necessity with all honors of war. The Americans could take only one cannon but all of their personal belongings. Two of Washington's captains would stay behind as hostages until the French prisoners from the earlier engagement were released in Virginia. Those generous terms carried a preamble, however. As rain continued to pour down, van Braam, whose knowledge of French was not infallible, stumbled through the text by candlelight under a leaking stockade roof. It claimed that the French raid had never been intended to disrupt the peace between France and England but only to avenge the assassination of a French officer. When he translated that phrase for Colonel Washington, van Braam rendered "*l'assassinat*" as "death." The error misled Washington about the magnitude of the confession he had just signed.

As Washington returned to Virginia, the Half-King gave his verdict on the battle. The French had been great cowards for not pressing their advantage, but the Americans had been fools. Other warriors from the Six Nations heard about the battle and agreed with him. Before Washington reached home, many of the tribes were turning away from the English, and by the year's end their warriors had either joined with the French or were staying neutral.

Washington's private journal was lost or stolen during his retreat. When it turned up in Europe, the French were already using his surrender terms to portray the British as murderers. A London magazine printed Washington's letter to his brother, and when King George II read that the young American commander had called the whistle of bullets charming he remarked, "He would not say so had he heard many." Among Britain's military officers, George Washington's name was becoming famous—as a byword for colonial incompetence.

In Williamsburg, Robert Dinwiddie, who had been the young colonel's patron, was separating himself from the defeat at Necessity. The authorities also refused to honor Washington's surrender terms and release the French prisoners. They said he had exceeded his authority. Youth and inexperience had contributed to Washington's defeat, but his bravery had been unmistakable, and the men who served under him valued it above an error in translation. Washington came back to Virginia under a haze, if not a cloud, but he was now a man to be taken seriously. He leased Mount Vernon from Lawrence's widow for fifteen thousand pounds of tobacco a year and took it as his country seat. He dined often at Belvoir, where Sally Fairfax remained charmingly impudent and instructed her seamstress to make shirts for him.

But Washington's military ambitions were effectively blocked. The new commander in chief for all royal forces in America openly criticized Washington's performance at Fort Necessity, and when the Virginia troops were reorganized

Colonel Washington was reduced to captain. Washington resigned.

EXPEDITION WITH BRADDOCK

He admitted that he left only because his honor had been affronted and that he was still strongly drawn to the soldier's life. In spring 1755 he offered to join a new expedition against the French. It would be led by Edward Braddock, a blunt-tongued major general sent from London. Washington avoided the troublesome matter of rank by volunteering to serve as a civilian and to pay his own expenses. Again, Mary Washington insisted that George not leave her, and her pleas delayed him one day. But Washington believed he could endure any amount of abuse—even from his mother—as long as he acted from decency and principle. Before he rode to join Braddock at Fredericksburg, he paused to write a fond but decorous letter to Sally Fairfax, assuring her that none of his friends could bring him more real delight than she. Mrs. Fairfax replied that although she wanted news of him, he should send it through mutual friends and not write to her directly. Washington accepted that reproach—he called it a gentle rebuke—and wrote to her anyway.

At the end of May 1755, one year after he had surprised Jumonville at breakfast, Washington set out with Braddock and more than two thousand British regulars, volunteers and militia for the French fort of Duquesne, one hundred and fifty miles away. During the expedition, Washington was handed one of his mother's rare letters. She asked him to send her a supply of butter and a Dutchman to help on her farm. "Honoured Madam," Washington began dutifully and went on to explain that where he was traveling both commodities were in short supply.

As they drew within a few miles of Duquesne, Braddock's advance guard was attacked by a band of Indians and Frenchmen who picked them off from behind trees. Washington had dysentery and was trailing at the end of Braddock's column. He had been disappointed when Braddock ordered him to stay back, but the commander had promised to summon him when the attack began.

Although he could barely mount his horse, Washington heard the first shots and rode to join the fray. French bullets tore into his coat, he endured waves of nausea, and two horses were shot from under him. Through it all, Washington fought on. Before the firing ended, the attackers had killed or wounded almost a thousand of Braddock's men—two thirds of the force sent into battle. Still the British officers would not change their traditional tactics and fight the French and the Indians on their own terms. Edward Braddock was shot through the lungs as he was giving the order to withdraw, and Washington helped carry him off the field in a silk sash. Braddock died during the retreat. His men buried him secretly in a grove a mile and a half from Fort Necessity.

For Washington, it had been another failure. Yet this time he reaped only praise for his gallantry. To his brother John he wrote that when he got back to the British camp he had heard stories of his death and even of his deathbed speech: "I take this early opportunity of contradicting the first and of assuring you I have not composed the latter." The governor of North Carolina wrote to congratulate him on the honor he had gained, and he was commissioned a militia colonel once again and named commander in chief of Virginia's forces. At twenty-three, George Washington had come through three military engagements without even a flesh wound and had begun to seem equally adroit, or lucky, in surviving the political wars.

CHAPTER 2

FARMER AND SLAVE OWNER

PEOPLE WHO MADE HISTORY

GEORGE WASHINGTON

Life at Mount Vernon

Robert F. Dalzell Jr. and Lee Baldwin Dalzell

When Washington's half-brother Lawrence died in 1752, his wife inherited the Mount Vernon estate, situated on the banks of the Potomac River in Virginia. When she remarried less than six months later, ownership of the estate transferred to George, who was then only twenty-two. Washington grew to love Mount Vernon, and throughout his lifetime he continually made changes and improvements to the house and its grounds.

When Washington married the widow Martha Custis in 1759, he brought her and her two children, Jackie and Patsy, to live at Mount Vernon. During the eight years of the Revolutionary War, Washington was able to spend only a few days at his estate. When he was finally able to return to his beloved home, he found contentment in farming, riding his horse around the grounds and fields, and partaking in an active social life that included entertaining many guests. The following reading by history professor Robert F. Dalzell Jr. and Williams College reference librarian Lee Baldwin Dalzell describes the kind of life, both public and private, that George Washington led at his home.

Like all gentry houses in Virginia, [Mount Vernon] was in some ways a very public place, which in turn is likely to seem odd to a modern consciousness. In our experience, houses have become private preserves devoted to family life. By the same token, any entertaining done "at home" is most often an intimate affair, with few if any public connotations. In eighteenth-century Virginia, however, houses were places of business as well as centers of family life, and that included the houses of the gentry, since the business of getting, keeping, and exercising power went on constantly at home. When Washington welcomed visitors to his home, he

Robert F. Dalzell Jr. and Lee Baldwin Dalzell, *George Washington's Mount Vernon: At Home in Revolutionary America.* New York: Oxford University Press, 1998. Copyright © 1998 by Oxford University Press, Inc. Reproduced by permission.

was welcoming fellow burgesses, fellow justices of the county court, fellow vestrymen, voters in local elections, influential citizens from other colonies, people bringing information he needed, people who owed him money, and people to whom he owed money. As a rule they were social equals, but even if they were not, it behooved him to treat them as such. So his door was always open, and his table was always full—even before he became a great and famous man.

It has been estimated that during the seven years between 1768 and 1775 roughly two thousand people were entertained at Mount Vernon, many of whom stayed for days on end and visited repeatedly. In April 1774, a typical month, an average of four to five guests joined the Washingtons every time they sat down to dinner. Guests were present all but five days of the month. Twice the couple dined at other houses in the neighborhood, which reduced to three the number of times they were, as Washington noted in his diary, "At home all day alone." Two thirds of the people who came to dinner also spent at least one night in the house, and thus had to be given tea and breakfast as well. The largest number of people at a single dinner was eleven, all of whom stayed the night.

A majority of the month's guests fell, in roughly equal proportions, into one of three categories: family members, neighbors and friends, and business associates of Washington's. . . .

The shad were running on the river that month, and on several occasions Washington took his guests to the fish landings to watch the catch being hauled in. There were also trips to Pohick Church and Alexandria, and in the middle of the month Washington spent a day hunting. Compared with these rather modest amusements, dinner must often have been the most interesting event of the day, a fact underscored by Washington's careful enumeration in his diary of those present. And making a house party of it, with the guests spending the night, would have provided yet another way of varying the daily routine. . . .

WASHINGTON'S SCHEDULE

After the Revolution, the constant coming and going of visitors at Mount Vernon resumed almost immediately. There were differences, however. Before the war Washington had chosen his guests; now they came whether he invited them or not, and often the group around the table at dinner included people he had never met before. Some arrived on specific errands; others made their way up the drive out of pure curiosity; many were individuals who themselves cut a large figure in the world. But high or low, famous or not, they all had to be received with appropriate courtesy.

In time, too, as the numerous surviving accounts of visits to Mount Vernon indicate, Washington developed a system for handling guests. Rising at five in the morning, he worked in his study until seven. At that point he joined his visitors and the rest of the household for breakfast, then went off alone on horseback to oversee work on one or more of the outlying farms. While he was away, it fell either to aides or to younger family members to amuse visitors. Most often they were given tours of the house and grounds, which seem to have been accompanied by a more or less standard running commentary, for the same facts appear again and again in the accounts—a few details about the history of the house, the dimensions of the new room and the piazza, the size of the estate, the number of slaves, something about their treatment, lists of plant species and livestock, the number of acres owned elsewhere by Washington. At two in the afternoon Washington returned and changed for dinner, which was at three. Tea was at six, and usually no supper at all was served. After bidding their guests good night, the Washingtons retired at nine.

On the standard tour, some parts of the house were bypassed completely. Not one of the visitors who left accounts mentioned having seen the Washingtons' bedchamber, for example. So it was possible to maintain a certain level of privacy. Similarly, Washington continued to be able to limit access to himself, either by retreating to his study or by riding off on plantation business. Most visitors, in fact, saw him only at meals and, if he chose, for brief periods afterward. Conversation at the table could be lively or slow, depending on his mood and, one suspects, his interest in the company present. The topic that seemed to appeal to him most was farming. Occasionally he would reminisce about the past. Contemporary politics were not discussed.

THE BOUNDARY BETWEEN PUBLIC AND PRIVATE LIFE

In all of this one senses a great deal of careful management. Thanks to his routine, Washington succeeded in preserving at least half of each day for his own purposes, even when visitors were present. Without undue awkwardness, some parts of the house remained off-limits to the curious. Keeping his innermost thoughts to himself, too, was a skill Washington had long since elevated to a minor art form. In each of these ways he could and did control the extent to which visitors impinged on his life and on the life of the rest of the household. On the essential point there was little if anything he could do, however. People had to be shown what they had come to see: the great hero of the Revolution, retired at last from his labors, with nothing more pressing on his mind than the business of everyday life.

Yet in reality Washington's situation was hardly that simple. If he was obliged to transform his private life into a perpetual performance for the touring public, surely the performance itself was a public act. Where, then, did the boundary lie? What was public and what was not, or had the two simply flowed together in a formless muddle? And this in the house that Washington had twice rebuilt as a palpable expression of his personal independence, his freedom. Yet plainly he felt that nothing less was demanded of him. By retiring to Mount Vernon he had proved that great power, assumed in the service of the people, could be relinquished when the need for it had passed. Now it fell to him to demonstrate that he could be content amid the quiet delights of life at home, and for that there had to be witnesses to observe him and to describe what they had seen. Hence the general welcome extended to the world at large. And on top of everything else, Washington was required to compose the entire performance from scratch. . . . Here too, as in so much else, he was first, without predecessor or peer, on the stage of history.

Such was life under Washington's vine and fig tree. Was he happy with it? The question is not one he was likely to have asked himself. Most visitors found him good-humored, if rather reserved. The pleasures Mount Vernon afforded were real enough, and if his existence there was interpreted as he hoped it would be, he could see it as a genuine service to the nation. He was also able to continue work on the house and grounds and had the satisfaction of seeing his plans for them come to fruition. At times there were signs of darker moods, but only rarely did anything resembling frustration or impatience disturb his outward calm. . . .

PRIVATE LIFE AT MOUNT VERNON

The public character of Mount Vernon had little in common, at least at first glance, with its private side. Full of guests or not, the house was the center of the Washingtons' life together. Over the years they lived in many different places but called no other home.

Mount Vernon was also where two generations of Custis children grew to maturity. After Jackie Custis died, cutting off the first generation, the Washingtons adopted his two youngest children, George Washington Parke Custis ("Wash") and Eleanor Parke Custis ("Nelly"). As a result, except for the years just before the Revolution, there were always young children in the house. Yet the children were not Washington's. How the couple dealt, together and separately, with the fact that their marriage was barren can only be imagined. For Washington the sense of deprivation, and quite possibly failure, must have been acute. As kind and thoughtful as she seems to have been, Martha would surely have done whatever she could to ease his pain, but she also devoted herself to nurturing her children and grandchildren with a passion that sometimes seemed to leave room for little else. She made them, if not the center of her life, the focus of unending worry and concern, and she indulged them with something approaching abandon.

Washington responded very differently to his responsibilities as a stepparent and step-grandparent. He managed the children's financial affairs (being careful to transfer to his own account whatever was due him for their expenses). He spent considerable time overseeing the boys' education, choosing their schools and eventually their colleges. He also tried to impose a certain amount of discipline on them, though with no great success. Jackie Custis seems to have been especially adept at eluding control. One of his teachers claimed never to have known anyone "so exceedingly indolent or so surprizingly voluptuous: one [would] suppose Nature had intended Him for some Asiatic Prince."

In all of this Washington can be seen as playing the role of traditional paterfamilias. It was the role he had watched his own father play, sending his sons off to England to be educated even before they reached their teenage years. Nor were Washington's relations with his mother such as to demonstrate the value of a more intimate approach to parenthood. Mary Washington professed to care deeply about her children, but she was demanding, difficult, and overprotective. Of course, Washington could have followed Martha's example, which as it happened had much in common with newer, less restrictive methods of childrearing being practiced by many of Virginia's leading families. Yet clearly he chose not to do so. Neither did he seem interested in endowing the young Custises imaginatively with his own paternity. They were not his children, and he would not (or could not) pretend otherwise.

MARTHA WASHINGTON

Washington's inability to share Martha's feelings for her children meant that their marriage lacked one of the bonds that customarily unites couples, but through the years the two formed other, equally strong ties. Good-natured and unpretentious, she was an accomplished hostess who quickly put people at ease, creating a more relaxed social atmosphere around him than he could achieve himself. While he was president it was an open secret that he preferred her teas to his own notoriously stiff "levées." At Mount Vernon, because he was so often away from the house supervising work being done elsewhere on the plantation, it frequently fell to Martha to entertain guests, and she did the honors with a cheerful graciousness regularly noted in letters and diaries. The architect Benjamin Latrobe wrote of her "good humored free manner that was extremely pleasing and flattering." "She has something very charming about her," commented Polish Army officer Julian Niemcewicz, who mentioned as well her "gay manner" and "bright eyes." And of all he found at Mount Vernon, Joshua Brookes, a young Englishman, wrote, "Mrs. Washington and Miss Custis pleased me most, especially the former."

Martha Washington

If Martha Washington brought to the couple's public activities the warmth and intimacy of private life, Washington in return gave her a public life full of interest and significance. He also helped her fashion, as he had himself, a persona suitable for that life. On meeting her, Abigail Adams commented: "She received me with great ease and politeness. She is plain in her dress, but that plainness is the best of every article.... Her hair is white, her teeth beautiful.... Her manners are modest and unassuming, dignified and feminine, not a tincture of hauteur about her." And later: "Mrs. Washington is one of those unassuming characters which create love and esteem.... I found myself much more deeply impressed than I ever did before their Majesties of Britain." However, the same woman who so impressed Abigail Adams never really mastered English grammar and spelling, at least on paper. The letters she wrote friends and relatives are lively and engaging, but in some circles her usual epistolary performance was likely to prove embarrassing. The solution, which seems to have been perfectly agreeable to her, was to have Washington draft those letters intended for people of consequence in the larger world (including Abigail Adams), after which Martha carefully copied his words in her own hand.

The letters produced in this way were more or less free of error, and not surprisingly, they also tended to express sentiments Washington himself repeatedly uttered. Thus Mercy Otis Warren—the wife of James Warren, the hero of the Battle of Bunker Hill and a woman with a keen sense of what it meant to stand before the bar of history—was told soon after Martha took up her duties as First Lady of her strong "predilictions for privet life," a point on which "the general's feelings" and her own were "perfectly in unison." It seemed unfortunate, therefore, the letter continued, "that I, who had much rather be at home should occupy a place with which a great many younger and gayer women would be prodigiously pleased.... I [know] too much of the vanity of human affairs to expect felicity from the splendid scenes of public life." Nonetheless she described herself as "determined to be cheerful and to be happy in whatever situation I may be."...

THE WASHINGTONS' RELATIONSHIP

In later life Martha Washington read several newspapers a day, and the spirited charge Edmund Pendleton remembered her giving her son as Washington was about to set out for the First Continental Congress, suggests that she was fully conversant with public affairs. And this may well have been the closest bond of all between the two. Washington had few close friends with whom he could share his thoughts, but he had a wife who was sympathetic, understanding, and discreet. It would be surprising if he had not confided in her. Moreover, the way he configured the spaces in his second rebuilding of Mount Vernon seems to point to just such a relationship. Each of the Washingtons had a separate room at the south end of the house, his study below and "Mrs. Washington's" chamber above. But there was also easy communication between the two rooms via the small stairway in the adjacent passage, a stairway visible from nowhere else in the house.

THE WASHINGTONS' CORRESPONDENCE

Another clue to the Washingtons' relationship is the fate of their correspondence. After his death Martha burned all but two of their letters to each other. Whether she took the step on her own initiative or because he had asked her to is unclear. It has been suggested that she did so in what amounted to a fit of pique—"a possessive reaction to having been forced to share her husband so extensively with the public." This seems unlikely. Martha Washington was not a vindictive person. The letters she and Washington had written to one another were part of the life they had shared away from public scrutiny. One imagines she destroyed them, if not at his request, knowing that it would have been his preference as much as it was hers. More than likely, too, in addition to being intimate and personal, the letters contained candid remarks about public events and personalities. And if they did, might they not also have cast the Washingtons in a rather different light from the one they took such care to train on themselves most of the time? If Martha Washington, longing for the forbidden delights of New York City, could joke in a letter to a friend about being a state prisoner, what feelings did she confide to Washington and he to her? Did she really miss Mount Vernon all that much when she was away? Did he? They both claimed to, certainly, but when duty called they left, time and again.

They also returned when duty required it, and in retirement Washington needed Martha every bit as much as he did in the larger world. Yet without children and the constant demands they made on her time and energy, there was less for her to do at Mount Vernon than away from it. In that sense, the death of Jackie Custis made it possible for her to establish, just as she was returning after the Revolution, a second family at Mount Vernon by bringing to it two of his children. At various times, too, the circle was enlarged even further with the addition of one or more of Washington's young nephews.

The Squire of Mount Vernon

Ralph K. Andrist

The primary cash crop for Virginians in the eighteenth century was tobacco, or "tobo" as it was often abbreviated. George Washington tried in vain for years to produce the kind of tobacco that demanded a high price when exported to England. He even went as far as dredging mud from the Potomac River and spreading it on his tobacco fields, hoping to enrich the soil that years of tobacco growing had depleted. In this manner, Washington experimented with several crops until he settled on wheat. He was, in fact, among the first Virginians to grow wheat as a cash crop.

This reading by Ralph K. Andrist, author and editor of many books dealing with American history, contains excerpts from Washington's diaries, many of them written in a kind of shorthand and using the arbitrary spelling that was fairly common in those days. The entries reveal Washington's frustrations with his crops and also reveal his dealings with his agent, Robert Cary. Colonists had to rely on agents to sell their crops in England. With the profits, the agents purchased goods for the colonists and shipped them to America. Sometimes the goods the colonists ordered cost more than they could get for their crops, and they racked up debts as a result. Washington was one of many who faced such financial problems.

Martha Custis and George Washington were married on January 6, 1759, on the Custis plantation. He was almost twenty-seven years old; she was a few months older. It was destined to be a happy marriage; she brought to it a cheerful nature, personal warmth, the ability to manage a large

Ralph K. Andrist, *The Founding Fathers: George Washington: A Biography in His Own Words*. New York: Newsweek, 1972. Copyright © 1972 by Newsweek, Inc. Reproduced by permission of the author.

plantation household—all the attributes of a good companion and an excellent hostess. She was considered pretty, but she was diminutive, as small as her husband was large and strong—the contrast must have been striking. Martha's late husband had left a large estate, 17,438 acres, with other property—cash, slaves, livestock, securities—worth some twenty thousand pounds sterling, or a little over half a million dollars, as nearly as it can be translated into today's terms. One third of this went to Martha and so became Washington's on marriage, subject to restrictions preventing him from alienating or encumbering her rights in the property. The other two thirds were the property of her two children, and Washington was made the administrator of their estate. Only in relation to her two children did Martha Washington fail to show common sense. At the time of her remarriage, her son, John Parke ("Jackie") Custis, was four; her daughter, Martha Parke ("Patsy") Custis, two. Their mother indulged them shamefully and had such a morbid anxiety about leaving them that she would not accompany George on trips unless the children went along. On February 22—the day he turned twenty-seven—Washington took his seat as a member in the [Virginia] House of Burgesses. He had been elected a member from Frederick County the previous July, even though he was on the Forbes expedition against Fort Duquesne at the time; his fame, the efforts of his friends, and his generous provision for potables (160 gallons of rum, punch, wine, and beer) made him an easy winner.

BRINGING HIS NEW FAMILY HOME

Leaving Williamsburg [Virginia's capital], Washington set out early in April for home with his bride, stepchildren, servants, and baggage. Not until he was almost at Mount Vernon did it occur to him that he had made no arrangements for their arrival, and he sent a messenger galloping on ahead with urgent instructions for his manager, John Alton.

> Thursday Morning [April 1, 1759]
> I have sent Miles on to day, to let you know that I expect to be up to Morrow, & to get the Key from Colo. Fairfax's which I desire you will take care of. You must have the House very well clean'd, & were you to make Fires in the Rooms below it wd. Air them. You must get two of the best Bedsteads put up, one in the Hall Room, and the other in the little dining Room that use to be, & have Beds made on them against we come. You must also get out the Chairs and Tables & have them very

well rubd. & Cleand. The Stair case ought also to be polishd in order to make it look well.

Enquire abt. in the Neighbourhood, & get some Egg's and Chickens, and prepare in the best manner you can for our coming. You need not however take out any more of the Furniture than the Beds Tables & Chairs in Order that they may be well rubd. & cleand.

FARMER WASHINGTON

In preparation for the arrival of his bride, Washington had added a story to the original story-and-a-half house at Mount Vernon, but he had found little time to furnish and decorate the enlarged mansion. Making this austere domain a home and managing a large household—there were eleven house slaves—was to be Martha's task. The land was George's responsibility. He accepted the challenge gladly; his diary entries early in the following year reveal that he was a man completely absorbed in his farming.

> January 1 [1760] Tuesday. Visited my Plantations and receivd an Instance of Mr. French's great Love of Money in disappointing me of some Pork because the price had risen to 22/6 [22 shillings, 6 pence] after he had engagd to let me have it at 20/.
>
> Calld at Mr. Posseys in my way home and desird him to engage me 100 Barl. of Corn upon the best terms he coud in Maryland.
>
> And found Mrs. Washington upon my arrival broke out with the Meazles.
>
> Jany. 2d. Wednesy. Mrs. Barnes who came to visit Mrs. Washington yesterday returnd home in my Chariot the Weather being too bad to Travel in an open Carriage—which together with Mrs. Washington's Indisposition confind me to the House and gave me an opportunity of Posting my Books and putting them in good Order.
>
> Fearing a disappointment elsewhere in Pork I was fein to take Mr. French upon his own terms & engagd them to be delivd. at my House on Monday next.
>
> Thursday Jany. 3d. The Weather continuing Bad & the same causes subsisting I confind myself to the House.
>
> Morris who went to work Yesterday caught cold, and was laid up bad again—and several of the Family were taken with the Measles, but no bad Symtoms seem'd to attend any of them.
>
> Hauled the Sein [fish nets] and got some fish, but was near being disappointd of my Boat by means of an Oyste[r] man

who had lain at my Landing and plaged me a good deal by his disorderly behaviour.

Friday Jany. 4th. The Weather continued Drisling and Warm, and I kept the House all day. Mrs. Washington seemg. to be very ill [I] wrote to Mr. Green [a clergyman-physician] this afternoon desiring his Company to visit her in the Morng.

Saturday Jany. 5th. Mrs. Washington appears to be something better. Mr. Green however came to see her abt. 11 Oclock and in an hour Mrs. Fairfax arrivd. Mr. Green prescribd the needful and just as we were going to Dinnr. Captn. Walter Stuart appeard with Doctr. Laurie.

The Evening being very cold, and the wind high Mr. Fairfax went home in the Chariot & soon afterwards Mulatto Jack arrivd from Fredk. with 4 Beeves.

Sunday Jany. 6th. The Chariot not returng. time enought from Colo. Fairfax's we were prevented from Church.

Mrs. Washington was a good deal better today, but the Oyster man still continued his Disorderly behaviour at my Landing I was obligd in the most preemptory manner to order him and his Compy. away which he did not Incline to obey till next morning. . . .

Tuesday Jany. 8. Directed an Indictment to be formd by Mr. Johnston against Jno. Ballendine for a fraud in some Iron he sold me.

Got a little Butter from Mr. Dalton—and wrote to Colo. West for Pork.

In the Evening 8 of Mr. French's Hogs from his Ravensworth Quarter came down one being lost on the way as the others might as well have been for their goodness.

Nothing but the disappoin[t]ments in this Article of Pork which he himself had causd and my necessities coud possibly have obligd me to take them.

Carpenter Sam was taken with the Meazles. . . .

Washington was not a skilled farmer at the outset. But unlike most of his fellow Virginians, he strove to preserve the land and its fertility. He ordered from London the latest books on agriculture, and he experimented with crops and farming methods, as these additional diary entries show.

Thursday April 3d [1760]. Sowd 17½ Drills of Trefoil seed in the ground adjoining the Garden, numbering from the side next the Stable (or Work shop) the residue of them viz [namely] 4 was sowd with Lucerne [alfalfa] Seed—both done with design to see how these Seeds answer in that Ground.

Sowd my Fallow Field in Oats today, and harrowd them in viz 10½ Bushels. Got done about three Oclock.

Cook Jack after laying of the Lands in this Field went to plowing in the 12 Acre Field where they were Yesterday as did the other plow abt. 5 Oclock after Pointing.

Got several Composts and laid them to dry in order to mix with the Earth brot. from the Field below to try their several Virtues.

Wind blew very fresh from South—Clouds often appeard, and sometimes threatned the near approach of Rain but a clear setting Sun seemd denoted the Contrary. . . .

Monday Apl. 14. Fine warm day, Wind Soly, and clear till the Eveng. when it clouded;

ORNAMENTAL TO THE FARM AND REPUTABLE TO THE FARMER

George Washington had an innate sense of order and was always concerned with maintaining a good reputation, and it showed in the way he designed Mount Vernon. Mac Griswold, who writes about the history of gardens, provides examples of how these two matters came together at Washington's estate in this excerpt from her book Washington's Gardens at Mount Vernon.

[As he grew older, Washington] increasingly cared about how his farm acres looked, as if they were testimony to his own character, a mirror of himself. To be a good farmer ranked with being a good commander, or a man whose personal honor was unstained by cowardice or treachery. He seemed almost as distressed by the news that his Potomac fishing operation had produced some bad barrels of salted herring as he was by the report of any political cabal against him. As much as he cared about his clothes, ordering in 1798 a fabulous new commander in chief's uniform of blue, "with yellow buttons and gold epaulettes (each having three stars) . . . and embroidered on the cape, cuffs, and pockets," he cared about how his hedges looked. He considered that they not only kept rooting hogs in bounds, but were "ornamental to the Farm and reputable to the Farmer."

He wrote to his manager, William Pearce, on October 6, 1793, "I shall begrudge no reasonable expense that will contribute to the improvement & neatness of my Farms, for nothing pleases me better than to see them in good order, and everything trim, handsome & thriving about them; nor nothing hurts me more than to find them otherwise."

Mac Griswold, *Washington's Gardens at Mount Vernon: Landscape of the Inner Man.* New York: Houghton Mifflin, 1999.

No Fish were to be catchd today neither.

Mixd my Composts in a box with ten Apartments in the following manner viz—in No. 1 is three pecks of the Earth brought from below the Hill out of the 46 Acre Field without any mixture—in No.

2. is two pecks of the said Earth and one of Marle [a type of crumby soil] taken out of the said Field which Marle seemd a little Inclinable to Sand.

3. Has 2 Pecks of sd. Earth and 1 of Riverside Sand.

4. Has a Peck of Horse Dung.

5. Has Mud taken out of the Creek.

6. Has Cow Dung.

7. Marle from the Gullys on the Hillside wch. seemd. to be purer than the other.

8. Sheep Dung.

9. Black Mould taken out of the Pocoson [a swamp usually dry in summer] on the Creek side.

10. Clay got just below the Garden.

All mixd with the same quantity & sort of Earth in the most effectual manner by reducing the whole to a tolerable degree of fineness & jubling them well together in a Cloth.

In each of these divisions were planted three Grains of Wheat 3 of Oats & as many of Barley all at equal distances in Rows & of equal depth (done by a Machine made for the purpose).

The Wheat Rows are next the Numberd side, the Oats in the Middle & the Barley on that side next the upper part of the Garden.

Two or three hours after sowing in this manner, and about an hour before Sun set I waterd them all equally alike with Water that had been standing in a Tub abt. two hours exposed to the Sun.

Began drawing Bricks burning Lime & Preparing for Mr. Triplet who is to be here on Wednesday to Work.

Finishd Harrowing the Clover Field, and began reharrowing of it. Got a new harrow made of smaller, and closer Tinings for Harrowing in Grain—the other being more proper for preparing the Ground for sowing.

Cook Jack's plow was stopd he being employd in setting the Lime Kiln.

DEALING WITH AGENTS

Managing a plantation had its problems, but hard work usually produced results; much more frustrating was Washington's relationship with the English merchants who were his agents in selling his tobacco and in buying the endless items not available in the Colonies. Washington complained that he was underpaid for his tobacco, overcharged for the goods sent him, given inferior merchandise, and taken advantage of in various other ways. Typical of scores of laments was one to Robert Cary and Company, which handled most of Washington's overseas business.

[Mount Vernon, August 10, 1760]

By my Friend Mr. Fairfax I take the Oppertunity of acknowledging the Receipts of your several favours that have come to hand since mine of the 30th. of November last, and observe in one of them of the 14 Feby. by Crawford that you refer to another by the same Ship, but this has never yet appeared. . . .

The Insurance on the Tobo. pr. Falman was high I think—higher than expected; And here Gentn. I cannot forbear ushering in a Complaint of the exorbitant prices of my Goods this year all of which are come to hand (except those packages put on board Hooper): For many Years I have Imported Goods from London as well as other Ports of Britain and can truely say I never had such a penny worth before. It woud be a needless Task to innumerate every Article that I have cause to except against, let it suffice to say that Woolens, Linnens, Nails &ca. are mean in quality but not in price, for in this they excel indeed, far above any I have ever had. It has always been a Custom with me when I make out my Invoices to estimate the Charge of them, this I do, for my own satisfaction, to know whether I am too fast or not, and I seldom vary much from the real prices doing it from old Notes &ca. but the amount of your Invoice exceeds my Calculations above 25 pr. Ct. & many Articles not sent that were wrote for.

I must once again beg the favour of you never to send me any Goods but in a Potomack Ship, and for this purpose let me recommend Captn. John Johnson in an annual Ship of Mr. Russels to this River. Johnson is a person I am acquainted with, know him to be very careful and he comes past my Door in his Ship: I am certain therefore of always having my Goods Landed in Good time and Order which never yet has happend when they come into another River: This year the Charming Polly went into Rappahannock & my Goods by her, recd. at different times and in bad order. The Porter entirely Drank out [by seamen during the voyage]. There came no Invoice of Mr. Dandridges Goods to me. I suppose it was forgot to be Inclosd.

Six weeks later Washington was penning a letter to the same agents, plaintively claiming that rapacious London shopkeepers were making Colonists their special victims.

[Mount Vernon, September 28, 1760]

By this conveyance, & under the same cover of this Letter, you will receive Invoices of such Goods as are wanting, which please to send as there directed by Capt. Johnston in the Spring—and let me beseech you Gentn. to give the necessary directions for purchasing of them upon the best Terms. It is needless for me to particularise the sorts, quality, or taste I woud choose to have them in unless it is observd; and you may believe me when I tell you that instead of getting things good and fashionable in their several kinds we often have Articles sent Us that coud only have been usd by our Forefathers in the days of yore. 'Tis a custom, I have some Reason to believe, with many Shop keepers, and Tradesmen in London when they know Goods are bespoke for Exportation to palm sometimes old, and sometimes very slight and indifferent Goods upon Us taking care at the same time to advance 10, 15 or perhaps 20 pr. Ct. upon, them. My Packages pr. the Polly Captn. Hooper are not yet come to hand, & the Lord only, knows when they will without more trouble than they are worth. As to the Busts a future day will determine my choice of them if any are wrote for. Mrs. Washington sends home a Green Sack to get cleand, or fresh dyed of the same colour; made up into a handsome Sack again woud be her choice, but if the Cloth wont afford that, then to be thrown into a genteel Night Gown. The Pyramid you sent me last year got hurt, and the broken pieces I return by this opportunity to get New ones made by them; please to order that they be securely Packd.

DEBT

Mount Vernon was badly run down when Washington inherited it; he built and repaired and bought parcels of land to round out his acres and then had to buy more slaves to work the additional land. Nor did he and Martha scrimp in satisfying their desires for fine clothes, furniture, and entertaining. As a result, Robert Cary and Company informed Washington early in 1764 that instead of having a balance in his account, he was indebted to the firm. Moreover, Jackie Custis's balance—the money from his father's estate separately deposited for him in London—had also shrunk. George Washington was quite bewildered.

Williamsburg, May 1, 1764.

The Copy of your Letter of the 13th. of February—by Falman—is come to hand, but for want of the Account Inclosed in the Original I am a loss to conceive how my balance can possibly be so much as £1811.1.1 in your favour, or Master Custis's so little as £1407.14.7 in his; however as the several Accts. will shew what Articles are charged and credited—without which there can be no judging—I shall postpone an explicit answer till they arrive. . . .

As to my own Debt I shall have no objections to allowing you Interest upon it untill it is discharged and you may charge it accordingly from this time forward, but had my Tobacco sold as I expected and the Bills been paid according to promise I was in hopes to have fallen very little in Arrears; however as it is otherwise I shall endeavour to discharge the Balle. as fast as I can, flattering myself there will be no just cause for com-plts. of the Tobacco this year.

TRYING TO IMPROVE HIS CROPS

Washington was forced to admit that the merchants' accounting was correct. He also at last faced up to a grim truth: no matter what he did, his Mount Vernon tobacco consistently received lower prices than that of his neighbors. Some of his 1765 diary entries reveal what he was doing about it.

[MAY]

12, 13 } Sowed Hemp at Muddy hole by Swamp.

Do [Ditto] Sowed Do above the Meadow at Doeg Run

15 Sowed Do at head of the Swamp Muddy H

16 Sowed Hemp at the head of the Meadow at Doeg Run & about Southwards Houses with the Barrel

JULY

22. Began to Sow Wheat at Rivr. Plantn.

23. Began to Sow Do. at Muddy hole

25. Began to Sow Do. at the Mill

AUGUST

9. Abt. 6 Oclock put some Hemp in the Rivr. to Rot. . . .

13. Finish'd Sowing Wheat at the Rivr. Plantn. i.e. in the corn ground 123 Bushels it took to do it.

15. The English Hemp i.e. the Hemp from the English Seed was picked at Muddy hole this day & was ripe.

15. Began to seperate Hemp in the Neck.

Master and Employer

Paul Leicester Ford

Like many southern plantation owners in the eighteenth century, Washington owned slaves, who worked on his farms. He often doubted whether such a practice was right and sometimes considered freeing his slaves and rehiring them to work for him, but until his death he continued to employ slaves at the farms he owned. In 1791, Washington decided never again to purchase a slave, and he seems to have kept that promise. This selection by nineteenth-century scholar, writer, and historian Paul Leicester Ford was first published in 1896, only thirty-one years after the end of the Civil War, and uses many of Washington's own words to describe the first president's life as a slave owner.

[When George Washington took] possession of the Mount Vernon estate in his twenty-second year, [twenty-eight slaves] came under [his] direction.... [By] 1774 [he had] one hundred and thirty-five besides ... the "dower slaves" of his wife. Soon after this there was [a surplus], and Washington in 1778 offered to barter for some land "Negroes, of whom I every day long more to get clear of," and even before this he had learned the economic fact that except on the richest of soils slaves "only add to the Expence."

In 1791 he had one hundred and fifteen "hands" on the Mount Vernon estate, besides house servants.... At this time Washington declared that "I never mean (unless some particular circumstance compel me to it) to possess another slave by purchase," but this intention was broken, for "The running off of my cook has been a most inconvenient thing to this family, and what rendered it more disagreeable, is that I had resolved never to become the Master of another slave by purchase, but this resolution I fear I must break. I have endeavored to hire, black or white, but am not yet supplied."

Paul Leicester Ford, *The True George Washington*. Freeport, NY: Books for Libraries Press, 1971.

complaint, and the doctor's prescription) sometimes a little wine, may be necessary to nourish and restore the patient; and these I am perfectly willing to allow, when it is requisite. My fear is, as I expressed to you in a former letter, that the under overseers are so unfeeling, in short viewing the negros in no other light than as a better kind of cattle, the moment they cease to work, they cease their care of them."

At Mount Vernon his care for the slaves was more personal. At a time when the small-pox was rife in Virginia he instructed his overseer "what to do if the Small pox should come amongst them," and when he "received letters from Winchester [Virginia] informing me that the Small pox had got among my quarters in Frederick [at one of Washington's farms]; [I] determin'd . . . to leave town as soon as possible, and proceed up to them. . . . After taking the Doctors directions in regard to my people . . . I set out for my quarters about 12 oclock, time enough to go over them and found every thing in the utmost confusion, disorder and backwardness. . . . Got Blankets and every other requisite from Winchester, and settl'd things on the best footing I cou'd, . . . Val Crawford agreeing if any of those at the upper quarter got it, to have them remov'd into my room and the Nurse sent for."

Other sickness was equally attended to, as the following entries in his diary show: "visited my Plantations and found two negroes sick . . . ordered them to be blooded;" "found that lightening had struck my quarters and near 10 negroes in it, some very bad but with letting blood they recover'd;" "ordered Lucy down to the House to be Physikd," and "found the new negro Cupid, ill of a pleurisy at Dogue Run Quarter and had him brot home in a cart for better care of him. . . . Cupid extremely Ill all this day and at night when I went to bed I thought him within a few hours of breathing his last."

This matter of sickness, however, had another phase, which caused Washington much irritation at times when he could not personally look into the cases, but heard of them through the reports of his overseers. Thus, he complained on one occasion, "I find by reports that Sam is, in a manner, always returned sick; Doll at the Ferry [one of Washington's farms], and several of the spinners very frequently so, for a week at a stretch; and ditcher Charles often laid up with lameness. I never wish my people to work when they are really sick, or unfit for it; on the contrary, that all necessary care should be taken of them when they are so; but if you do not examine into their complaints, they will lay by when no more ails them, than all those who stick to their business, and are not complaining from the fatigue and drowsiness which they feel as the effect of night walking and other practices which unfit them for the duties of the day." And again he asked, "Is there anything particular in the cases of Ruth, Hannah and Pegg, that they have been returned sick for several weeks together? Ruth I know is extremely deceitful; she has been aiming for some time past to get into the house, exempt from work; but if they are not made to do what their age and strength will enable them, it will be a bad example for others—none of whom would work if by pretexts they can avoid it."

PUNISHING THE SLAVES

Other causes than running away and death depleted the stock. One negro was taken by the State for some crime and executed, an allowance of sixty-nine pounds being made to his master. In 1766 an unruly negro was shipped to the West Indies (as was then the custom), Washington writing the captain of the vessel,—

> "With this letter comes a negro (Tom) which I beg the favor of you to sell in any of the islands you may go to, for whatever he will fetch, and bring me in return for him
> "One hhd of best molasses
> "One ditto of best rum
> "One barrel of lymes, if good and cheap
> "One pot of tamarinds, containing about 10 lbs.
> "Two small ditto of mixed sweetmeats, about 5 lbs. each.
> And the residue, much or little, in good old spirits. That this fellow is both a rogue and a runaway (tho' he was by no means remarkable for the former, and never practised the latter till of late) I shall not pretend to deny. But that he is exceeding healthy, strong, and good at the hoe, the whole neighborhood can testify, and particularly Mr. Johnson and his son, who have both had him under them as foreman of the gang; which gives me reason to hope he may with your good management sell well, if kept clean and trim'd up a little when offered for sale."

Another "misbehaving fellow" was shipped off in 1791, and was sold for "one pipe and Quarter Cask of wine from the West Indies." Sometimes only the threat of such riddance was used, as when an overseer complained of one slave, and his master replied, "I am very sorry that so likely a fellow as Matilda's Ben should addict himself to such courses as he is pursuing. If he should be guilty of any atrocious crime, that would affect his life, he might be given up to the civil authority for trial; but for such offences as most of his color are guilty of, you had better try further correction, accompanied with admonition and advice. The two latter sometimes succeed where the first has failed. He, his father and mother (who I dare say are his receivers) may be told in explicit language, that if a stop is not put to his rogueries and other villainies, by fair means and shortly, that I will ship him off (as I did Wagoner Jack) for the West Indies, where he will have no opportunity of playing such pranks as he is at present engaged in."

It is interesting to note, in connection with this conclusion, that "admonition and advice" were able to do what "correction" sometimes failed to achieve, that there is not a single order to whip, and that the above case, and that which follows, are the only known cases where punishment was approved. "The correction you gave Ben, for his assault on Sambo, was just and proper. It is my earnest desire that quarrels may be stopped or punishment of both parties follow, unless it shall appear *clearly*, that one only is to blame, and the other forced into [a quarrel] from self-defence." In one other instance Washington wrote, "If Isaac had his deserts he would receive a severe punishment for the house, tools and seasoned stuff, which has been burned by his carelessness." But instead of ordering the "deserts" he continued, "I wish you to inform him, that I sustain injury enough by their idleness; they need not add to it by their carelessness."

This is the more remarkable, because his slaves gave him constant annoyance by [what he considered to be] their wastefulness and sloth and dishonesty. Thus, "Paris has grown to be so lazy and self-willed" that his master does not know what to with him; "Doll at the Ferry must be taught to knit, and *made* to do a sufficient day's work of it—otherwise (if suffered to be idle) many more will walk in her steps;" "it is observed by the weekly reports, that the sewers make only six shirts a week, and the last week Carolina (without being sick) made only five. Mrs. Washington says their usual task was to make nine with shoulder straps and good sewing. Tell them therefore from me, that what *has* been done, *shall* be done;" "none I think call louder for [attention] than the smiths, who, from a variety of instances which fell within my own observation whilst I was at home, I take to be two very idle fellows. A daily account (which ought to be regularly) taken of their work, would alone go a great way towards checking their idleness." And the overseer was told to watch closely "the people who are at work with the gardener, some of whom I know to be as lazy and deceitful as any in the world (Sam particularly)."

Furthermore, the overseers were warned to "endeavor to make the Servants and Negroes take care of their cloathes;" to give them "a weekly allowance of Meat . . . because the annual one is not taken care of but either profusely used or stolen;" and to note "the delivery to and the application of nails by the carpenters, . . . [for] I cannot conceive how it is possible that 6000 twelve penny nails could be used in the corn house at the River Plantation; but of one thing I have no great doubt, and that is, if they can be applied to other uses, or converted into cash, rum or other things there will be no scruple in doing it.". . .

CONCERN FOR HIS SLAVES' WELL-BEING

Whatever his opinion of his slaves, Washington was a kind master. In one case he wrote a letter for one of them when the "fellow" was parted from his wife in the service of his master, and at another time he enclosed letters to a wife and to James's "del Toboso," for two of his servants, to save them postage. In reference to their rations he wrote, "whether this addition . . . is sufficient, I will not undertake to decide;—but in most explicit language I desire they may have plenty; for I will not have my feelings hurt with complaints of this sort, nor lye under the imputation of starving my negros, and thereby driving them to the necessity of thieving to supply the deficiency. To prevent waste or embezzlement is the only inducement to allowancing of them at all—for if, instead of a peck they could eat a bushel of meal a week fairly, and required it, I would not withhold or begrudge it them." At Christmas-time there are entries in his ledger for whiskey or rum for "the negroes," and towards the end of his life he ordered the overseer, "although others are getting out of the practice of using spirits at Harvest, yet, as my people have always been accustomed to it, a hogshead of Rum must be purchased; but I request at the same time, that it may be used sparingly."

A greater kindness of his was, in 1787, when he very much desired a negro mason offered for sale, yet directed his agent that "if he has a family, with which he is to be sold; or from whom he would reluctantly part, I decline the purchase; his feelings I would not be the means of hurting in the latter case, or *at any rate* be incumbered with the former.". . .

WILLIAM

A single one of these slaves deserves further notice. His body-servant "Billy" was purchased by Washington in 1768 for sixty-eight pounds and fifteen shillings, and was his constant companion during the war, even riding after his master at reviews; and this servant was so associated with the General that it was alleged in the preface to the "forged letters" that they had been captured by the British from "Billy," "an old servant of General Washington's." When Savage painted his well-known "family group," this was the one slave included in the picture. In 1784 Washington told his Philadelphia agent that "The mulatto fellow, William, who has been with me all the war, is attached (married he says) to one of his own color, a free woman, who during the war, was also of my family. She has been in an infirm condition for some time, and I had conceived that the connexion between them had ceased; but I am mistaken it seems; they are both applying to get her here, and tho' I never wished to see her more, I cannot refuse his request (if it can be complied with on reasonable terms) as he has served me faithfully for many years. After premising this much, I have to beg the favor of you to procure her a passage to Alexandria."

When acting as chain-bearer in 1785, while Washington was surveying a tract of land, William fell and broke his knee-pan, "which put a stop to my surveying; and with much difficulty I was able to get him to Abington, being obliged to get a sled to carry him on, as he could neither walk, stand or ride." From this injury Lee never quite recovered, yet he started to accompany his master to New York in 1789, only to give out on the road. He was left at Philadelphia, and [his secretary] Lear wrote to Washington's agent that "The President will thank you to propose it to Will to return to Mount Vernon when he can be removed for he cannot be of any service here, and perhaps will require a person to attend upon him constantly. If he should incline to return to Mount Vernon, you will be so kind as to have him sent in the first Vessel that sails for Alexandria after he can be moved with safety—but if he is still anxious to come on here the President would gratify him, altho' he will be troublesome—He has been an old and faithful Servant, this is enough for the President to gratify him in every reasonable wish."

By his will Washington gave Lee his "immediate freedom or if he should prefer it (on account of the accidents which have befallen him and which have rendered him incapable of walking or of any active employment) to remain in the situation he now is, it shall be optional in him to do so—In either case however I allow him an annuity of thirty dollars during his natural life which shall be independent of the victuals and *cloaths* he has been accustomed to receive; if he *chuses* the last alternative, but in full with his freedom, if he prefers the first, and this I give him as a testimony of my sense of his attachment to me and for his faithful services during the Revolutionary War."

Two small incidents connected with Washington's last illness are worth noting. The afternoon before the night he was taken ill, although he had himself been superintending his affairs on horseback in the storm most of the day, yet when his secretary "carried some letters to him to frank, intending to send them to the Post Office in the evening," Lear tells us "he franked the letters; but said the weather was too bad to send a servant up to the office that evening." Lear continues, "The General's servant, Christopher, attended his bed side & in the room, when he was sitting up, through his whole illness. . . . In the [last] afternoon the General observing that Christopher had been standing by his bed side for a long time—made a motion for him to sit in a chair which stood by the bed side."

WASHINGTON'S WILL

A clause in Washington's will directed that

"Upon the decease of my wife it is my will and desire that all the slaves which I hold in *my own right* shall receive their freedom—To emancipate them during her life, would, tho earnestly wished by me, be attended with such insuperable difficulties, on account of their intermixture of marriages with the Dower negroes as to excite the most painful sensations—if not disagreeable consequences from the latter, while both descriptions are in the occupancy of the same proprietor, it not being in my power under the tenure by which the dower Negroes are held to manumit them—And whereas among those who will receive freedom according to this devise there may be some who from old age, or bodily infirmities & others who on account of their infancy, that will be unable to support themselves, it is my will and desire that all who come under the first and second description shall be comfortably cloathed and fed by my heirs while they live and that such of the latter description as have no parents living, or if living are unable or unwilling to provide for them, shall be bound by the Court until they shall arrive at the age of twenty five years.... The negroes thus bound are (by their masters and mistresses) to be taught to read and write and to be brought up to some useful occupation."

In this connection Washington's sentiments on slavery as an institution may be glanced at. As early as 1784 he replied to [his friend the Marquis de] Lafayette, when told of a colonizing plan, "The scheme, my dear Marqs., which you propose as a precedent to encourage the emancipation of the black people of this Country from that state of Bondage in wch. they are held, is a striking evidence of the benevolence of your Heart. I shall be happy to join you in so laudable a work; but will defer going into a detail of the business, till I have the pleasure of seeing you." A year later, when [Methodist Bishop] Francis Asbury was spending a day in Mount Vernon, the clergyman asked his host if he thought it wise to sign a petition for the emancipation of slaves. Washington replied that it would not be proper for him, but added, "If the Maryland Assembly discusses the matter; I will address a letter to that body on the subject, as I have always approved of it."

When South Carolina refused to pass an act to end the slave-trade, he wrote to a friend in that State, "I must say that I lament the decision of your legislature upon the question of importing slaves after March 1793. I was in hopes that motives of policy as well as other good reasons, supported by the direful effects of slavery, which at this moment are presented, would have operated to produce a total prohibition of the importation of slaves, whenever the question came to be agitated in any State, that might be interested in the measure." For his own State he expressed the "wish from my soul that the Legislature of this State could see the policy of a gradual Abolition of Slavery; it would prev't much future mischief." And to a Pennsylvanian he expressed the sentiment, "I hope it will not be conceived from these observations, that it is my wish to hold the unhappy people, who are the subject of this letter, in slavery. I can only say, that there is not a man living, who wishes more sincerely than I do to see a plan adopted for the abolition of it; but there is only one proper and effectual mode by which it can be accomplished, and that is by legislative authority; and this, as far as my suffrage will go, shall never be wanting."

WASHINGTON'S OTHER EMPLOYEES

Washington by no means restricted himself to slave servitors. Early in life he took into his service John Alton at thirteen pounds per annum, and this white man served as his body-servant in the Braddock campaign, and Washington found in the march that "A most serious inconvenience attended me in my sickness, and that was the losing the use of my servant, for poor John Alton was taken about the same time that I was, and with nearly the same disorder, and was confined as long; so that we did not see each other for several days." As elsewhere noticed, Washington succeeded to the services of Braddock's body-servant, Thomas Bishop, on the death of the general, paying the man ten pounds a year. . . .

Of Washington's general treatment of the serving class a few facts can be gleaned. He told one of his overseers, in reference to the sub-overseers, that "to treat them civilly is no more than what all men are entitled to, but my advice to you is, to keep them at a proper distance; for they will grow upon familiarity, in proportion as you will sink in authority if you do not." To a housekeeper he promised "a warm, decent and comfortable room to herself, to lodge in, and will eat of the victuals of our Table, but not set at it, or at any time *with us* be her appearance what it may; for if this was *once admitted* no line satisfactory to either party, perhaps could be drawn thereafter."

Chapter 3
Military Leader

PEOPLE WHO MADE HISTORY

GEORGE WASHINGTON

Appointment as Commander

Douglas Southall Freeman

In early 1775, many Americans began to realize that a war with Britain over American independence was inevitable. In May, delegates from thirteen colonies met in Philadelphia for the Second Continental Congress. Their primary goal was the establishment of an army to defend the colonies against British intervention. Their mission was an urgent one—the British were occupying Boston, and Congress needed soldiers to surround the city to prevent the British from taking further control of the colonies.

    In the following selection, noted Washington biographer Douglas Southall Freeman tells how and why the delegates chose George Washington to lead the Continental army. Freeman points out that one reason Washington was named was that, until that time, most of those involved in the revolutionary cause had been from Massachusetts. Selecting the man from Virginia, the delegates thought, would result in both getting more backing from that powerful colony and showing colonial unity to the British and to the other American colonies. When made aware of the strong possibility that he would be named as commander in chief, Washington was not enthusiastic. Instead, he regretted being removed from his home, Mount Vernon, and he feared what failure might do to his reputation.

In the [plan] for raising the [army of "expert riflemen" to march to Boston], it was specified that when these troops reached Boston they should be employed as Light Infantry "under the command of the chief officer in that army." Correspondence of the Massachusetts Delegates had contained

Douglas Southall Freeman, *George Washington: A Biography. Volume Three: Planter and Patriot.* New York: Charles Scribner's Sons, 1951. Copyright © 1951 by Charles Scribner's Sons. Reproduced by permission.

warnings of a possible crumbling of the lines around Boston unless the troops there had assurance that the United Colonies would support them. Although the letters from New England did not so state in clear-cut words, it was becoming manifest that the retention of a sufficient force to confine the British to Boston depended in large part on assurance that all the Colonies would stand behind the men in Roxbury and around Cambridge. Action to this end had been postponed from week to week in the hope of winning to a strong, positive course of unanimous action the few Delegates who still clung to the hope that the final appeal to [England's] King [George III to move his troops out of Boston] would be answered favorably if the Colonies did not resort to common violence and defiant rebellion before they laid their petition at the foot of the throne. The majority were weary now of deferring to what they regarded as the illusion of this element of their membership. Necessity could not wait any longer on diplomacy. Americans must demonstrate by their acts what they so often had asserted—that the cause of Massachusetts was the cause of all. Compulsion was absolute. A leader of ability and character must be commissioned in the name of the United Colonies and must be sent to Boston to take command of troops paid and fed by "the continent" and reenforced promptly with volunteers from every province.

Such a leader must personify the unity of Americans, their character, their resolution, their devotion to the principles of liberty: Who should that leader be? Perhaps a majority of the New Englanders favored the selection of Artemas Ward, Commander-in-Chief of the Massachusetts troops in front of Boston. If, as some feared, Ward's health would not permit his continued service in the field, one or another of several general officers familiar with their own region was preferred by most of the Delegates from the Northeastern Colonies. John Adams, who increasingly was the spokesman of the best judgment of Massachusetts, thought it politic to name a man from a different part of America and thereby to dissipate the suspicion some were supposed to nurture that New Englanders wished to impose their will on the other Colonies. [Congressional delegates] Elbridge Gerry and Joseph Warren favored Charles Lee. If he was unacceptable because he had not been born in America, they looked with favor on "the beloved Colonel Washington."

Washington's Reaction

Washington of course had heard all of this and had known for days that he was being advocated by some Delegates. They regarded him as the most experienced of the younger soldiers, the member of Congress who had displayed in committee the greatest familiarity with military matters and, as far as they could ascertain, the best judgment. One after another had told him, in effect, "You are the man." Every such expression alarmed and depressed him. He enjoyed so much happiness in the life he had been leading at Mount Vernon that he could not think of exchanging it for army command otherwise than with dismay. He felt, also, that he did not have the training, and he did not believe he had the ability to discharge so overwhelming a task. His reluctance was manifest to his colleagues. He did not once "insinuate"—the verb was of his choosing—that he wished the command, and he did his utmost to restrain his friends from advocating his election.

Soon he had to face the possibility that in spite of wish and inclination, he might be subjected to so strong an appeal by Congress that he might be compelled to yield. On the 16th of May, he had written the Fairfax Committee [in Virginia] to name someone to serve in his stead, should a Virginia Convention be called in his absence, but he had inserted "pro tem" with reference to his substitute as if he felt sure he would return soon to Virginia. Now, because of the stronger prospect of a call to military duty for the Congress, he had [Virginia delegate] Edmund Pendleton draft a will for him; and in his letters to Martha, he avoided any mention of the probable time of his home-coming. As the pressure on him continued, he urged his friends to help him resist it and he probably prevailed upon Edmund Pendleton openly to oppose his election, but as the middle of June approached, he began to feel that destiny and nothing less than destiny, was shaping his course.

Nominated

On the 14th, Washington went to the Congress and listened to discussion of the number and type of troops that should be raised, a subject of liveliest interest to him. At length John Adams rose. In the eyes of those who believed reconciliation [with England] still possible, Adams was a convinced advocate of separation from Great Britain; but his reputation as a revolutionary did not weaken his position as perhaps the wisest and most influential representative of New England. He proceeded now to show the need of action to save the New England army in front of Boston. If it dissolved, said he, through despair or lack of supplies and ammunition, the organization of another force of like numbers would be extremely difficult. Before a new army could be collected, the British, no longer under siege, might march out of the city and spread desolation. The colonial forces already in service, Adams argued, must have heartening evidence that the whole of British North America was behind them; this could best be done by placing the army under the direction of a man who represented the Congress and the continent.

Washington of course approved without interrupting to say so. Then he heard Adams admit that this might not be the proper time to nominate a General, and that the choice of a particular individual probably was going to be the question that presented the largest difficulty. For his part, Adams went on, he did not hesitate to say that he had one person in mind, one only. At the words [Massachusetts delegate] John Hancock, who was in the chair, showed manifest pleasure, as if he were certain Adams was about to call his name. Washington, fearing otherwise, felt embarrassment creep over him. Adams did not prolong the suspense: The commander he had in mind, he said, was a gentleman from Virginia. On the instant John Hancock's expression changed: his disappointment was beyond concealment; the tightening of his lips and the flash of his eye showed that he felt Adams had betrayed his expectations. Adams observed this but went straight on: he referred, he said, to one whose skill and experience as an officer, whose independent fortune . . . With that, Washington bolted for the adjoining library: Adams could be talking of no other than of him.

He went out; he stayed out; but after adjournment, he of course was told of what happened: John Adams paid high tribute to Washington and predicted that the choice of the Virginian would be approved by "all America" and would be a means of uniting the efforts of the Colonies more cordially than would be possible under any other leader. Somewhat to John Adams's surprise and to the deepened mortification of John Hancock in the chair, Samuel Adams [another delegate from Massachusetts] seconded his cousin's recommendation. Mild dissent was immediate, though not general. Several members reasserted the familiar argument that as the whole of the army came from New England and had succeeded in confining the British in Boston, the men were entitled to a General of their own. In this view, Edmund Pendleton concurred. All the Delegates who expressed this opinion were careful to state that their objection was not to Washington personally but to the employment of any other commander than one who was known to the men and had shared their hardships.

The debate ended that day without any decision, but now that Washington's name had been proposed on the floor, those who advocated him did not hesitate in seeking to convert their friends. Southerners who cherished regional pride but had deferred to New England needed to hear no other argument than that the choice of Washington would be acceptable to Massachusetts and Connecticut; men from the threatened Colonies had no answer to those of their neighbors who told them the election of Washington was politically expedient, because it would assure full Southern support of the struggle against the British. No advocate of Washington's preferment showed any disposition at the outset, to attribute superlative military qualities to him. The Virginian veteran was admired; he was accounted, able and experienced; he was of unchallenged character and rectitude; reliance could be placed on his sound judgment and on his wide acquaintance with business affairs. Eliphalet Dyer probably spoke the mind of numerous Delegates when he said of Washington: "He is a gentleman highly esteemed by those acquainted with him, though I don't believe, as to his military and real service, he knows more than some of ours . . ." Expediency prevailed even where the impression of Washington's martial ability did not convince some of the members that he was preeminently the man to head the army. Within a few hours after Adams spoke, the opposition to Washington evaporated.

UNANIMOUSLY CHOSEN

On Thursday, June 15, 1775, when the discussion was resumed in Congress, everything pointed to the selection of Washington. He stayed away and knew nothing of the deliberations until, about dinner time, the Delegates left the hall and, as they met him, shook his hand, congratulated him, greeted him as "General," and told him how, when the Committee of the Whole finished its debate and went through the formality of reporting, Congress resolved "that a General be appointed to command all the continental forces, raised, or to be raised, for the defence of American liberty." Then Thomas Johnson of Maryland rose to his feet and proposed Washington. No other name was put forward; election was unanimous; adjournment followed almost immediately.

Washington was overwhelmed, but he had so many duties to discharge that he did not have time that afternoon to think at length of the immense task he had taken upon himself. Following dinner at Burns's [Tavern] "in the fields," he had to attend a meeting of the committee to draft rules and regulations for the government of the army. Some hours had to be found during the evening, also, for the preparation of a reply to the formal notification he was to expect the next day. In this labor he probably had the aid of Edmund Pendleton, who wrote more readily than Washington did, but he doubtless specified that Pendleton make it plain he did not seek the command and did not feel qualified for it. With all his old anxiety to avoid censure, Washington wanted it understood, also, that he did not accept the position for the pay of $500 a month that Congress had attached. Were he to take the salary, critics would complain of the amount and would say he wanted to make money rather than to serve his country. If he waived all pay and failed later, he could not be accused of having acted from mercenary motives, and, if he won, he would have the warmer praise and gratitude because he had no monetary compensation.

ACCEPTANCE

The answer to Congress was shaped accordingly and, no doubt, was in Washington's pocket when, the next day, he walked to the State House for the ceremonies. John Hancock, President of the Congress, by this time had recovered somewhat from his disappointment over his failure to receive the command and he made the best of the vote that left him in the chair when he had thought of himself, perhaps, as being addressed from the chair. Solemnly Hancock began: The President had the order of Congress to inform George Washington, Esq., of the unanimous vote in choosing him to be General and Commander-in-Chief of the forces raised and to be raised in defence of American liberty. The Congress hoped the gentleman would accept.

Washington bowed, took out the paper and read:

> Mr. President: Tho' I am truly sensible of the high Honour done me in this Appointment, yet I feel great distress from a

consciousness that my abilities and Military experience may not be equal to the extensive and important Trust: However, as the Congress desires I will enter upon the momentous duty, and exert every power I Possess In their Service for the Support of the glorious Cause: I beg they will accept my most cordial thanks for this distinguished testimony of their Approbation.

But lest some unlucky event should happen unfavourable to my reputation, I beg it may be remembered by every Gentn. in the room, that I this day declare with the utmost sincerity, I do not think my self equal to the Command I am honoured with.

As to pay, Sir, I beg leave to Assure the Congress that as no pecuniary consideration could have tempted me to have accepted this Arduous employment [at the expence of my domestt, ease and happiness] I do not wish to make any profit from it: I will keep an exact Account of my expences; those I doubt not they will discharge and that is all I desire.

There was applause, no doubt, and widely voiced gratification that he was willing to serve his country without pay, but, of course, so plain and personal an answer made no deep-cutting impression on men accustomed to eloquence in every utterance on the floor. With no more ado, Congress agreed to name a committee of three to draft a commission and formal instructions for the General; and then, after some discussion of Indian relations in New York, the Congress decided that it later would choose two Major Generals, five Brigadiers and various staff officers whose pay was fixed forthwith. Next—as if deliberately exhibiting the range of the perplexities with which it wrestled—Congress debated the means whereby the troops in New York could be reenforced. At the end of a long session, Washington went to dine with Dr. Thomas Cadwalader.

The Commission

The next day, Washington's commission was reported by the committee—Richard Henry Lee, Edward Rutledge and John Adams—who had framed it. The paper ran in the name of "The Delegates of the United Colonies," each of which was specified. It proceeded to assign him the command of all the forces for the defence of American liberty and for repelling invasion; "and you are hereby vested with full power and authority to act as you shall think for the good and welfare of the service." Obedience and diligence were enjoined on Washington's subordinates; he was himself exhorted to "cause discipline and order to be observed in the army," to see that the soldiers were exercised, and to provide them "with all convenient necessities." In every particular, he was to regulate his conduct "by the rules and discipline of war ... and punctually to observe such orders and directions, from time to time, as you shall receive from this, or a future Congress of these United Colonies, or committee of Congress." When they had approved this document, the members unanimously declared in a vigorous resolution that "they [would] maintain and assist him, and adhere to him, the said George Washington, Esq., with their lives and fortunes in the same cause."

All this was as well done as members knew how to do it and it could not be otherwise than acceptable to Washington. If his experience as a soldier made him realize that it would be difficult for a committee of Congress to direct a military campaign, his common sense told him there was at the time no source of authority other than Congress, which had to act through committees. Besides, his own troubles during the French and Indian War had not been with members of the General Assembly but with the Governor, Robert Dinwiddie. In the best of circumstances, with the most sympathetic consideration by the wisest of committees, the morrow of organization, discipline, supply, training, combat and all the contingency of war would be dark, dark, dark! Washington knew that and he agonized over it. As he talked with [Virginia delegate] Patrick Henry of his lack of training for the task assigned him, the new General had tears in his eyes. "Remember, Mr. Henry," he said, "what I now tell you: from the day I enter upon the command of the American armies, I date my fall, and the ruin of my reputation." His friends did not take so pessimistic a view but they sympathized. At a dinner given Washington by some of the leaders at a tavern on the Schuylkill [River] below the city, the first toast was to "The Commander-in-Chief of the American Armies." [Patriot Dr.] Benjamin Rush recorded later: "General Washington rose from his seat, and with some confusion thanked the company for the honor they did him. The whole company instantly rose and drank the toast standing. This scene, so unexpected, was a solemn one. A silence followed it, as if every heart was penetrated with the awful but great events which were to follow the use of the sword of liberty which had been put into General Washington's hands by the unanimous voice of his country."

Assessing Washington's Strategy and Leadership

John E. Ferling

> History professor John E. Ferling analyzes Washington's role as commander in chief of the Continental army in this reading. In doing so, Ferling points out not only Washington's positive leadership qualities and acts of bravery but also his weaknesses. He compares what Washington did after conferring with his officers to what he did when he acted on his own, and concludes that Washington preferred an aggressive, offensive stance over a conservative, defensive one—despite often adopting the latter to save his army. Furthermore, Ferling agrees with many other historians that Washington's concern for his reputation and his drive to succeed, as well as his firm belief in American independence, were important elements in his strategies. Ferling teaches at the State University of West Georgia and has written extensively on early America.

What manner of military commander was General Washington? Moreover, what was the relationship between Washington's character and his leadership? Was he the man that [Washington's second-in-command General] Charles Lee saw, a "puffed up charlatan . . . extremely prodigal of other men's blood and a great oeconomist of his own." Was he the man that one of his young officers saw, the "last stage of perfection to which human nature is capable of attaining." Or, with more information and greater detachment, can the historian see still a different Washington?

In most respects it is difficult to imagine Washington pursuing alternative military strategies. Not only did his army's tactics generally conform to the martial wisdom of the age,

John E. Ferling, *The First of Men: A Life of George Washington.* Knoxville: The University of Tennessee Press, 1988. Copyright © 1988 by The University of Tennessee Press. Reproduced by permission of The University of Tennessee Press.

his decisions normally reflected the collective wisdom of his general officers as expressed in the frequent councils of war. Yet the manner in which he longed to act can be revealing, as can be those episodes when he shook loose of the counsel of his officers and struck out on his own path. Always Washington seemed to view a conservative, defensive strategy with disdain. During the siege of Boston he yearned to assail [British General William] Howe. He fretted over losing the "esteem of mankind" if he remained inactive, and even though he acknowledged that to attack might be "to undertake more than could be warranted by prudence," he nevertheless sought to secure his officers' backing for an assault. Washington similarly exhibited a penchant for standing and fighting on Long Island and Manhattan, and once again in the contest for Fort Washington. Only at Long Island, where congressional pressure probably hectored Washington into a duel with the British and Hessian forces, did he lack a free hand; in the other instances there were compelling reasons to have retreated and fought a "war of posts," a strategy which he had articulated but infrequently pursued. In the year and a half that followed the debacle at Fort Washington, he again and again lashed out at his adversary, making dangerous assaults at Trenton and Princeton, at Germantown and Monmouth. Once again, safer, more cautious courses might have been embraced, yet he always seemed to equate retreat with personal weakness. He seemed mesmerized by the "honor of making a brave defense," by which, curiously, he meant resolutely fighting his foe in a pitched battle. On the other hand, he feared he would be subject to "reproach" if he adopted a [cautious] strategy. "I see the impossibility of serving with reputation," he remarked in frustration, often speaking of the certainty that he would "lose my Character" in this war, sometimes seeming to equate the destruction of his reputation with the policy of inaction which circumstances often made unavoidable. Thus to preserve his honor he leaned toward defiant action, toward bold and vigorous conduct, and when he succeeded in the pursuit of a daring and grandiose plan his response was relief, not just for the victory but because "my reputation stands firm."

His conduct in this war was not uncharacteristic. This was the same man who had stood at Fort Necessity [in the French and Indian War], who repeatedly had urged an assault on Fort Duquesne, who had carped incessantly at the "string of forts" concept. Always he longed to execute a brilliant stroke, always he thought in terms of the grand and audacious gesture. To imagine George Washington thinking any other way is not only to fail to understand the man but to fail to comprehend that it was his inescapable quest for esteem that governed and dictated the life-and-death choices he made.

RELATIONS WITH HIS OFFICERS

What of his relations with his principal officers? When Charles Lee remarked that Washington was a "dark designing" man bent upon the destruction of every man whom he considered to be a threat to his station, he may have come closer to the truth than most historians have cared to admit. Washington perhaps put it most succinctly. While he sought talent and dedication in his officers, he also wanted "attachment" and the "purest affection" from those about him. He valued the sort of behavior perhaps best exemplified by [French officer Marquis de] Lafayette, who acted, in the commander's opinion, "upon very different principles" from those of men like Lee and [General Horatio] Gates. But one did not have to be servile to win Washington's support. Lafayette and [Washington's aid, Joseph] Reed, and, one suspects, [General Nathaniel] Greene and probably [Alexander] Hamilton, among others, were not above playing that role. A man like [General Benedict] Arnold was not so inclined, however, and Washington respected him. Washington's relationships with his general officers worked on several levels. Some men provided the adoration and support that he required. Some officers—Lafayette and Arnold, and probably, [General John] Sullivan, Hamilton, and Reed—served almost as models, embodying the virtues that Washington longed to manifest, whether it was intelligence, education, urbanity, eloquence, courage, or daring. But finally, and most importantly, General Washington had to be in total control, or, at least, he needed to believe that his powers of control were in no way jeopardized. From the very outset his control over Ward, for example, was questionable, and Washington immediately was cool, even hostile, toward him. When he discovered that Reed had questioned his judgment, he turned implacably cold. When he grew to believe that his control of Gates and Lee had diminished, he ruthlessly turned against them.

Washington's Personality

Washington's personality and temperament were that of a self-centered and self-absorbed man, one who since youth had exhibited a fragile self-esteem. His need for admiration and affirmation was considerable, for only thus could his nagging doubts about his capabilities and his competence be overcome. Lest his imagined inadequacies be discovered, he adopted an aloof and formal manner. The result was that he had no friends in the real sense of the word, and he was at ease with—and closest to—only those who accommodated his needs, principally aspiring young men who basked in his presence and women who, in the custom of the times, treated him with deference. His attitude was a prescription for judging all men as either threatening or amicable.

Many contemporaries seemed unable to understand Washington. Some observers ascribed almost superhuman virtues to him, and they fretted over America's fate should his presence be lost. He came to be regarded as the indispensable man of the War of Independence, the one person upon whom the success—indeed, the very continuation—of the war depended. Washington's absence would lead to "the ruin of our Cause," the president of Congress, Henry Laurens, told his son, whereas the commander's "magnanimity, his patience, will save the Country. . . ." Lafayette, more characteristically, expressed the same thoughts directly to Washington. If "you were lost for America, there is nobody who could keep the army and the Revolution [intact] for six months." But was General Washington truly the linchpin of the Revolution?

Washington's Symbolic Value

Washington's continued presence as commander of the Continental army was important, if only for symbolic reasons. By 1778, as Laurens and Lafayette had said, Washington already had come to symbolize the Revolution. To a degree that was unrivaled, Washington continued to embody those noble traits that had comprised the Revolutionary outlook at the outset of the war. His honesty, courage, and selfless service seemed beyond question, and even after three years as the commander of the Continental army, he continued to be seen, not as a hardened soldier, but as a trustworthy civilian who had been called to arms. In addition, it was crucial for the success of the war effort that no attempt be made to remove Washington from command. Had Congress deposed Washington in 1777 or 1778—or had that body even attempted to remove him—the act surely would have been seen as venal and narrowly factious, indeed as an antirevolutionary blow. Any move against Washington would have resulted in an atmosphere of ill-feeling and uncertainty that would surely have jeopardized the war effort.

But was Washington's continued presence essential only for symbolic and political reasons? The Washington who had ridden to Cambridge to assume command was a man of many talents. His earlier soldiering had helped prepare him for the administrative responsibilities he would bear, no small matter when it is remembered that the management of the military machine was a constant concern, whereas the army actually was thrust into battlefield situations only infrequently. Washington's years as a Virginia soldier also provided him with valuable experience in dealing with politicians, teaching him how to get his way, when to push and when it was expedient to let matters lie. He was wise enough not to ally himself with one faction in Congress, and he knew that it would be counterproductive to appeal over that body's head to the general public. He additionally knew better than to revert to the whining, petulant behavior that had tarnished his relationship with [Virginia Governor Robert] Dinwiddie. . . . Since boyhood Washington had been a careful student of behavior, watching to see what fashion dictated, then striving to shape his own conduct to conform. By the war years his plain, sober, vigilant, hard-working life style was too deeply rooted in his temperament to have been superficial or contrived. Even so, he understood the public temper in a way that leaders such as [Major General Philip] Schuyler or Lee could never have fathomed, and that intuitive genius led him to disdain a salary, to jettison certain pastimes—hunting and gaming, for instance—that long had been his habit as a Virginia planter, and scrupulously to avoid the public appearance of indulgences that smacked of intemperance or indifference toward his responsibilities.

On the other hand, there was little in Washington's background to prepare him for the strategic and tactical decisions he would have to make, and he was even more a greenhorn when it came to commanding under fire. As a Virginia soldier he never had commanded more than a thousand men, nor had he ever led his men against a professional European army. His combat experience consisted of three engagements: the ten-minute ambush of Jumonville [in the French and Indian War], and the one-day fights at Fort Necessity and alongside Braddock on the Monongahela.

LUCK PLAYED A PART

Nevertheless, by 1778 he had survived—and succeeded—on the battlefield. In part, Washington's achievements were due to luck. Four times in 1776 his inexperience, his penchant for standing and fighting, and his early inability to resist the demands of powerful politicians, led him into nearly fatal traps. On Long Island, at Manhattan, at Fort Washington, and when [British General] Cornwallis had him pinioned between the Assunpink and the Delaware [Rivers], Washington seemingly had blundered into fighting in areas from which retreat would be difficult, perhaps impossible. But only at Fort Washington did he suffer for his errors. From the other traps he escaped, largely through fortuitous occurrences: sudden rainstorms, unanticipated fog, felicitous nightfalls that seemed to come on when he most needed them, although Washington was also sufficiently resourceful to seize the good fortune that fate offered. Between 1775 and 1778, however, his best stroke of luck was not only to have had an adversary such as the indolent, cautious Howe, but to have been fighting an enemy that entered the conflict unprepared for the kind of war this was certain to be, a struggle that would require a huge commitment of manpower, men that would have to be supplied against almost insurmountable obstacles.

A DRIVE TO WIN

But Washington's accomplishments transcended luck. Essentially he understood this struggle. He knew what could win the war, as well as what might lose it. He could be cautious, resorting to ... tactics that ran counter to his grain, retreating to preserve his army for another day, all the while protracting the conflict, buying time for war weariness to set in and eat away at Britain, time that would eventually induce America's friends in Europe to intervene. But he could be— he longed to be—unpredictably daring as well. At Dorchester Heights [in Massachusetts] and again at Trenton and Princeton [in New Jersey], at Germantown [in Pennsylvania] and still again at Monmouth [in New Jersey], he lashed out in hazardous undertakings that so bore the imprint of his militant, activist, venturesome character that it is difficult to conceive of many other high American officers even contemplating such steps. Indeed, he alone seems to have planned the Trenton-Princeton operations; he had to nudge his general officers repeatedly to gain their consent to act at Dorchester; he obtained their approval for the strike at Germantown through what amounted to outright trickery; and he acted at Monmouth despite almost everyone's advice to remain inert. It was his nature to think in grandiose terms and to act in a daring manner. In fact, he was driven toward this behavior, for to act otherwise was to raise the specter of inadequacy and self-contempt. It was his good fortune to escape the blunders into which his temperament might have led him, but it was due to these same compelling drives that he had reaped for America its greatest victories in this war.

A Historic Decision

While Washington stated several times during his lifetime that he was not comfortable with the idea of slavery, many historians agree that he was racist, as most aristocrats were during his time. His belief that African Americans were inferior influenced him not only on his plantations but also as he led the Continental army. Here, historian Fritz Hirschfeld explains the events that led up to Washington's decision to allow African Americans into the army.

[Immediately after he began to serve as commander in chief of the Continental army,] Washington was confronted with a novel and perplexing situation. Before his arrival, Massachusetts authorities had permitted the enlistment of black volunteers into the state militia. Now, the additional recruitment of African Americans—both free and slave—implied that the bondsmen among them would have to be given their freedom and that all African Americans, while serving in the military, would be eligible for rights and privileges equivalent to those enjoyed by whites. Washington was not prepared to grant these concessions to a race he had always deemed inferior. Indeed, he and his subordinate commanders, after duly debating the issue at a council of war in Cambridge on October 8, 1775, opted unanimously to keep the army white and to bar African Americans from being recruited or from volunteering. Only a surprise tactical move by the enemy forced Washington to re-

NOT ALWAYS ENDEARING

The insecurities that led Washington to his quest for self-esteem, as well as to his venturesome proclivities, his remoteness, and his suspicious, distrusting nature were not always endearing qualities. Nor did they always serve him well. His search for self cohesion led him into clashes with good general officers, perhaps even to the ruination of men like Ward and Lee; it prompted him to tolerate an essential mediocrity such as Sullivan, while blinding him to the inexperience and failures of a lad like Lafayette, and it almost certainly influenced his negative reaction to the plan to invade Canada, a strategy with considerable potential merit. But at the same time his makeup helped him find daring and capable officers like Arnold and [Anthony] Wayne and [Henry] Knox. Indeed, qualities that might have been deleterious in almost any other pursuit became virtues when ex-

consider this exclusionary policy.

Lord Dunmore, the last royal governor of Virginia, in an effort to bolster his Tory forces at the expense of the rebellious American slaveholders, announced in November 1775 that the British would free all slaves who were prepared to take up arms against their former masters. With approximately five hundred thousand slaves living within the borders of the thirteen colonies, the British offer of emancipation was something Washington could not afford to ignore. He promptly countered by reversing himself and rescinding most of his earlier discriminatory pronouncements. African Americans were now officially allowed to enroll in the Continental army.

With that historic decision, whether or not he realized at the time its far-reaching implications, and whatever face-saving rationalizations he put forward to justify his turnabout, Washington became directly responsible for setting in motion a momentous and irreversible progression of events. African American soldiers—carrying weapons, trained in the art of war, and seasoned in combat—would no longer be considered meek and submissive slaves; nor would they be satisfied to return to a condition of abject servitude after the war had ended. Military service was the first major step taken after almost 150 years of slavery to legitimatize the enslaved Americans' long march toward full equality with white Americans.

Fritz Hirschfeld, *George Washington and Slavery: A Documentary Portrayal.* Columbia: University of Missouri Press, 1997.

ercised by the commander of an army, for his character steeled him for difficult decisions, drove him to action, and even isolated him, contributing to his larger-than-life aura.

Lee and Hamilton saw the dark side of George Washington. But those who esteemed this man also were correct, for he exhibited many admirable qualities. He combined courage with diligence. The first came naturally, but industry and perseverence were traits that he had been compelled to learn in his long ascent from [his boyhood at] Ferry Farm [in Virginia]. . . .

Now, an amateur soldier confronted by a professional adversary, Washington once again called upon those strategies that always had served him so well. To compensate for his inexperience he studiously read the best military manuals. Realizing his own inadequacies, he sought and listened to advice. He worked hard, putting in one long day after another. He learned from his mistakes, and, above all, he learned the folly of indecision.

A Beloved Leader

Washington's greatest asset, a French officer once noted, was his faculty for understanding "the art of making himself beloved." Not only did Washington seem untainted by the corruptibility that his countrymen perceived as the inevitable accompaniment of royalty, but, even more, his actions seemed to manifest the greatest virtues of republicanism. Again, his refusal of a salary, his eschewing of a sumptuous lifestyle, his sacrifice in the public cause, his willingness as commander to abide by the general will of his civilian governors, his very embodiment of what John Adams once called the "great, manly, warlike virtues" captured the popular imagination. He knew what was expected of him. His office, he once said, required that he behave with "the strictest rectitude, and most scrupulous exactness." As usual in such matters he was correct. Perhaps, as some scholars have suggested, his grasp of what was required of him arose from some innate genius. Yet Washington was a man well practiced in the art of understanding others. At the core of his being lay the compelling drive that led to his search for self-enhancement, and all his life Washington had sought to learn the techniques that would facilitate his yearnings.

Perhaps it would have been preferable for another man to have commanded the Continental army, but few contemporaries—and still fewer historians—would have hazarded that opinion. To swap Washington for an elderly "Artemas" Ward, an indolent Schuyler, a rustic [Israel] Putnam, a temperamental and acerbic Lee hardly seems a bargain. What if Gates had supplanted Washington? He was ambitious, political, vain, and manipulative, but so was Washington. Gates also was more experienced militarily; he too was a good administrator, his compassion for his men was at least equal to that of Washington, and his commitment to the principles of the Revolution was above question. Thus, he was a reasonable candidate for the job, though we cannot know how Gates would have performed as the commander of the Continental army any more than we can know how Washington would have acted had he initially been appointed to serve under Gates.

By 1778, Washington had lived up to his countrymen's expectations, and by 1778 he had come to symbolize the Revolution, embodying the republican virtues of courage and selfless public service. On the other hand, his generalship was laudatory, but not brilliant. While his leadership had resulted in one extraordinary triumph (Trenton-Princeton), as well as one estimable maneuver that produced an apparent victory (Dorchester Heights), he was also largely responsible for one crushing defeat (Fort Washington [in New York]). His daring almost led to another sensational victory at Germantown, but by the same token his risk-taking nearly had resulted in losses both in the New York and the Monmouth engagements, and his shoddy attention to military intelligence contributed to his army's losses at Brandywine [in Pennsylvania].

By 1778, therefore, it is difficult to disagree with John Adams's assessment. The Revolution was too big to hang on the performance of one man, he had told [the patriot] Dr. [Benjamin] Rush. Washington's contribution to the war effort were obvious and crucial, but Adams was correct to suggest that success or failure hinged on many men and many variables. Moreover, given his own genius at understanding the events of his time, Adams realized what many have been unable to accept: through the summer of 1778 Britain itself was more responsible for its own military woes than was any American leader.

Washington the Spymaster

Thomas Fleming

The use of espionage, or spying, has been a part of military strategy for thousands of years. And while today espionage usually relies on complicated technology, in Washington's era it was done through letters, codes, invisible ink, and eavesdropping. When Washington decided to prolong the Revolutionary War with the goal of weakening the British commitment over a long period of time, he turned to the use of espionage. By using spies to infiltrate the British army and discover their plans, Washington was able to frustrate some of their efforts. In this reading, author and historian Thomas Fleming describes how spies were used by both Washington and his officers as well as by the British.

George Washington a master of espionage? It is commonly understood that without the Commander in Chief's quick mind and cool judgment the American Revolution would have almost certainly expired in 1776. It is less well known that his brilliance extended to overseeing, directly and indirectly, extensive and very sophisticated intelligence activities against the British.

Washington had wanted to be a soldier almost from the cradle and seems to have acquired the ability to think in military terms virtually by instinct. In the chaos of mid-1776, with half his army deserting and the other half in a funk and all his generals rattled, he kept his head and reversed his strategy. The Americans had started with the idea that a general action, as an all-out battle was called, could end the conflict overnight, trusting that their superior numbers would overwhelm the presumably small army the British could afford to send to our shores. But the British sent a very big, well-trained army, which routed the Americans in the

Thomas Fleming, "George Washington, Spymaster," *American Heritage*, vol. 51, February/March 2000. Copyright © 2000 by American Heritage Publishing Company. Reproduced by permission.

first several battles in New York. Washington sat down in his tent on Harlem Heights and informed the Continental Congress that he was going to fight an entirely different war. From now on, he wrote, he would "avoid a general action." Instead he would "protract the war."

In his 1975 study of Washington's generalship, *The Way of the Fox*, Lt. Col. Dave Richard Palmer has called this reversal "a masterpiece of strategic thought, a brilliant blueprint permitting a weak force to combat a powerful opponent." It soon became apparent that for the blueprint to be followed, Washington would have to know what the British were planning to do, and he would have to be able to prevent them from finding out what he was doing. In short, espionage was built into the system.

Washington had been acquainted with British colonial officials and generals and colonels since his early youth, and he knew how intricately espionage was woven into the entire British military and political enterprise. Any Englishman's mail could be opened and read if a secretary of state requested it. Throughout Europe every British embassy had its intelligence network.

Thus Washington was not entirely surprised to discover, shortly after he took command of the American army in 1775, that his surgeon general, Dr. Benjamin Church, was telling the British everything that went on in the American camp at Cambridge, Massachusetts. He was surprised to find out, not long after he had transferred his operations to New York in the spring of 1776, that one of his Life Guard, a soldier named Thomas Hickey, was rumored to be involved in a plot to kill him.

By that time Washington had pulled off his own opening gambit in a form of intelligence at which he soon displayed something close to genius: disinformation. Shortly after he took command in Cambridge, he asked someone how much powder the embryo American army had in reserve. Everyone thought it had three hundred barrels, but a check of the Cambridge magazine revealed most of that had been fired away at Bunker Hill. There were only thirty-six barrels—fewer than nine rounds per man. For half an hour, according to one witness, Washington was too stunned to speak. But he recovered and sent people into British-held Boston to spread the story that he had eighteen hundred barrels, and he spread the same rumor throughout the American camp.

NATHAN HALE IN NEW YORK

In chaotic New York, grappling with a large and aggressive British army, deserting militia, and an inapplicable strategy, Washington temporarily lost control of the intelligence situation. That explains the dolorous failure of Capt. Nathan Hale's mission in September 1776. Hale, sent to gather information behind British lines, was doomed almost from the moment he volunteered. He had little or no contact with the American high command, no training as a spy, no disguise worthy of the name, and an amorphous mission: to find out whatever he could wherever he went.

There is little evidence that Washington was even aware of Hale's existence. He was involved in something far more serious: figuring out how to burn down New York City in order to deprive the British of their winter quarters, despite orders from the Continental Congress strictly forbidding him to harm the place. He looked the other way while members of Hale's regiment slipped into the city; they were experts at starting conflagrations thanks to a tour of duty on fire ships—vessels carrying explosives to burn enemy craft—on the Hudson.

On September 21, a third of New York went up in flames. The timing was disastrous for Hale, who was captured the very same day. Anyone with a Connecticut accent became highly suspect, and the British caught several incendiaries and hanged them on the spot. They gave Hale the same treatment: no trial, just a swift, humiliating death. Hale's friends were so mortified by his fate, which they considered shameful, that no one mentioned his now-famous farewell speech for another fifty years. Then an old man told his daughter about it, and Yale College, seeking Revolutionary War heroes among its graduates, quickly immortalized him.

Washington never said a word about Hale. His only intelligence comment at the time concerned New York. The fire had destroyed Trinity Church and about six hundred houses, causing no little discomfort for the British and the thousands of Loyalist refugees who had crowded into the city. In a letter, Washington remarked that "Providence, or some good honest fellow, has done more for us than we were disposed to do for ourselves."

One of Hale's best friends, Maj. Benjamin Tallmadge, never got over his death. He probably talked about it to Washington, who assured him that once they got the protracted war under control, all espionage would be handled from Army headquarters, and no spy's life would be wasted the way Hale's had been.

JOHN HONEYMAN AT TRENTON

Surviving long enough to fight an extended conflict was no small matter. In the weeks after Hale's death, disaster after disaster befell the American army. Washington was forced to abandon first New York and then New Jersey. On the other side of the Delaware, with only the shadow of an army left to him, he issued orders in December 1776 to all his generals to find "some person who can be engaged to cross the river as a spy" and added that "expense must not be spared" in securing a volunteer.

He also rushed a letter to Robert Morris, the financier of the Revolution, asking for hard money to "pay a certain set of people who are of particular use to us." He meant spies, and he had no illusion that any spy would risk hanging for the paper money the Continental Congress was printing. Morris sent from Philadelphia two canvas bags filled with what hard cash he could scrape together on an hour's notice: 410 Spanish dollars, 2 English crowns, 10 shillings, and 2 sixpence.

The search soon turned up a former British soldier named John Honeyman, who was living in nearby Griggstown, New Jersey. On Washington's orders Honeyman rediscovered his loyalty to the king and began selling cattle to several British garrisons along the Delaware. He had no trouble gaining the confidence of Col. Johann Rail, who was in command of three German regiments in Trenton. Honeyman listened admiringly as Rail described his heroic role in the fighting around New York and agreed with him that the Americans were hopeless soldiers.

On December 22, 1776, having spent about a week in Trenton, Honeyman wandered into the countryside, supposedly in search of cattle, and got himself captured by an American patrol and hustled to Washington's headquarters. There he was publicly denounced by the Commander in Chief as a "notorious" turncoat. Washington insisted on interrogating him personally and said he would give the traitor a chance to save his skin if he recanted his loyalty to the Crown.

A half-hour later the general ordered his aides to throw Honeyman into the guardhouse. Tomorrow morning, he stated, the Tory would be hanged. That night Honeyman escaped from the guardhouse with a key supplied by Washington and dashed past American sentries, who fired on him. Sometime on December 24 he turned up in Trenton and told Colonel Rail the story of his narrow escape.

The German naturally wanted to know what Honeyman had seen in Washington's camp, and the spy assured him that the Americans were falling apart. They were half-naked and freezing, and they lacked the food and basic equipment, such as shoes, to make a winter march. Colonel Rail, delighted, prepared to celebrate Christmas with no military worries to interrupt the feasting and drinking that were traditional in his country. He never dreamed that Honeyman had given Washington a professional soldier's detailed description of the routine of the Trenton garrison, the location of the picket guards, and everything else an assaulting force would need to know.

At dawn on December 26 Washington's ragged Continentals charged through swirling snow and sleet to kill the besotted Colonel Rail and capture most of his troops. New Jersey had been on the brink of surrender; now local patriots began shooting up British patrols, and the rest of the country, in the words of a Briton in Virginia, "went liberty mad again."

SPIES AND THEIR TECHNIQUES

Washington set up a winter camp in Morristown and went to work organizing American intelligence. He made Tallmadge his second-in-command, though he was ostensibly still a major in the 2d Continental Dragoons. That regiment was stationed in outposts all around the perimeter of British-held New York, and Tallmadge visited these units regularly, supposedly to make sure that all was in order but actually working as a patient spider setting up spy networks inside the British lines. His methods, thanks to Washington's tutelage, could not have been more sophisticated. He equipped his spies with cipher codes, invisible ink, and aliases that concealed their real identities. The invisible ink, which the Americans called "the stain," had been invented by Dr. James Jay, a brother of the prominent patriot John Jay, living in England. It was always in short supply.

Two of the most important American agents operating inside British-held New York were Robert Townsend, a Quaker merchant, and Abraham Woodhull, a Setauket, Long Island, farmer. Their code names were Culper Jr. and Culper Sr. As a cover, Townsend wrote violently Loyalist articles for the *New York Royal Gazette;* this enabled him to pick up information from British officers and their mistresses, and he sent it on to Woodhull via a courier named Austin Roe.

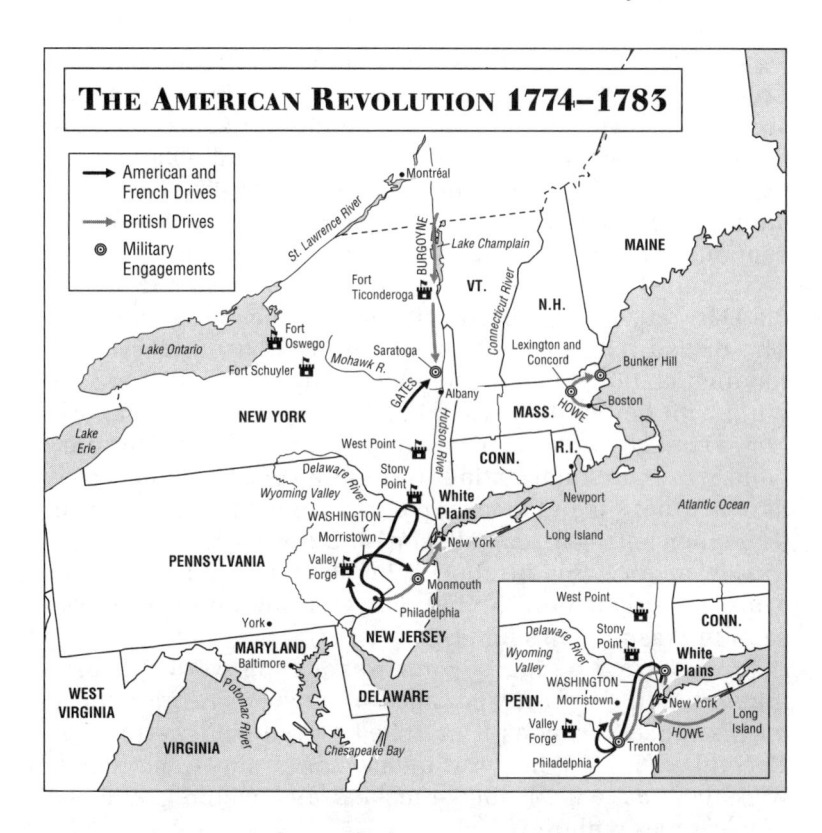

Woodhull would then have a coded signal hung on a Setauket clothesline that was visible through a spyglass to Americans on the Connecticut shore. A crew of oarsmen would row across Long Island Sound by night, collect Townsend's letters, and carry them to Tallmadge's dragoons, who would hurry them to Washington. The general applied a "sympathetic fluid" to reveal the secret messages written in Dr. Jay's "stain."

When the British occupied Philadelphia, in 1777, Washington salted the city with spies. His chief assistant there was Maj. John Clark, a cavalryman who became expert at passing false information about American strength at Valley Forge to a spy for the British commander General Howe.

Washington laboriously wrote out muster reports of the Continental Army, making it four or five times its actual size; the British, recognizing the handwriting, accepted the information as fact and gave the spy who had obtained it a bonus. Washington must have enjoyed this disinformation game; at one point, describing a particularly successful deception, Clark wrote, "This will give you a laugh."

The most effective American spy in Philadelphia was Lydia Darragh, an Irish-born Quaker midwife and undertaker. The British requisitioned a room in her house to serve as a "council chamber" and discussed their war plans there. By lying with her ear to a crack in the floor in the room above, Mrs. Darragh could hear much of what they said. Her husband wrote the information in minute shorthand on scraps of paper that she hid in large cloth-covered buttons. Wearing these, her fourteen-year-old son would walk into the countryside to meet his brother, a lieutenant in the American army. He snipped off the buttons, and the intelligence was soon in Washington's hands.

Mrs. Darragh's biggest coup was getting word to Washington that the British were about to make a surprise attack on his ragged army as it marched to Valley Forge in early December 1777. When the attack came, the Continentals were waiting with loaded muskets and cannon, and the king's forces withdrew.

The British returned to Philadelphia determined to find whoever had leaked their plan. Staff officers went to Mrs. Darragh's house and demanded to know exactly when everyone had gone to bed the previous night—except one person. "I won't ask you, Mrs. Darragh, because I know you retire each night exactly at nine," the chief interrogator said. Lydia Darragh smiled and said nothing. After the war she remarked that she was pleased that as a spy she had never had to tell a lie.

British Spies

The British, of course, had a small army of spies working for them as well, and they constantly struggled to penetrate Washington's operations. Toward the end of 1779, one of their Philadelphia spies wrote to Maj. John Andre, the charming, witty, artistically talented director of British intelligence: "Do you wish to have a useful hand in their army and to pay what you find his services worth? The exchange is 44 to 1." The numbers refer to the vertiginous depreciation of the Continental dollar; British spies, too, wanted to be paid in hard money.

The Americans did their best to make trouble for Andre by spreading around Philadelphia and New York the rumor that he was given to molesting boys. It is not clear whether Washington was involved in these particular smears, and they hardly chime with Andre's reputation for charming women, notably a Philadelphia belle named Peggy Shippen, who eventually married Gen. Benedict Arnold.

In any event, Andre was very successful at keeping tabs on the Americans. Surviving letters from his spies show him obtaining good estimates of American army strength in 1779. At one point Gen. Philip Schuyler made a motion in the Continental Congress that it leave Philadelphia because "they could do no business that was not instantly communicated" to the British. Andre's most successful agent was a woman named Ann Bates, a former schoolteacher who married a British soldier while the army was in Philadelphia. Disguised as a peddler, she wandered through the American camp, counted the cannon there, overheard conversations at Washington's headquarters, and accurately predicted the American attack on the British base in Newport, Rhode Island, in 1778.

The intelligence war reached a climax, or something very close to one, between 1779 and 1781. American morale was sinking with the Continental currency, and trusting anyone became harder and harder. Washington could never be sure when a spy had been "turned" by British hard money, and the British tried to accelerate the decline of the paper dollar by printing and circulating millions of counterfeit bills.

Soon an astonished American was writing, "An ordinary horse is worth twenty thousand dollars." In despair Congress stopped producing money; this brought the army's commissary department to a halt. The Continental desertion rate rose, with veterans and sergeants among the chief fugitives.

Washington struggled to keep the British at bay with more disinformation about his dwindling strength. His spies had achieved such professionalism that he had to appeal to Gov. William Livingston of New Jersey to spare three men arrested in Elizabethtown for carrying on an illegal correspondence with the enemy. That was exactly what they had been doing—as double agents feeding the British disinformation.

The three spies stood heroically silent. Washington told

Livingston they were willing to "bear the suspicion of being thought inimical." But realism could not be carried too far; the Continental Army could not hang its own agents. Would the governor please do something? Livingston allowed the spies to escape, and intelligence documents show that three years later they were still at work.

A Close Call at Morristown

By June 1780 agents had given the British high command accurate reports of the American army's weakness in its Morristown camp. The main force had diminished to four thousand men; because of a shortage of fodder, there were no horses, which meant the artillery was immobilized. The British had just captured Charleston, South Carolina, and its garrison of five thousand, demoralizing the South. They decided a strike at Washington's force could end the war, and they marshaled six thousand troops on Staten Island to deliver the blow.

A few hours before the attack, a furtive figure slipped ashore into New Jersey from Staten Island to warn the Continentals of the enemy buildup. He reached the officer in command in Elizabethtown, Col. Elias Dayton, and Dayton sent a rider off to Morristown with the news. Dayton and other members of the New Jersey Continental line, backed by local militia, were able to slow the British advance for the better part of a day, enabling Washington to get his army in motion and seize the high ground in the Short Hills, aborting the British plan.

It was a very close call. Without the warning from that spy, the British army would certainly have come over the Short Hills, overwhelmed Washington's four thousand men in Morristown, and captured their artillery. This probably would have ended the war.

After the royal army retreated to New York, word reached them that a French expeditionary force was landing in Newport, Rhode Island, to reinforce the struggling Americans. The British commander, Sir Henry Clinton, decided to attack before the French had a chance to recover from the rigors of the voyage and fortify.

This was the Culper network's greatest moment. Robert Townsend, alias Culper Jr., discovered the plan shortly after Clinton put six thousand men aboard transports and sailed them to Huntington Bay on the north shore of Long Island.

They waited there while British frigates scouted Newport Harbor to assess the size of the French squadron.

Townsend's warning sent Washington's disinformation machine into overdrive. Within twenty-four hours a double agent was in New York, handing the British top-secret papers, supposedly dropped by a careless courier, detailing a Washington plan to attack the city with every Continental soldier and militiaman in the middle states.

The British sent horsemen racing off to urge Sir Henry Clinton in Huntington Bay to return to New York with his six thousand men. Clinton, already discouraged by the British admiral's lack of enthusiasm for his plan to take Newport, glumly agreed and sailed his soldiers back to their fortifications. There they waited for weeks for an assault that never materialized.

While Clinton was in Huntington Bay, he and two aides were made violently ill by tainted wine they drank with dinner aboard the flagship. He ordered the bottle seized and asked the physician general of the British army to examine the dregs in the glasses. The doctor said the wine was "strongly impregnated with arsenic." During the night the bottle mysteriously disappeared, and Clinton was never able to confirm the assassination attempt or find the perpetrator. This may have been Washington's way of getting even for the Hickey plot.

BENEDICT ARNOLD

The main event in the later years of the intelligence war was the treason of Benedict Arnold in 1780. However, the American discovery of Arnold's plot to sell the fortress at West Point to the British for six thousand pounds—about half a million dollars in modern money—was mostly luck. There was little that Benjamin Tallmadge or his agents could claim to their credit except having passed along a hint of a plot involving an American general a few weeks before.

There is no doubt that West Point would have been handed over and Benedict Arnold and John Andre given knighthoods if three wandering militiamen in Westchester County had not stopped Andre on his return to New York with the incriminating plans in his boot. The motive of these soldiers was not patriotism but robbery; Westchester was known as "the neutral ground," and Loyalists and rebels alike wandered there in search of plunder.

Hanging John Andre was one of the most difficult things Washington had to do in the intelligence war. The major was the object of universal affection, and Alexander Hamilton and others on Washington's staff urged him to find a way to commute the sentence. Washington grimly replied that he would do so only if the British handed over Arnold. That of course did not happen, and Andre died on the gallows. In the next twelve months, Washington made repeated attempts to capture Arnold. He ordered an American sergeant named Champe to desert and volunteer to join an American legion that Arnold was trying to create. To give Champe a convincing sendoff, Washington ordered a half a dozen cavalrymen to pursue him, without telling them he was a fake deserter. Champe arrived in the British lines with bullets chasing him.

Washington would seem to have liked these little touches of realism. Unusually fearless himself, he had once said as a young man that whistling bullets had "a charming sound." One wonders if spies such as Honeyman and Champe agreed.

Soon Champe was a member of Arnold's staff, living in the former general's house on the Hudson River in New York. Through cooperating agents, Champe communicated a plan to knock Arnold unconscious when he went into his riverside garden to relieve himself one moonless night. A boatload of Americans would be waiting to carry him back to New Jersey and harsh justice.

On the appointed night the boat was there, and Arnold went to the garden as usual, but Champe was on a troopship in New York Harbor. Clinton had ordered two thousand men, including Arnold's American legion, south to raid Virginia. Champe had to watch for an opportunity and deserted back to the American side.

Arnold's defection badly upset American intelligence operations for months. He told the British what he knew of Washington's spies in New York, and they made several arrests. Townsend quit spying for six months, to the great distress of Washington and Tallmadge.

The intelligence war continued during the year remaining until Yorktown. Washington's reluctant decision to march south with the French army to try to trap a British army in that small Virginia tobacco port was accompanied by strenuous disinformation efforts intended to tie the British army to New York for as long as possible. In the line of march as the allied force moved south through New Jersey were some thirty large flatboats. British spies reported that the Americans were constructing large cooking ovens at several points near New York. Both seemed evidence of a plan to attack the city.

Benedict Arnold, now a British brigadier, begged Sir Henry Clinton to ignore this deception and give him six thousand men to attack the long, vulnerable American line of march. Clinton said no. He wanted to husband every available man in New York. By the time the British commander's Philadelphia spies told him where Washington was actually going, it was too late. The royal army under Charles Lord Cornwallis surrendered after three weeks of pounding by heavy guns, the blow that finally ended the protracted war.

After the War

Even after the fighting wound down, intelligence activity went on. In the fall of 1782, a year after Yorktown, a French officer stationed in Morristown wrote, "Not a day has passed since we have drawn near the enemy that we have not had some news of them from our spies in New York." For a final irony, the last British commander in America, Sir Guy Carleton, sent Washington a report from a British agent warning about a rebel plot to plunder New York and abuse Loyalists as the British army withdrew, and Washington sent in Major Tallmadge and a column of troops—not only to keep order but also to protect their agents, many of whom had earned enmity for appearing to be loyal to George III.

Among the American spies in New York was a huge Irish-American tailor named Hercules Mulligan who had sent Washington invaluable information. His greatest coup was a warning that the British planned to try to kidnap the American commander in 1780. Mulligan reported directly to Washington's aide Col. Alexander Hamilton.

Another of the deepest agents was James Rivington, editor of the unctuously loyal *New York Royal Gazette*. He is believed to have stolen the top-secret signals of the British fleet, which the Americans passed on to the French in 1781. The knowledge may have helped the latter win the crucial naval battle off the Virginia capes that September, sealing Cornwallis's fate at Yorktown.

The day after the British evacuated New York, Washington had breakfast with Hercules Mulligan—a way of announcing that he had been a patriot. He also paid a visit to James Rivington and apparently gave him a bag of gold coins. When he was composing his final expense account for submission to the Continental Congress with his resignation as Commander in Chief, Washington included from memory the contents of the bag of coins Robert Morris had rushed to him in late December 1776: 410 Spanish dollars, 2 English crowns, 10 shillings, and 2 sixpence. The circumstances under which he received it, Washington remarked, made it impossible for him ever to forget the exact amount of that crucial transfusion of hard money. It is another piece of evidence, barely needed at this point, that intelligence was a centerpiece of the strategy of protracted war—and that George Washington was a master of the game.

General Washington and the Progress of the Revolutionary War

Mackubin Owens

In this article, Mackubin Owens, professor of strategy and force planning at the United States Naval War College, analyzes the strategies used by George Washington during the Revolutionary War. After acknowledging that Washington is not considered by historians to be an expert strategist, Owens says that he disagrees and goes on to explain why. He points out that because Congress provided little financial support for the Continental army and because the British had the advantage of a powerful navy and a well-trained and disciplined army, Washington and his army were forced to fight a primarily defensive war. The "fight and retreat" strategies he used are described by military historians as being "Fabian"—in other words, following the tactics used by the Roman general Fabius Maximus Cunctator when he fought Hannibal in the first century B.C. During various phases of the war, however, Washington adapted his strategy to take advantage of all opportunities to smite the enemy, all the while keeping his eyes on the political objective of the war: to gain independence from Great Britain.

[Washington] has not often been studied as a strategist, and when he has, his reputation usually has not fared very well. . . . Those who study the U.S. military tradition prefer the Civil War or World War II. For most, [Generals] Grant, Lee, Pershing, Marshall, Eisenhower, and Patton, not Washington, epitomize the American military tradition. . . .

Many recent and contemporary historians have come to view [Washington] as a general of, at best, only mediocre mil-

Mackubin Owens, "General Washington and the Military Strategy of the Revolution," *Patriot Sage: George Washington and the American Political Tradition*, edited by Gary L. Gregg II and Matthew Spalding. Wilmington, DE: ISI Books, 1999. Copyright © 1999 by ISI Books. Reproduced by permission.

itary talents. Thus George Athan Billias remarks that "Washington's gifts as a general were more political than military and that his unique contribution to the Continental army resulted not from his grasp of strategy and tactics but rather from his skill in handling America's military leaders." . . . Richard Ketchum asserts that "he was less than a brilliant strategist . . . his method can only be described as persistence.". . .

These views do a great injustice to Washington. Examining his conduct of the war in light of the modern understanding of strategy reveals a different story. Washington was indispensable to American success. The principles of the Revolution had to be vindicated on the field of battle, and it was mostly Washington's strategic sense that made this vindication possible. . . .

ON STRATEGY

Strategy is both a process and product. As such, it is dynamic. It must be adapted to changing conditions, e.g., geography, technology, and social conditions. A strategy that works under one set of conditions may not work under different ones. To develop and execute a strategy requires that one be able to comprehend the whole and bring the right instrument to bear at the right time and in the right place in order to achieve the object of the war. . . .

Before we can evaluate Washington's strategy, . . . we must articulate criteria for making our judgment. These can be seen as a series of questions.
- Was the strategy adequate for achieving the end? Did it fit with the character of the war?
- Did it take account of the strengths and weaknesses of the enemy and tactical, operational, logistical, and geographical constraints?
- Were the means appropriate to the political objective? . . .
- What were the costs and risks of pursing the strategy?
- *Were there better alternatives than the one chosen?*

When we apply these criteria to Washington's strategic sense, especially considering the paucity of his means, we begin to see how unfair many previous assessments of his generalship have been.

WASHINGTON'S STRATEGIC SENSE

Strategy is a plan of action for using available means to achieve the ends of policy. Although at least at the beginning of hostilities, some Americans entertained the possibility of reconciliation with Britain, the goal of the war as Washington understood it by the end of 1775 was the *independence* of the United States as a *republican union* not hemmed in *geographically* by other powers. But as [military theorist Carl von] Clausewitz observes, war is the violent clash between two opposing wills. Thus Washington's strategy had to take account of not only American goals, but also the strategy of the British.

BRITISH GOALS AND STRATEGY

The Americans faced an adversary in possession of a multitude of advantages. First among these was Britain's sea power, which enabled British forces to strike at will anywhere along America's substantial coast and inland as far as deep-draft ships could navigate. The second was a well-trained and disciplined army of long-term professionals, both British regulars and German mercenaries. These soldiers were competent practitioners of eighteenth-century tactics, which involved intricate battlefield maneuvers designed to gain a positional advantage over an adversary, or if necessary, close with the bayonet. Third, no matter how divisive the conflicts resulting from party factions in British politics may have been, [Britain's King] George III and his ministers possessed a unity of effort that the Americans in Congress and the States could only envy.

The British, of course, faced problems of their own. To begin with, they had to overcome the "tyranny of distance." Despite its naval supremacy, the projection of power by Britain into North America required a major effort. Second, to win, the British had to occupy all of the colonies. However, the expanse of territory and low population density of North America made it difficult to maintain armies in the field anywhere away from the major population centers. When operating in the American interior away from their naval support, e.g., [when] British General John Burgoyne [was] at Saratoga, British armies were at a major disadvantage....

Third, British commanders fought the war with a sword in one hand and an olive branch in the other, believing that popular support for the war was minimal. This often prevented British commanders from delivering the *coup de grace* when they had the opportunity. A case in point is the Long Island–New York campaign of the summer and fall of 1776, during which [British] General William Howe failed to exploit several opportunities to annihilate Washington's force.

Fourth, economic reality and the need to address its other security problems limited the resources Great Britain could bring to bear against the American insurgents. This reality affected the way British commanders fought in North America: they could not afford to accept high casualties because losses could not easily be replaced. This problem of allocating resources was exacerbated when France entered the war in 1778.

Finally, British strategy was constrained by the dictates of eighteenth-century warfare. Battles fought according to the tactics of the time could be costly. Because these casualties could not be replaced, British commanders usually sought to avoid battle, attempting instead to maneuver their adversary into hopeless situations, in which the latter's only options were surrender or dissolution of the army.

AMERICAN GOALS AND STRATEGY

A successful strategy always focuses on the object of the war. For America, the *political* objective was to maintain the cause of liberty and secure the independence of the American colonies. It quickly became apparent to Washington that to achieve this political object he must achieve a *military* object as well, which was not the defense of places, but the maintenance of the army as an effective force. This was [necessary because, while Americans supported the war when it began in 1775, as time passed] . . . enthusiasm for the war waned as subsequent British military success rendered the outcome questionable.

Washington believed that more than republican virtue and moral ardor would be required to defeat the British. . . . Accordingly, his primary means for achieving the ends of policy was . . . the Continental Line: well-trained and well-disciplined citizen-soldiers under national control rather than the control of individual states. But this was easier said than done: national control ultimately resided in the Continental Congress, which could not act without the approval of the individual states, each of which was jealous of its own sovereignty and prerogatives.

In general, there are two types of war-fighting strategies: strategies of *annihilation* and strategies of *attrition* or *exhaustion*. Strategies of annihilation focus on the cataclysmic battle and are usually associated with [Carthaginian general] Hannibal and [French general] Napoleon. Strategies of attrition can be further subdivided into attrition by strategic *offensive* and attrition by strategic *defensive*.

A paucity of means forced Washington to assume the strategic defensive for most of the war. While it may have been the only alternative open to him given the circumstances he faced, this strategic choice created a dilemma for him and the Revolution. The fact that neither the militia nor the Continental Line was able consistently to defeat the British in the open field meant that he had to avoid combat except under the most favorable circumstances. By thus protracting the war, he hoped to wear the British out before they achieved success.

But there was always the danger that this strategy would cause the Americans to give out first. A strategy based on constant avoidance of battle and ceaseless retreat risked an adverse psychological impact on the American people at large.... [Washington] recognized the dilemma he faced: if he fought and lost his army, he could lose everything, but if he refused to fight, he could still lose everything as the people he defended lost heart.

Washington's strategy is often described as Fabian in character. But while [Roman general] Fabius Maximus Cunctator always avoided battle with Hannibal when the latter invaded Italy, Washington sought to deliver an offensive stroke whenever possible, as he did at [the New Jersey towns of] Trenton, Princeton, and Monmouth. Yet he consistently took pains to ensure that when he did fight he would be able to disengage to fight another day.

It should be noted that Washington shared with Congress the responsibility for the conception, if not the execution, of strategy during the War of American Independence. During the early years of the war, Congress generally deferred to Washington, but after the setbacks of 1776, it attempted to take on a more active and assertive role. Washington ... went out of his way to allay the concerns of Congress and to inform that body of his actions.

By 1778, Washington had once again begun to take the lead in developing as well as implementing American strategy, with Congress focusing on providing Washington what he needed.... By the end of the war, economic problems and the weakness of the Articles of Confederation had combined to render Congress nearly impotent....

It is possible to divide the War of American Independence into four periods: (1) April 1775–June 1776—*From Rebellion to Revolution and Independence;* (2) July 1776–December 1777—*Defending American Independence Against Superior Force;* (3) January 1778–October 1781—*The American War Becomes World War;* and (4) November 1781–December 1783—*Winning the Peace.* During each period, Washington kept the ultimate goal in view but, balancing potential outcomes against possible risks, adapted his strategy to meet changing conditions.

FROM REBELLION TO REVOLUTION AND INDEPENDENCE

The first fourteen months of the War of American Independence may be called the revolutionary period. This was the war's *offensive* phase as well, during which the Revolutionaries successfully seized control of the institutions of governance and ejected British power and authority. In most respects, it was a spontaneous uprising of the people in which the militia played the prominent role. Militia engaged the British regulars at Lexington and Concord [, and] it was militia that subsequently surrounded the British in Boston....

The magnitude of the popular uprising against the British in New England surprised even the most ardent American Revolutionaries. Most were simply swept along by the tide of events. The Continental Congress created the Continental Army in June, appointing Washington as commander in chief. But... before Washington could assume command of the newly created army around Boston, the militia had precipitated another battle. The British drove the rebels off Bunker (Breed's) Hill [near Boston], but at a staggering price. This British victory had important consequences for the future—British commanders rarely again risked a frontal assault against even untrained American forces.

Washington realized that the situation prevailing in the summer of 1775—with the British bottled up in Boston—was unlikely to improve. He hoped that by acting quickly and decisively and by threatening to make a costly and protracted war, the Revolutionaries could deter British military action and convince Britain to recognize the colonists' "rights as Englishmen."...

Many of the plans he developed for attacking Boston involved risky operations probably beyond the capabilities of

WASHINGTON THE COMMANDER

As commander in chief of the Continental army, Washington demanded respect, but in turn he respected those under him. In this excerpt, award-winning writer James Thomas Flexner, a leading expert on George Washington, describes Washington's demeanor as the leader of the first American army.

Washington did not regard his military eminence as an excuse for self-indulgence, but rather as the opposite. In this, he was very different from the highborn British generals with their mistresses, their hangovers and gaming tables. Washington asked nothing of his men that he was unwilling to do himself. Probably not another soldier in the entire army served so unrelentingly as did the Commander in Chief, who year after year did not allow himself a single day's furlough. And, although he kept up enough dignity at headquarters so that the men did not have to be ashamed of meanness, he shared their shortages and physical hardships whenever crisis made that reasonable....

Although Washington was by no means an equalitarian who slapped his social inferiors on the back, he responded to all men who came into his focus—however lowly their rank—as individuals whose personal interests should be considered, who had rights as well as duties. In the conventional sense Washington was not a reformer, because when intolerance of human weakness emerged among his emotions, he did not make it a basis of action but did his best to suppress it. He expected men to be weak and fallible, regarding this condition, like the infertile soil at Mount Vernon, as the essential ground on which fine effects would have to be achieved.

James Thomas Flexner, *George Washington in the American Revolution: 1775–1783*. Boston: Little, Brown, 1968.

---

his untrained army. One option, however, enabled him to take offensive action against the British without the risk associated with the other alternatives: moving captured artillery from Fort Ticonderoga [in New York] to Boston. Once the guns were emplaced [just outside Boston] on Dorchester Heights, the British position in Boston became untenable.

The British evacuated Boston in March 1776, leaving no forces in the American colonies. Since, for the most part, Revolutionaries also had seized colonial governments and ousted and defeated Loyalists, the Americans had achieved important military objectives. . . . But the primary political objective—acceptance by the British of American demands—remained elusive. George III refused to budge from the principles he had established in his August 1775 "Proclamation for Suppressing Rebellion and Sedition" in the colonies.

Washington's strategy during this period was strongly influenced by his certainty that time would not improve the situation for the Revolutionaries around Boston. British power, he believed, could only increase. Thus, Washington had an incentive to act quickly and decisively in order to maintain the advantage.

Another factor that caused him to proceed aggressively was the fact that most of his soldiers had enlisted for short terms and that many of these enlistments would be up before sustained operations realistically could be undertaken. This accounts for his offensive-mindedness despite the precariously low level of military supplies and equipment and what many commentators consider to be the rash nature of some of his plans, e.g. his idea to attack Boston across the harbor had it frozen. . . .

The first fourteen months of the war generally favored the American cause. The decision by General Howe, the British commander in America, to concentrate his available forces in Boston stripped Loyalists in the remaining northern colonies of the Crown's protection, leaving them at the mercy of the Patriots. The Loyalists in the South were able to put up more resistance, but Patriot militia soon overthrew them as well. By the time the British evacuated Boston, the Revolutionaries had seized the institutions of power in all thirteen colonies.

Defending American Independence

During the second phase of the war, three major elements changed. First, the political goal of the war changed from reconciliation—the insistence that Britain merely recognize the Americans' equal rights as Englishmen—to the demand for independence. Second, the magnitude of the British effort increased substantially. Finally and consequently, the British took the offensive, actively trying to suppress the rebellion in America. Washington was forced to adapt his strategy to these changing circumstances.

The Americans initially justified armed resistance to Britain on the basis of the demand that the Crown and Parliament recognize their equal rights as Englishmen. But as it became increasingly difficult for the Americans to war against British forces while maintaining their allegiance to the Crown, they had, for the most part by the summer of 1776, changed their political goal in the war to outright independence. This was important for Washington, because in order to raise the volunteer recruits necessary to man the Continental Army—the instrument he needed to implement his strategy—the political goal had to be seen by veterans and potential recruits alike as worthy of considerable effort and risk. . . .

[In July 1776], he had the Declaration of Independence read to the troops. He expressed the hope that "this important Event will serve as a fresh incentive to every officer, and soldier, to act with Fidelity and Courage, as knowing that now the peace and safety of his country depended (under God) soley on the success of our arms: And that he is now in the service of a State, possessed of sufficient power to reward his merit, and advance him to the highest Honors of a free Country."

But Washington recognized that while patriotism was necessary, it was not sufficient if America was to vindicate its independence on the battlefield. . . . The sort of army he would need to outlast the British was a long-term force of regulars who would have to be compensated for their service.

Washington and a committee of the Continental Congress had assumed that the British would send a force of about 23,000 soldiers to America, 10,000 to Canada, and the remainder to New York, which Washington assumed to be the British objective. Given the expected superiority of trained British troops over an American force, their "net assessment" projected a requirement for a force twice the size of the invader's army.

Unfortunately, Congress overestimated its own ability to raise troops and underestimated the ability of the British to do the same. In particular, they did not count on the Crown's access to German soldiers [Hessian mercenaries], 30,000 of whom eventually were employed in America.

By the end of the summer of 1776, General Howe commanded the largest expeditionary force that Britain had ever sent anywhere up to that time: 30,000 British and German troops, with 5,000 more Hessians on the way, backed by a fleet of seventy warships and hundreds of other vessels under his brother, Admiral Richard Howe. To defend New York,

Washington could muster fewer than 10,000 troops, most of whom were new recruits. Appeals to Congress and nearby states doubled the force by the time Howe attacked in August.

THE NEW YORK CAMPAIGN

British strategy for 1776 centered on controlling the Hudson River and eliminating the rebellion in New England, where it appeared to be strongest. To do this required Howe to seize New York and, if possible, destroy the Continental Army. Because Washington was slow to modify his strategy to take account of the new conditions, Howe nearly succeeded.

To be fair to Washington, his choices during the New York campaign of 1776 were severely constrained by political considerations. Foremost among these limitations on his freedom of action was the demand by Congress that he defend New York, despite British operational advantages. Nonetheless, Washington remained committed to an offensive posture long after it should have been clear that the tactical instrument he possessed did not meet the requirements of this posture.

During the New York campaign of the summer and fall of 1776, Washington rashly invited head-to-head engagements with the British. As a result of his aggressiveness, he nearly was trapped on Long Island and Manhattan when Howe used the mobility afforded by the Royal Navy to sail up the Hudson River and interdict Patriot communications with New Jersey. He subsequently was surprised and outflanked by Howe on Long Island and his forces routed. When Howe prepared to besiege Washington's entrenchments on Brooklyn Heights, Washington executed a skillful withdrawal to Manhattan. But twice more, Howe almost trapped him on Manhattan, once on the southern end of the island and again at Harlem Heights. He refused to abandon Fort Washington after he finally evacuated Manhattan. This failure cost the Patriots 3,000 troops killed or captured.

At this point, Washington recognized that because he could not prevail against a force the size of Howe's possessing the mobility it was afforded by the Royal Navy, he needed to change his strategy. Political considerations had required that he at least attempt to defend New York, but strategic necessity now required that he give it up or the cause might be lost. [Patriot general] Nathanael Greene had provided the rationale for this strategy:

> The City and Island of New York are no objects for us; we are

not to bring them into competition with the general interests of America. Part of the army has already met with a defeat; the country is struck with a panick; any capital loss at this time may ruin the cause. 'Tis our business to study to avoid any considerable misfortune, and to take post where the enemy will be obliged to fight us; and not us them.

Washington accepted the thrust of Greene's argument and laid out in a letter to Congress the strategy he would pursue for the remainder of the year:

> ... We should on all occasions avoid a general action, or put anything to the risque, unless compelled by a necessity into which we ought never to be drawn, [is evident]. ... When the fate of America may be at stake on the issue; when the wisdom of cooler moments and experienced men have decided that we should protract the war if possible; I cannot think it safe or wise to adopt a different system when the season for action draws so near a close.

This was Washington's blueprint for the Fabian phase of his strategy.

Though Howe and his subordinates tried to bring him to battle, Washington adhered to his strategy. He maintained constant contact with Howe's army, retreating when Howe advanced, advancing cautiously when he fell back. In the late fall, Washington abandoned New York and retreated into New Jersey. As winter approached, he informed Congress that he would have to retreat beyond the Delaware River, causing panic in Philadelphia.

Howe originally had no intention of driving as far as the Delaware. ... But then Howe made an error that undid all that he had accomplished up to that point. Giving in to his more aggressive subordinates, he authorized an advance to the Delaware. ... Howe was now overextended, exposing himself to a counterstroke, which Washington delivered with stunning suddenness against the Hessian outpost at Trenton on Christmas night and a British brigade at Princeton [New Jersey] less than a fortnight later.

Battles must be judged not only according to tactical outcome, but also in terms of their strategic and political effects. This is the case with Trenton and Princeton. In less than two weeks, an army on the verge of disintegration won two unexpected victories, forced Howe to abandon New Jersey, and revived the revolutionary cause teetering on the brink of extinction. Strategically, Howe was back where he had started in the summer—holding bases at New York and

Newport [Rhode Island] but little more. . . .

Meanwhile Washington positioned his army where it could respond no matter what Howe did. Moving into the hills of northern New Jersey and the Hudson highlands, Washington took up a position that was easily defended, easily resupplied, and most importantly, sat astride Howe's communications in New Jersey. No matter whether Howe moved north toward Albany or south toward Philadelphia, Washington, by holding the Hudson [River], could counter his thrust by taking advantage of interior lines of operation. . . . In order to maintain his strategic advantage, he vociferously opposed Congress's attempt to force him to disperse his force along the Delaware River.

Washington's strong strategic position was probably one factor that influenced Howe's decision to move by sea to [invade] the middle colonies rather than up the Hudson to support [General] Burgoyne. The prospect of rooting Washington's forces out of their defenses in the Hudson highlands could not have appealed to Howe, "in whose mind was indelibly etched that horrible scene on Bunker Hill."

Washington moved to delay Howe's army as it approached Philadelphia, fighting sharp clashes at Brandywine Creek and White Horse Tavern, and then attacking a part of Howe's force at Germantown. Though all were tactical setbacks for the Americans that failed to prevent Howe's occupation of Philadelphia, the strategic effect of the campaign as a whole was to convince Howe to end the war effort for 1777.

Indeed, the strategic outcome of the second phase was to make it increasingly clear to the British that they could not prevail against the Patriots. As 1777 ended, the British had nothing to show for their effort but enclaves at New York, Newport, and Philadelphia. Meanwhile, the cost had been ruinous: Burgoyne's entire army and a third of Howe's irreplaceable troops had become casualties. Most importantly, by maintaining his army intact and delivering a blow whenever possible, Washington's strategy helped to create the conditions that convinced France to join the war on the side of America. France's entry completely changed the character of the war, and once again Washington adapted his strategy to fit the circumstances.

The French alliance had a number of effects, not the least of which was to neutralize Britain's greatest single advantage over the Americans—sea power. "Next to the loan of money," wrote Washington, "a constant naval superiority on these coasts is the object most interesting. . . . This superiority, with an aid of money, would enable us to convert the war into a vigorous offensive.". . .

With France's entry into the war . . . Britain was now forced to follow a policy of limited liability, hoping to pacify the colonies but refusing to commit any more resources to the effort. Sir Henry Clinton, who had replaced Howe at the end of 1777, was ordered to abandon Philadelphia, and even New York if need be, in order to free up troops for operations elsewhere.

Clinton evacuated Philadelphia on June 18, 1778, and began a march north to New York. He was hounded along the way by Washington's army, which had improved greatly under the tutelage of the Prussian captain Friedrich Wilhelm von Steuben during the winter at Valley Forge [Pennsylvania]. The Continentals fought splendidly at Monmouth Court House [New Jersey] and by July, Washington was back where he had started two years earlier, but this time in an offensive posture. . . .

WASHINGTON TRIES TO SEIZE THE INITIATIVE

In the fall of 1778, Washington attempted to divine Clinton's moves for the campaign season of 1779. He concluded that his adversary had only three options: attempt to destroy Washington's army, attempt to defeat the French fleet, or attempt to seize West Point on the Hudson. In fact, Washington was wrong, for once. Clinton had in mind a southern campaign, descending on Savannah [Georgia] at the end of December 1778. . . .

The year 1779 was a year in which political and economic problems outweighed military ones. Inflation was rampant, speculation was widespread, and political factions were emerging to make Congress even less effective than it had been previously. Financial problems limited the military options. . . .

[Militarily] 1780 was a disaster [for the Americans]. British troops launched a vigorous campaign in the South, seizing Charleston [South Carolina] and inflicting the bloodiest defeat of the war on the Americans at Camden [South Carolina]. British forces overran Georgia and the Carolinas and threatened Virginia. Worst of all, Benedict Arnold, America's best-known combat commander, turned traitor and nearly succeeded in betraying West Point to the British. Because of economic paralysis and political infighting, Washington was unable to organize a summer campaign. Additionally, Patriot morale reached a low point in 1780.

But there was some good news, delivered by the [French general] Marquis de Lafayette. A French expeditionary force, including a ground force, was en route. Given that the Patriot cause was teetering on the brink of collapse, Washington immediately began to plan a major combined-force effort against the British. . . .

New York was his preferred objective, but circumstances combined to prevent the necessary preponderance of force to ensure success. He laid out the general conditions that would have to prevail if the allies were to defeat the British. The most important of these was naval superiority. . . .

Despite his efforts, there was not to be a major combined offensive in 1780. But Washington recognized that the perilous state of the American cause required activity somewhere. Accordingly, Washington looked south, sending Nathanael Greene, his most aggressive subordinate, to the Carolinas to try to redeem the situation there in the aftermath of Gates's debacle at Camden.

Greene . . . was a proponent of the strategy of protracted war practiced by Washington and put that strategy into action immediately. Greene never won a battle in the South, but the strategic effect of his campaign was to force the British to abandon the Carolinas because they could not afford the casualties they suffered in gaining their tactical successes.

Meanwhile, the French decided to increase their effort in America. [French King] Louis XVI dispatched a fleet under the Comte de Grasse and provided the financial support that would permit the Americans to sustain a major effort against the British. De Grasse was instructed to cooperate with Washington and the French army under [General] Rochambeau.

Washington and Rochambeau agreed to attack the British wherever the prospects for success were greatest. Washington still preferred to attack New York, but when de Grasse informed him of his intention to sortie into the Chesapeake Bay and remain there from early September through mid-October, Washington seized this opportunity to destroy the British army in Virginia.

In a flawless operation, coordinated with Rochambeau, he executed a march from New York to Virginia before the

British could react. His well-known preference for an attack on New York worked to his advantage, permitting him to deceive the British about his intentions until it was too late. A feint at Staten Island fixed Clinton in place until the main body of the combined force had cleared Philadelphia on its way to its rendezvous with de Grasse on the Chesapeake.

Cornwallis's position at Yorktown, Virginia, was invested by Washington and Rochambeau, and de Grasse fought off a British fleet in the Battle of the Capes, sealing the British commander's fate. On October 17, Cornwallis asked for terms [of surrender].

By ending British efforts to subdue the colonies and thereby ensuring the independence of the United States, the Yorktown campaign ranks as one of the most decisive in history. It was also a tribute to Washington's persistence in pursuit of his strategic vision.

WINNING THE PEACE

Euphoria swept the country after Cornwallis's surrender. The end of the war at last seemed to be at hand. But Washington understood that the war was not yet won and that a relaxation of vigilance could undo all that had been accomplished over six years of war. Indeed, the period from Yorktown to the Treaty of Paris was a time of great peril for the new Republic.

Washington had to hold the Continental Army together to ensure that the peace would favor the United States. At the same time, he had to ensure that this army would not become an instrument for overthrowing the Republic. The obstacles he faced in achieving these goals were substantial. . . .

New York remained the main strategic objective for Washington. Sending forces south to reinforce Greene, Washington himself rejoined the forces he had left to guard the Hudson. Washington continued to hope for French cooperation and began to plan for a subsequent campaign.

It is well he did. Despite what his countrymen may have thought, the war was not yet over. George III had no intention of giving up his claim to the colonies. The King's ministers proposed a return to a strategy based on naval blockade, supported by Loyalists and regulars. . . . But a series of reverses in the Caribbean, at [the island of] Minorca [off the coast of Spain] and in South Florida finally convinced the King that he should cut his losses in America.

As peace negotiations progressed, Washington pursued a "conciliatory war," never letting down his guard and treating every British proposal with skepticism. After de Grasse was defeated [by the British] at the Battle of the Saintes [in the Caribbean] in April 1782 and Rochambeau's army embarked at Boston for the Indies in the fall, Washington was once again left to his own devices. He proposed to concentrate his forces against the British in New York.

While there were to be no more campaigns, it seems clear that Washington's vigilance helped to ensure a favorable outcome in the peace negotiations. . . . The American diplomats, led by Benjamin Franklin, deserve tremendous credit for their negotiating skill, but the fact that the Americans gained both independence and generous territorial concessions can be attributed in part to Washington's refusal to permit the military situation to deteriorate. He had won the war, and his vigilance now strengthened the hand of the American negotiators, enabling them to win the peace.

Chapter 4
President

People Who Made History
George Washington

The Washington Administration

Forrest McDonald

In the following selection, University of Alabama research professor of history Forrest McDonald recounts the presidency of George Washington. He begins with Washington's reaction to his election, then explains how Washington's first months put to test the powers relegated to the president by the Constitution. He also details the extent to which Washington was concerned with establishing protocol. In addition, McDonald elaborates on Washington's declaration of American neutrality with regard to the French Revolution (which took place from 1789 to 1795 and was greatly influenced by the American Revolutionary War). Finally, McDonald discusses Washington's handling of the Whiskey Rebellion.

It was a foregone conclusion, from the moment the Constitution was published, that Washington would be the choice of the electoral college. Students who encounter contemporary documents for the first time are amazed at the adulation lavished upon the man. In Europe as well as in America he was heralded as the Greatest Character of the Age. His customary designation as the Father of His Country was an appellation far more exalted than the Father of His People that was applied to monarchs. It is no exaggeration to say that Americans were willing to venture the experiment with a single, national republican chief executive only because of their unreserved trust in George Washington.

THE RELUCTANT PRESIDENT

Less certain was whether he would answer the call. He had announced when he resigned as commander in chief that he would never again hold public office, and he regarded that

Forrest McDonald, *The American Presidency: An Intellectual History.* Lawrence: University Press of Kansas, 1994. Copyright © 1994 by the University Press of Kansas. Reproduced by permission.

pledge as a sacred promise. He sincerely questioned his ability to fill the presidential office effectively, for even though he had successfully commanded the army and administered his vast plantations with great system and skill, he had had virtually no experience in governing. Beyond these reservations, he positively dreaded the thought of leaving the serenity of his beloved Mount Vernon to take up the cares of renewed public service. Compounding the uncertainty was his reluctance to discuss the matter lest that "be construed into a vainglorious desire of pushing myself into notice as a candidate."

A number of friends and associates broached the subject in letters, but it was probably his former aide-de-camp Alexander Hamilton whose persuasion was decisive. Hamilton initiated an exchange of letters [in late 1788] in which he argued that by signing and recommending ratification of the Constitution Washington had pledged himself to do everything he could to give it life. "It is to little purpose to have *introduced* a system," he wrote, "if the weightiest influence is not given to its firm *establishment*, in the outset." Then Hamilton rather presumptuously said, "It would be inglorious in such a situation not to hazard the glory however great," which Washington had "previously acquired." This appeal to a combination of duty and courage was irresistible. . . .

Washington . . . agreed to serve. But he expressed his misgivings poignantly in a letter to [South Carolina politician] Edward Rutledge, written [on May 5, 1789] shortly after his inauguration. "I greatly apprehend that my Countrymen will expect too much from me. I fear, if the issue of public measures should not corrispond with their sanguine expectations, they will turn the extravagant (and I may say undue) praises which they are heaping upon me at this moment, into equally extravagant (though I will fondly hope unmerited) censures."

It seemed, during the first term, that Washington's misgivings had been unjustified. The executive departments and the federal court system were established, the president filled government offices with men of high quality, the public debts (which had been devastating) were ordered in a way that increased the nation's prosperity, and the divisions left by the ratification process had been bridged. In 1792, the uncertainty of affairs in Europe, combined with the fact that the presidential experience had not been especially unpleasant, made it possible for supporters to prevail upon Washington to serve a second term. His luster untarnished, he was elected again by the unanimous vote of the electoral college. The second term, however, proved to be a nightmare. As would happen in most two-term presidencies, the second term saw the country imperiled by foreign wars and rent by violent political confrontations at home. The Father of His Country was indeed beset by "unmerited censures" of the vilest kind, and the psychic cost of the second term was more than any person could reasonably be expected to bear. That would be true of most of his successors.

But Washington had defined the presidency, grounded it on firm foundations, and made it central to the survival of the republic by the time he retired in 1797. Not all the precedents he established would last, not even until the end of the century. Yet he made the office viable, an institution of great flexibility and energy that could exert its will while remaining under the ultimate control of the law.

The Nascent Government

The new government started inauspiciously. Congress, scheduled by the Confederation Congress to convene in New York on March 4, 1789, did not obtain a quorum until April 6. Any man other than Washington might have been on the scene, ready to launch the ship of state, for he and everyone else knew that he had been elected president, but to avoid seeming eager he remained at home awaiting official notice. Congress accordingly counted the votes and dispatched a messenger to notify him; even then he made a leisurely trip northward, gratified but somewhat distressed by the overwhelming popular acclaim shown him along the way. He finally arrived—to be inaugurated on April 30.

During the week before he got to the city, and for two weeks afterward, the Senate was engaged in a debate over an appropriate form of address for the president. John Adams, having spent many years as American minister in the courts of Europe, had acquired a taste for royal pomp and had convinced himself that something approaching regal "dignity and splendor" would be necessary if people were to respect the new government. He insisted to the senators, to whom he regularly pontificated, that only an exalted system of titles would infuse the people with adequate awe and veneration to lend permanence and weight to the government. A goodly number of senators, thinking of their body as an American

House of Lords, seemingly agreed. Richard Henry Lee, who had earlier been as ardent a radical republican as Adams had been, was among this group: [According to William Maclay, who kept a diary of early senate proceedings] at one point Lee rose and "read over a list of the Titles of all the Princes and Potentates of the Earth, marking where the Word Highness occurred." Oliver Ellsworth observed that the "appellation of President" was too common for the chief executive of a nation, inasmuch as there were presidents "of Fire Companies & of a Cricket Club." Various titles were proposed, including "his elective majesty" (the title of the king of Poland), until the Senate fixed upon "His Highness the President of the United States and Protector of the Rights of the Same." The House of Representatives balked, refusing to accept any title but the simple constitutional formulation, "President of the United States."

President Washington was mightily embarrassed by this, not least because the debate and other indicators revealed the existence of a "court party" in the Senate that wanted to make the presidency quasi-monarchical; he himself was searching for rules of comportment suitable to a republican executive. He had scarcely taken up residence in a large rented house when throngs of visitors began to call, most come to gape at the Great Man or to solicit jobs. All acted as if they had a constitutional right to be there. From breakfast to bedtime, Washington complained [in a letter to David Stuart] it was impossible to be "relieved from the ceremony of one visit before I had to attend to another." Upon inquiring about the practice of the presidents of the Confederation Congress, he learned that they had been "considered in no better light than as a Maitre d'Hôtel . . . for the table was considered as a public one." After two days of harassment, Washington published a notice in the newspapers that he would thereafter receive "visits of compliment" between 2:00 and 3:00 P.M. on Tuesday and Friday and that he would "neither return visits nor accept any invitations."

That elicited complaints in some quarters. Pennsylvania senator William Maclay grumbled that Washington proposed "to be seen only in public on Stated times like an Eastern Lama." Washington sought the advice of Madison, Jay, Adams, and Hamilton. He needed rules of behavior, he told them, that would strike a balance between "too free an intercourse and too much familiarity," which would reduce the dignity of the office, and "an ostentatious show" of monarchical aloofness, which would be improper in a republic. A "line of conduct" was worked out. Dinners were to be held every Thursday at 4:00 P.M. for government officials and their families on a regular system of rotation to avoid favoritism. Two occasions a week were established for greeting the general public, a levee for men on Tuesdays from 3:00 to 4:00 P.M. and tea parties for men and women on Friday evenings. Anyone respectably dressed could attend without invitation or prior notice.

Matters of Protocol

Three other matters of protocol were given careful attention. One concerned the president's salary. Washington had refused to accept a salary during the Revolutionary War, and in his inaugural address he asked not to be compensated except by an expense account. Congress, however, took the position that the Constitution mandated a "fixed compensation" for the president and voted a salary of $25,000 per year. . . .

A second concern was the inauguration ceremony. Washington took the oath of office in the Senate chamber, where both houses of Congress had gathered, and then he delivered his address. This procedure was consciously patterned after the arrangements in England, where the king, at the beginning of each session of Parliament, addressed both houses in the chamber of the Lords. Each house of Congress completed the ritual by calling on the president later with a formal answer, as the Lords and Commons customarily did. That pattern was repeated annually on the occasion of the State of the Union address. But Washington took some of the monarchical edge off the proceedings by wearing a suit of brown broadcloth made in Connecticut.

A third matter had to do with the niceties of federal-state relations. After the first session of the First Congress adjourned in the fall of 1789, Washington made a good-will tour through New England, avoiding Rhode Island, which had not yet ratified the Constitution, and Vermont, which was governing itself as an independent republic. As he approached Cambridge, Massachusetts, he was invited to review the militia troops there; he declined, "otherwise than as a private man," because they were under state jurisdiction. Having deferred to state sensibilities in that regard, he similarly refused John Hancock's invitation to stay in the governor's residence in Boston but agreed to have dinner together—on the assumption that Hancock would acknowledge the subordinate position of governors by first paying the president a courtesy call. Hancock instead sent a message that he was crippled with gout and could not leave home, whereupon Washington flatly refused to see him except in Washington's own lodgings. Next day the governor, heavily swathed in bandages, called upon the president.

Establishing Protocol for the Head of State

Such concerns can be regarded as trivial—some contemporaries thought them pretentious or comical—but Washington did not so view them, and he was right. He fully understood, if only intuitively, that the presidency, if properly established, would be dual in nature, chief executive officer but also ritualistic and ceremonial head of state, and that the latter function was quite as vital as the more prosaic administrative one. Moreover, it was his task to enable the American people to make the transition from monarchy to republicanism by serving as the symbol of nationhood and to institutionalize that symbol by investing it in the office, not in the man. To that end, he behaved as if his every move was being closely scrutinized, which to a considerable extent it was. He even opened a correspondence with a Virginia friend who could mingle with ordinary folks and inform him how people were responding to the president's doings. When the correspondent wrote that certain actions had led some people to endorse [Virginia politician] Patrick Henry's assertion that the presidency "squinted toward monarchy," Washington made appropriate adjustments in his behavior.

Washington was able to succeed, partly because of a natural gravity and dignity combined with simplicity of tastes and manners, but more importantly because he was a consummate actor who had self-consciously been role-playing throughout his adult life. Lest that observation be taken as pejorative, additional observations are in order, particularly in regard to the eighteenth-century concept of character. The word was rarely used to denote internal qualities. Its most common signification meant reputation: One had a character for honesty, fickleness, perspicacity. But it also meant, in polite society and in public life, a persona that one deliberately selected and always wore; it was conventional practice to pick a role, like a part in a play, and attempt to act it consistently, always to "be in character." If one chose a character that one could play comfortably and played it long enough and well enough, by degrees it became a "second nature" that superseded one's primary nature, which was generally thought to be base. One became, in other words, what one pretended to be. Washington differed from ordinary mortals by picking a progression of characters during his lifetime, each nobler and grander than the last, and by playing each so well that he ultimately transformed himself into a man of extrahuman virtue. . . .

DEFINING THE CONSTITUTIONAL GOVERNMENT

Preoccupation with ritual was appropriate during the first few months, for until Congress enacted the legislation, there were almost no laws to be executed, no executive departments to administer them, and no courts to adjudicate them. As the first session unfolded, the doings in the Congress amounted almost to a second constitutional convention, for they organically defined, shaped, and gave life to a government that the Constitution only authorized.

Washington had thought of actively directing the process, but then he decided it would be prudent to let others lead. He had written a sixty-two-page statement of maxims, principles, and proposals but scrapped it and instead presented a handful of legislative recommendations in his inaugural address. These concerned his duties in treaty-making or as commander in chief: a proposal for bringing the minuscule existing military establishment into conformity with the Constitution, one establishing a temporary commission to treat with southern Indians, and one authorizing the calling of the militia in the Ohio country if needed. All three were acted upon. Perhaps it was Congress' apparent willingness to grant him blanket authority in such matters, together with the demonstrated court-party inclinations of the Senate and the advice of the people he consulted most frequently (Madison, Hamilton, Jay), that induced him to play a passive role in the definition of the executive power in 1789. In any event, most people in government seemed anxious to clothe the president with adequate powers, which spared him the unpleasant necessity of seeking the powers himself. . . .

A significant decision regarding executive power arose in the House debates concerning the creation of the executive departments. William Loughton Smith of South Carolina, citing Hamilton's *Federalist* 77, contended that senatorial approval would be necessary for presidential removal of executive officeholders just as it was for appointment. Madison, who had rapidly emerged as the principal court-party spokesman in the First Congress, summarized the arguments. Four general positions had been advanced: that the matter was for Congress to decide; that "no removal can take place otherwise than by impeachment"; that the power was "incident to that of appointment, and therefore belongs to the President & Senate"; and that the power of removal was vested solely in the president. The last of these prevailed by a sizable majority.

That decision did not bind future congresses or presidents; the question would be raised again on several pivotal occasions in American history. But the constitutional reasoning underlying the decision became established doctrine. The Constitution, Madison declared, vested the executive power in the president, with the exception that the Senate shares the appointment and treaty-making powers. Congress is not authorized to add other exceptions. Madison then asked [in a speech he made to Congress on June 16 and 17, 1789], "Is the power of displacing an executive power? I conceive that if any power whatsoever is in its nature executive it is the power of appointing, overseeing, and controlling those who execute the laws." If the Constitution had not required senatorial approval of appointments, the president "would have the right by virtue of his executive power to make such appointment." This was an endorsement of the view that the president has certain unspecified but real powers that he exercises by virtue of the vesting clause; the vesting clause was a positive grant, not an abstract generalization.

Senator Maclay was unhappy with the House's decision, perceiving it as undercutting the Senate's special relationship with the executive. Indeed, he objected to the creation of departments by ordinary legislative process. The proper way, he contended in his diary, was for the president to communicate "to the Senate that he finds, such & such officers necessary in the Execution of the Government. and nominates the Men. if the Senate approve they will concur in the Measure. if not refuse their Consent." When the appointments are made, Maclay went on, the president should notify the House and request adequate salaries. The House could then "shew their concurrence or disapprobation by providing for the Officer or not.". . .

WASHINGTON CONSULTS THE SENATE

The course of . . . Indian negotiations strained relations between president and Senate further and established an important precedent. On Saturday, August 22, after several days of interchange about who would sit where when the president called on the Senate for consultation, Washington appeared with Henry Knox, the acting superintendent of war. Knox handed Washington a paper with seven points on which advice and consent was being sought; Washington handed it to Adams, who read it aloud, rapidly. Carriages outside made such a noise that no one understood "one Sentence of it." After the doorkeeper closed the windows, Adams read the first point, which contained several references to the whole paper. [Pennsylvania Senator] Robert Morris rose to say he had not been able to hear the paper and asked that it be read again. It was. Then Adams put the question on the first point, yes or no. An embarrassed silence followed. Maclay broke it by requesting that before an answer be given the treaties involved should be read, along with the instructions issued by the old Congress to the negotiators. The senators then raised a cacophony of voices, speaking of every manner of thing, at which Washington grew progressively angrier. Finally, he "started up in a Violent fret" and declared, "*This defeats every purpose of my coming here.*" Tempers gradually cooled, but following another fruitless session on Monday Washington resolved never to enter the Senate for a consultation again.

He kept that vow, and thus the idea that the Senate would serve as an executive council was stillborn. In future Washington consulted with senators occasionally in his own office, individually or in small groups, and he received committees of the Senate, but by and large he dealt formally with the whole Senate only in writing, and he sought its consent after he had initiated and concluded negotiations with foreign powers. (Most of his successors followed his example.)

Yet he continued to regard the Senate as constitutionally more important than the House because of its share of the executive authority, an attitude that led him to consider exercising the veto. Early in September he sent a letter asking Madison's advice on a variety of matters, including the query, "Being clearly of opinion that there ought to be a difference in the wages of the members of the two branches of the Legislature"—the appropriations bill had provided equal pay—"would it be politic or prudent in the President when the Bill comes to him to send it back with his reasons for nonconcurring?" Apparently Madison advised against the veto, for it was not exercised. Thereafter Washington grew extremely reluctant to veto legislation and did not use the power until April of 1792, on a bill that was patently unconstitutional and only after Jefferson urged him to veto something lest the power fall into disuse, as it had in England. He vetoed but one more bill during his presidency, on the eve of his departure from office. . . .

CONSULTING HIS ADVISERS

Perhaps because Washington sensed that his chief administrators were not especially compatible as a group, he did not consult them collectively during his first term. When his perceived need for an advisory body increased, upon the outbreak of the French revolutionary wars, he began to consult them, but he also turned to the Supreme Court. In the summer of 1793 he framed (actually [Secretary of the Treasury Alexander] Hamilton framed for him) a series of questions about international law and treaty obligations, and he forwarded these to the Court for an opinion. Chief Justice Jay had been a frequent presidential adviser, and he and the other justices would have been eager to become an ex officio advisory council—but for a flukish circumstance. Shortly before, Congress had assigned the Court the administrative duty of reviewing pension claims of war veterans. The justices, not wishing to take on the onerous and somewhat demeaning task, indignantly refused, saying that they were already overworked, that the function was not judicial, and that it violated the principle of the separation of powers. Now, asked to assume an executive role, the Court could not with good grace reverse its stand. It accordingly refused. Thereafter, Washington regularly called the department heads together for meetings—and thus was born the presidential cabinet. . . .

[A disagreement between Washington's secretary of state, Thomas Jefferson, and the secretary of the treasury, Alexander Hamilton, over how Hamilton was handling the nation's finances resulted in the formation of an opposing political party. In reaction to what they felt was Hamilton's attempt to make the U.S. government more like the British monarchy, Jefferson and James Madison organized what they called the "Republican" party.]

Declaring Neutrality

The timing of the formation of an opposition party was unfortunate, for it coincided with revolutionary France's intrusion into American affairs. The United States was tied to France by gratitude for its help in winning independence and by the "perpetual" treaty of alliance of 1778. Most Americans cheered when the French Revolution began in 1789, perceiving it as a reform movement approved by [French king] Louis XVI, whom they regarded as a great champion of liberty; most, except the more ardent republican ideologues, had stopped cheering by the time they learned of the king's execution in 1793. Meanwhile, France declared war against Prussia and Austria, and shortly afterward it dispatched Citizen Edmond Genet as a special minister to enlist the United States in the cause of liberating the world. The Americans were not expected to join France as a belligerent—the alliance extended only to defensive wars—but to work in concert to extend the "empire of liberty" and to punish colonial powers by cutting off trade with them. Genet was assigned three specific duties: obtain American foodstuffs for France, use American ports as bases for privateering, and enlist American citizens in private expeditions to reconquer Canada, Florida, and Louisiana. Genet arrived in Charleston in April, 1793, and began a tour northward toward Philadelphia, handing out privateering commissions along the way.

Washington, understanding that to incur the hostility of Great Britain could be catastrophic, asked his cabinet for ideas about how to preserve neutrality. Jefferson, who usually took the position that the management of foreign affairs was exclusively an executive function, now let francophilia sway his judgment, arguing that since only Congress could declare war, it alone could declare neutrality; a presidential proclamation of neutrality would be unconstitutional. Hamilton and Knox urged that such a proclamation could and should be issued. (Hamilton even reduced Jay to draft one. So much for protestations about the separation of powers.) Washington agreed with them, and on April 22 he issued the proclamation. . . .

To proclaim neutrality was one thing, to enforce it quite another. French agents boldly used American ports to equip privateers, and French consuls, on Genet's instructions, acted as prize courts. The obvious agents for policing such activity were the customs collectors, but when Hamilton proposed employing them Jefferson protested vehemently, saying that to do so would make them "an established corps of spies or informers against their fellow citizens." Instead, Jefferson proposed using grand juries, an ineffectual method. [Virginia governor Edmund] Randolph did bring proceedings against two Americans who were serving on board a French privateer, but absent a federal law against recruiting and given his uncertain grasp of the law of nations Randolph based the prosecution on the common law offense of disturbing the peace. Both Americans were acquitted. Washington thought it best to employ the state governors to enforce the neutrality proclamation. The governors were inadequate to the task, and in August Washington adopted Hamilton's original suggestion.

THE WHISKEY REBELLION

Genet's activities were tangentially connected with another law enforcement problem. He had promoted the organization of about three dozen "democratic-republican societies," political action clubs that formed the extreme left wing of the republican party. The most radical societies were in western Pennsylvania, a hotbed of resistance to the collection of the federal excise on whiskey. In the summer of 1794 the members and assorted hooligans engaged in a good deal of violence, launching an armed attack against and burning the house of the excise inspector, robbing the mails, tarring and feathering collectors, defying court orders, and organizing a march on Pittsburgh by a mob of five or six thousand armed men. County and state officials, when they did anything, supported the insurgents.

Orders to desist being ignored, Washington determined to suppress the rebellion by force. Under the Militia Act of 1792, the president was authorized to call out the militia if a federal judge certified that the laws of the United States were being opposed "by combinations too powerful to be suppressed by the ordinary course of judicial proceedings." Justice James Wilson so certified in August, and Knox, on the president's instructions, wrote to the governors of New Jersey, Pennsylvania, Maryland, and Virginia to mobilize a total of 12,950 men. In September the forces were assembled and began marching westward with Washington himself in command. He stayed with the troops for three weeks, then turned them over to Gov. Henry "Light-Horse Harry" Lee.

Resistance disappeared; several thousand men fled down the Ohio to Kentucky, a few score people were arrested, twenty were taken to Philadelphia and tried for treason, and two were convicted. Washington pardoned them.

Though Jefferson, who had long since left the government, scoffed that "an insurrection was announced and proclaimed and armed against, but could never be found," Washington's handling of the episode was skillful. The guiding principle was, as Hamilton put it in another context, "Whenever the Government appears in arms it ought to appear like a *Hercules,*" for the respect it thus inspires is likely to prevent the necessity for bloodshed. Presidents who followed that maxim in suppressing rebelliousness generally succeeded. Washington also set a key precedent in the aftermath of the Whiskey Rebellion. Through General Lee, he granted a blanket amnesty to the insurgents—thereby simultaneously indicating that the president's pardoning power extends to a general dispensing of the laws and showing a magnanimity that strengthened his administration in the eyes of the public.

Establishing Precedents for the Executive Office

David E. Maas

> When he became president, George Washington wrote, "I walk on untrodden ground. There is scarcely any part of my conduct which may not hereafter be drawn into precedent." And during his presidency, Washington remained conscious of his groundbreaking role and set many precedents that presidents continue to follow to this day. In this reading, history professor David E. Maas enumerates several of these precedents and explains why Washington thought each one was important to the office.

There has been a tendency for historians to summarize presidents with a few words. For example, Nixon hoped his would be, "he went to China", but admits historians will probably say, "He resigned the office." If I were to play this game I might summarize FDR with "solved the depression and began the welfare system." Or JFK, "charismatic Camelot leader and lover." My summary for George Washington would be "Founding Father of the American Presidency."

Why this title? Because if one rated the question which president had the greatest impact on the office, one could make a case for George Washington. First and most importantly, the framers of the Constitution gave extensive powers to the presidency because they knew George Washington would be the first president and could be trusted. Second, because he was first and therefore everything he did set a precedent. . . .

George Washington agreed and realized that his every action would set precedent. Once as president Washington refused a request of Congress for diplomatic correspondence

David E. Maas, "George Washington: The Founding Father of the American Presidency," *George Washington in and as Culture*, edited by Kevin L. Cope. New York: AMS Press, 2001. Copyright © 2001 by AMS Press, Inc. Reproduced by permission.

with England. His stated reason: it "would be to establish a dangerous precedent."

Washington set at least 25 precedents. The details of a few of these will serve to illustrate how he shaped the office of President for all future occupants.

The Private President

First precedent: a president of the United States is often an unknowable person. George Washington's unknowable quality came from his reserve and his personal desire to put a gap between himself and others. Mrs. Henrietta Liston, the wife of the British ambassador, told President Washington that she could read in his facial expressions the pleasure he expected from retirement from the presidency. Washington replied, "You are wrong; my countenance never yet betrayed my feelings." The secretary of the British ambassador observed President Washington and then wrote, "he possesses the two great requisites of a statesman, the faculty of concealing his own sentiments and of discovering those of other men." Almost every later president has opted for privacy and concealment over an open, folksy approach.

Part of the unknowable quality of Washington comes from the impossibility of separating the real person from the myth or public image. George Washington was America's first great hero. Babies were christened after him as early as 1775 and while he was still president he was made into a wax figure. After his death in December 1799, he passed still further into legend. Mason Weems in his early biography of Washington added the false stories of the cherry tree and the dollar across the Potomac. Today Washington's surname has been appropriated for one American state, seven mountains, eight streams, ten lakes, 33 counties, nine American colleges, 121 American towns. When I was a youth in Washington, D.C. there was even a baseball team named after him, the Washington Senators, now known as the Minnesota Twins. They were such poor players that my father said the team was "First in walks, first in errors, and last in the American League." Washington's birthday is a national holiday; his visage appears on the one dollar bill, our quarter, and on postage stamps. He is one of four presidents carved in Mt. Rushmore where his head is 60 feet from chin to scalp. There are statues of him all over America. In Washington, D.C., a town named after him, there is a 555-foot-high monument.

It is hard to know what the real Washington was like. At the University of Virginia a team of historians are working on publishing the 135,000 documents produced by Washington. Editor William Abbot, who has read all the documents, observed: "Washington is a man of action, not of introspection. He didn't discuss his innermost thoughts. Washington was practical and reserved. He was not interested in revealing things about himself." Scholars learn little of George Washington from the correspondence between him and his wife, since Martha destroyed all but two of his letters to her. His diaries tell little of the inner man, but are more concerned with barometer readings.

WASHINGTON'S PHYSICAL STATURE

Second precedent: the presidency is often a beauty contest with voters influenced by an impressive physical persona. In the twentieth century, the tallest candidate has won all but four presidential elections. George Washington was an impressive person. He stood a full head and shoulders taller than most of his contemporaries. The average height for men who fought in the American Revolution was five feet five and one-half inches. When George Washington died the medical doctors measured him and recorded his height at six feet three and one-half exact inches. . . .

In 1760 a fellow member of the Virginia House of Burgesses, George Mercer, described Washington as "straight as an Indian, measuring 6 feet 2 inches in his stockings, and weighing 175 pounds when he took his seat in the assembly in 1759. His frame is padded with well developed muscles, indicating great strength. . . . His head is well shaped though not large, but is gracefully poised on a superb neck. A large and straight rather than a prominent nose; blue-gray penetrating eyes, which are widely separated and overhung by a heavy brow. His face is long rather than broad, with high round cheek bones, and terminates in a good firm chin. He has a clear though rather colorless pale skin, which burns with the sun. A pleasing, benevolent though a commanding countenance, dark brown hair, which he wears in a queue. His mouth is large and generally firmly closed, but which from time to time discloses some defective teeth." George Washington got his poor teeth from the practice of cracking walnuts with his teeth when he was young. After losing his teeth, he wore dentures. He had numerous sets of dentures made variously from lead, ivory, and the teeth of humans, cows, and other animals, but not from wood, as was popularly believed.

PRESIDENTIAL PRECEDENTS

Third, most presidents live high at taxpayers' expense and leave the office with even more potential for income. The Continental Congress on 15 June 1775 offered George Washington $500.00 per month, but Washington only asked for expenses. It turned out that such patriotism can be profitable. If Washington had accepted a general's pay, he would have earned a total of $48,000.00. In 1783, he submitted vouchers totaling $414,108.21 plus $7,488.00 in interest, representing a 6% annual. In addition, Washington claimed $27,665.30 in travel expenses for his wife Martha. Next to money spent for spies, the largest single expenditure was for his housekeeping costs. The nation's commander-in-chief lived exceedingly high on tax-payer dollars. He dressed in the latest military fashions, transported himself in expensive carriages, and never skimped on food or liquor. When he became president, Washington received $25,000.00 year. A high salary in 1789 since a skilled artisan in New York City earned $250 a year and unskilled laborers as little as $115 a year.

Fourth, George Washington as president toured all 13 states. Subsequent presidents regularly emulate this practice when they campaign for the presidency. A male admirer described Washington's visit to Salem in 1789. "I have had the happiness . . . of seeing this incomparable President. You may laugh but he has a most beautiful face. Did you ever see a countenance a thousandth part so expressive of that goodness, benevolence, sensibility, and modesty which characterize him? . . . His appearance as he passed thorough Court Street in Salem was far from gay, or making anyone else so. He looked oppressed by the attention that was paid him, and as he cast his eye around, I thought he seemed to sink at the notice he attracted. When he had got to the Court House, and had patiently listened to the ditty they sung at him, and heard the shouts of the multitude, he bowed very low, and as if he could bear no more turned hastily around and went into the house.". . .

Fifth, Washington set the precedent that a president staffs the White House with his own people. When on 16 April 1789 Washington left Mount Vernon for New York City to take the oath of office, he took with him Tobias Lear, Harvard '83, his secretary, and Colonel David Humphreys, a Yale graduate and his speech writer. He staffed the White House with the best graduates of Ivy League schools. He further staffed his home in New York City with slaves from Mount Vernon. . . .

THE FIRST INAUGURATION

Sixth, presidents have inaugurations and give addresses. On Thursday, 30 April 1789, on the balcony of Federal Hall in New York City, Robert R. Livingston, chancellor of state of New York, administered the oath. William Maclay, senator from Pennsylvania, as an eyewitness to the inaugural address wrote, "This great man was agitated and embarrassed more than ever he was by the leveled cannon or pointed musket. He trembled, and several times would scarce make out to read, though it must be supposed he had often read it before."

The inaugural illustrates the problems of a new administration with no precedents. The event stirred a flurry of questions concerning proper protocols. Vice President [John] Adams, as presiding officer of the Senate, worried over how should Washington be received so as to preserve a proper balance between dignities of the presidency and the legislature. Adams asked senators, "How shall I behave? How shall we receive it? [Washington's inaugural address] Shall it be standing or sitting?" George Washington wisely scrapped his original 73-page speech and gave an address that lasted less than 20 minutes. The most remarkable part of his address is that more than a third of it contained religious phrases. He was not striking a popular position, as a modern-day politician might, by paying lip service to religion and simply making sure that the address contained few Christian terms without concern for theological content (or the lack thereof). He did not mention "Christ" or even use the word "God." Instead he referred to God in deistic terms such as "the invisible hand which conducts the affairs of men" or "the benign parent of the human race." Although Washington delivered the address in a very low tone and with ill-timed gestures, every one in the audience was moved to tears. The one exception was Senator Maclay. The ever caustic Maclay evaluated Washington's address as "heavy, dull, stupid." Maclay, upset by Washington's inept delivery and clumsy elocution, added, "I felt hurt that he was not first in everything."

146 George Washington

During the evening and the next day the Senate engaged in a heated debate over how to reply to George Washington's speech. Some delegates wanted to refer to it as "the most gracious speech," words traditionally used by parliament in replying to addresses of the king. Senator Maclay objected as "we have lately had a hard struggle for our liberty against Kingly Authority." Finally the Senate dropped the word "gracious" as some felt it represented the first step toward royalty.

George Washington then sent the Senate a note thanking its membership for their acknowledgment. Vice President Adams responded to Washington in kind, delivering to George Washington the Senate's thank you for George Wash-

Washington (shown at his inauguration) strengthened the government and shaped the office of president for all future occupants.

ington's thank you. George Washington then responded with another note. This escalating process of mutual appreciation at last ended when, fortunately, the Senate decided not to thank him for thank you on their thank you.

WASHINGTON AND GOD

Precedent seven: a close identification of our presidents with Christianity or the blessing of God the Creator. A New Jersey resident wrote the following on the event of Washington's first inauguration: "That God by his peculiar grace chose thee to rule the state." A New Hampshire citizen wrote an ode for singing on Washington's inauguration and included the observation that the unanimous choice of President Washington proved "nothing but a pure effort of divine Providence, could have produced such a union of sentiment." Another admirer from Boston using Washington's name as an acrostic included the phrases, "Of every virtue and each gift possest, religion reigns triumphant in his breast, Grant him, Almighty God! Thy aid and health.". . .

When Washington as president visited every state in the Union, his visits prompted similar outpourings of odes, songs, and addresses, many tinged with religious sentiments. He was praised for "God like deeds," an ode contained a chorus with the phrase "See the godlike Washington.". . .

Ironically, in contrast to the public perception, Washington was one of our most non-religious presidents. He never took communion in any church. This is the testimony of his granddaughter Eleanor Parke "Nelly" Custis. Furthermore, Dr. James Abercrombie, assistant rector of Christ Church in Philadelphia, testified that George Washington always left before communion was served. On one occasion Dr. Abercrombie preached a sermon against the evil of those who by example discourage others from taking communion, the message clearly aimed at George Washington. Washington took it well and ever after simply stayed away on communion Sundays. . . .

ESTABLISHING PROTOCOL

Eight precedent: It was in Washington's first term that he received the title "president of the United States." A key issue in the first Congress was the fact that it had the important task of setting precedents! One issue occupying a lot of time was what title to call senators and the president. Most senators led by Vice President John Adams wanted exalted titles and a Senate committee proposed that the President should have the title "His Highness the President of the United States and Protector of the Rights of the Same." The Senate favored this and argued "a decent respect for the opinion and practice of civilized nations," required such a title. . . .

Ninth, Washington established protocol for White House socials. George Washington consulted with [James] Madison, [Alexander] Hamilton, Adams, and [John] Jay on the proper procedure and frequency of socials, since the precedent once established might long continue. On one hand he noted that he needed to avoid "the inconveniences as well as reduction of respectability by too free an intercourse and too much familiarity." On the other hand, it was essential to avoid giving the impression "of an ostentatious show of mimicry of sovereignty."

Ultimately he decided on two socials a week: one was the President's tea for men only on Tuesdays from 3 to 4 pm. The other was Martha's tea for men and women held on Friday evenings. At the first president's tea, all the guests were in the room and then Humphreys, one of his secretaries, threw open the door and shouted "The President of the US." This so surprised and upset George Washington that ever after Washington arrived first in the room and then the guests entered. George Washington always stood wearing his most formal clothes, with a hat under his arm, and his dress sword. He bowed to each guest in turn, but never shook hands with anyone during his eight years as president.

At Martha's tea, Mrs. Washington normally remained seated while servants stood at the door and announced the guests' names. Then an aide would escort the ladies to Mrs. Washington. After a curtsey and a brief moment of conversation, each lady was conducted to a chair where she was to sit till George Washington came up to her. Then she was free to go into the other room for refreshments: ice cream, tea, coffee, cakes, candy, fruit, punch. No liquor was ever served at these parties.

Soon the Washingtons added a third social each week: a dinner by invitation starting at 4:00 pm on Thursdays. President and Mrs. Washington sat opposite each other in the middle of the dinner table with men on George Washington's side and women at Martha's side. Senator Maclay, who disliked George Washington, recorded his first invitation to one of these dinners. "It was the most solemn dinner ever I eat at, not an health drank, scarce a word said!" Then after dinner, "The President filling a glass of wine with great formality drank the health of every individual by name round the table. Everybody imitated him, changed glasses, and such a buzz of health, sir and madam, . . . never had I heard before.". . .

George Washington decided against attending the funerals of private persons. On Sunday 15 November 1789 George Washington received an invitation to attend the funeral of Isaac Roosevelt (an ancestor of Theodore Roosevelt), but declined as in his diary he wrote: "first because the propriety of accepting any invitation of this sort appeared very questionable—and secondly, (though to do it in this instance might not be improper,) because it might be difficult to discriminate in cases which might thereafter happen."

Tenth precedent: Presidents are the most "visible" citizens and subject to a barrage of criticism. George Washington did have the trappings of monarchy for Democratic Republicans to criticize. He rode to work in a carriage drawn by six horses and escorted by uniformed outriders. A former friend, Thomas Paine, in 1796 wrote in a public pamphlet that George Washington was a bad general during the war because his sole strategy consisted of "doing nothing." Increasingly in his second term, some newspapers attacked George Washington as a "political hypocrite," and not the father but "step-Father" of his country. George Washington was so deeply concerned about his press image that he subscribed to twelve newspapers. Most of his successors have a similar fascination with their public image, going Washington one better, when they hire spindoctors.

Eleventh precedent: a man should not cling to power. Because of disgruntled American army officers General Washington in March 1783 had the opportunity to make himself the first monarch of America. Instead he personally quelled the rebellion and then "The gallant hero sheathed the deathful sword.". . . In 1789 he reluctantly chaired the Constitutional Convention and with equal reluctance became our first president. As he arrived in New York to take the oath of office, a poet wrote, "No Alexander's mad career,/No Caesar's dictatorial reign,/No dazzling pomp that scepters wear." After two terms as president, he retired, thus establishing a precedent-setting two-term presidency. George Washington was fed up with politics and upset by personal attacks in the press. He decided not to run again, even though there was no two-term limitation (as set by the twenty-second amendment passed in 1951), or precedent.

Other precedents that deserve notice, but because of brevity can only receive brief mention include: ...

13. Created the Executive Branch or cabinet.

14. Very partisan in appointments to government positions; very few anti-Federalists or Democratic Republicans received an office.

15. Established the principle of balancing geographical sections of the country in his cabinet and Supreme Court appointments.

16. Delivered an annual message to Congress, in person.

17. Made the president responsible for recognizing the legality of new governments.

18. Likewise, determined that the president decides on issues of American neutrality or engagement during foreign wars.

19. In 1796, refused to give the House some diplomatic correspondence, thereby establishing the right of the executive branch to withhold information from legislative bodies.

20. In 1791, sent Gouverneur Morris to Europe, establishing a precedent for presidents commissioning special envoys without Senate approval.

21. Demonstrated that politics happen at social events by sponsoring dinners and sailing parties to convince Congressmen to move the nation's capitol to D.C. (in 1790, Washington took Hamilton and Jefferson on a three-day fishing trip off Sandy Hook). . . .

24. Monuments in D.C. for famous presidents: the House of Representatives, after his death, resolved that a marble monument be built and he should be buried there, although the 555-foot Washington Monument wasn't constructed until 100 years later.

25. Elaborate public funerals, instead of private ones, on the grounds that presidents are public figures. Although Washington's body was never moved to D.C. but remained at Mt. Vernon, the funeral service, by Rev. Thomas Davis, on 18 December 1799, was not as simple as Washington had wanted. A procession of mourners filed between two long rows of soldiers, a band played music, guns boomed from a ship anchored in the Potomac, and the Masonic order to which George Washington belonged sent a large contingent.

Washington's Role in the Controversy over Slavery

Dorothy Twohig

The institution of slavery in America was controversial from the day it began. But while many agreed that it was an unjust practice, few were willing to give it up. The economy of the southern states depended on slavery, and to many it seemed that without it, the new nation's financial framework would collapse.

When George Washington became president, he was concerned not only with maintaining financial stability in the United States but also with keeping the states together in a unified whole. Before the founding of the United States, the colonies had been separate, independent entities, each with its own interest; now the union of states was embarking upon a new venture—the creation of a central government. As the first leader of that government, Washington realized just how fragile the bonds that held the states together were. This article by Washington scholar and University of Virginia professor Dorothy Twohig explains that Washington did not attack the issue of slavery while president primarily because he realized that it was the one issue that could tear the new nation apart.

On April 16, 1789, Washington left Mount Vernon to begin his journey to New York City to assume the presidency. He went, he said, "to the chair of government, with "feelings not unlike those of a culprit who is going to the place of his execution, so unwilling am I, in the evening of a life nearly consumed in public cares, to quit a peaceful abode for an Ocean of difficulties." Over the preceeding months he had conducted an

Dorothy Twohig, "'That Species of Property': Washington's Role in the Controversy over Slavery," *George Washington Reconsidered*, edited by Don Higginbotham. Charlottesville: University Press of Virginia, 2001. Copyright © 2001 by The Rector and Visitors of the University of Virginia. Reprinted by permission of the publisher.

extensive correspondence with friends, countering their unanimous urgings that he accept the presidency with his own agonizing reluctance to risk his hardwon reputation on the uncertainties of the new government. All along the route to the capital, he passed through cheering throngs to whom he seemed the embodiment of the patriot leader. Gouverneur Morris probably echoed the views of most Americans when he wrote Washington in 1788 that "You alone can awe the Insolence of opposing Factions & the greater Insolence of assuming Adherents. . . . You will become a Father to more than three Millions of Children." Washington brought with him from his service in the Revolution an unblemished reputation for honor and integrity, for being above the struggles of political life, for dedication to duty and to the state. Both at home and abroad he was the man of the century.

Critics of Washington have insisted that if there was a time before the Civil War when slavery as an institution might have been successfully attacked, Washington could have seized this moment if he had given leadership to the antislavery forces. There is no indication that he ever considered any such course. No one understood better than he the fragility of the framework that bound the states together. During the [Articles of] Confederation years his faith in the new nation he had given almost ten years of his life to create had faltered. "I see," he wrote [his former military subordinate the French Marquis de] Lafayette, "one head gradually changing into thirteen." He confided to John Jay in 1786 that in his opinion virtue had "in a great degree, taken its departure from our Land." "We have probably had too good an opinion of human nature in forming our confederation," he wrote in in the mid-1780s, adding that men would not "adopt & carry into execution, measures the best calculated for their own good without the intervention of a coercive power." The convention of 1787 restored his optimism. "I begin to look forward," he wrote Sir Edward Newenham in 1788, "with a kind of political faith, to scenes of National happiness, which have not heretofore been offered for the fruition of the Most favoured Nations. The Natural, political, and Moral circumstances of our Nascent empire justify the anticipation."

LITTLE SUPPORT FOR ABOLITION

But Washington was a political realist. Presiding over the Constitutional Convention [in 1787] left him fully aware of the specter slavery had presented at the convention. Although it had not seemed an important factor when sessions began in Philadelphia, by the end of the summer it had permeated every phase of the deliberations. In the convention the strongest supporters of the Constitution were willing to take a stand on matters they felt essential to the success of the enterprise—to the making of a new government; but, as Washington had observed, they were not willing to sink their ship by taking on North and South Carolina and Georgia on the subject of slavery. In many of the debates the delegates trod so delicately that they employed euphemisms to avoid even the use of the word; slaves were disguised as "persons," or "persons held to Service or Labour"; the slave trade became "migrations." Day after day Washington sat in the president's chair listening attentively to the debates, although there is no evidence he spoke out on slavery or indeed on many other matters. The reception given to the strong antislavery speeches of Gouverneur Morris of New York and the diatribes against slavery by George Mason of Virginia were not lost on Washington. Delegates such as Charles C. Pinckney contended that "the property of the Southern States was to be as sacredly preserved, and protected to them, as that of land, or any other kind of property in the Eastern States were to be to their citizens. Property in slaves should not be exposed to danger under a government instituted for the protection of property." Even staunch supporters of the Constitution [such as] Pierce Butler of South Carolina retrenched when slavery was threatened. "The security the Southern States want," Butler said, "is that their negroes may not be taken from them, which some gentlemen within or without doors have a very good mind to do."

The experience of the Convention may well have shown Washington that there would be little substantive support from antislavery spokesmen if he had decided to take a vigorous position on the question....

In return for their support of the new government, the slave-owning southerners got most of what they wanted in the convention. The three-fifths clause [which stated that representation in the lower house of Congress would be determined by the free population of a state, plus three-fifths of all other persons in the state—meaning slaves] gave them extra representation in Congress.... The slave trade clause guaranteed their right to import new slaves for at least twenty years and the fugitive slave clause gave slave owners the right to repossess runaway slaves in free states.

The climate of the presidential years was equally unpromising. By the mid-1780s it was evident that the idealism of the 1770s had turned out to be an illusion. As Washington well knew, the last decades of the century witnessed a reversal in states like Virginia, where during the war there had been widespread public attacks on slavery and embryonic plans for the aboliton of the institution. Proslavery petitions proliferated in Virginia; over twelve hundred signatures appearing in such petitions to the assembly, testifying to considerable opposition to manumission [the freeing of slaves] and to deepening hostility toward the antislavery activities of the Quakers, Methodists, and others. The Deep South tightened legislation regarding slaves. There were sporadic objections to slavery on moral grounds, some northerners pointing out as early as 1790 the immorality of aristocrats living off the sweat of their slaves. On occasion northern intellectuals may have espoused a free-labor ideology, but they failed to advance their cause by overt action. Even the North profited by slavery in terms of its economic connections with the South, and except for occasional lip service from societies to promote manumission, there was little mainstream opposition from that quarter. In considering ratification of the Constitution, not one state which held conventions in the late 1780s introduced any amendment concerning slavery. And in fact there was little vocal support for the antislavery movement. Among Washington's peers, critics of slavery like [Alexander] Hamilton and Jay were active in manumission societies but offered few public comments. [James] Madison, a lifelong opponent of the institution, confined his musings on the contradictions between the ideals of the Revolution and the existence of slavery to his memoranda. [Thomas] Jefferson made relatively few public statements on the institution, except for his agonized soul-searching concerning the eligibility of blacks for full citizenship. Benjamin Franklin, especially through the Pennsylvania Abolition Society, gave more impressive leadership. Patrick Henry opposed slavery but kept his own slaves because, as he said, of the "general Inconvenience of living here without them."

Washington was aware [that] organized opposition to slavery had never come from a wide spectrum of the population. Postwar . . . arguments against slavery [made by church leaders] had made little headway and [had little] impact on southern owners. Certainly such mainstream questioning of the validity of the institution as did exist tended to center on the contention that slavery had been foisted by Great Britain on unwilling colonies who now had to deal with the resulting evils. Washington, like many others of his post-Revolutionary generation, still blamed Britain for hanging slavery around colonial necks.

Even the opposition itself was fragmented. Most of the opponents of slavery were Quakers and members of other benevolent religious groups, and slavery was only one of their interests. Early in the eighteenth century Quaker opponents of slavery had concentrated their efforts on the conditions of slavery and on the sect's religious duties toward the slaves. Not until the late 1760s and early 1770s was there strong opposition to the foreign and domestic slave trade, and recent research has suggested serious conflicts among Quakers regarding the freeing of slaves. Quakers generally shared Washington's strongest objection to the institution—that the buying and selling of slaves broke up families. The fact that by the end of the Revolution, slaveholders had an enormous economic stake in the preservation of the institution while advocates of abolition had nothing to lose was certainly not lost on Washington.

THE ROLE OF THE NEW PRESIDENT

Washington shared the determination of most of his own generation of statesmen not to allow slavery to disturb their agenda for the new Republic. Antislavery sentiment came in a poor second when it conflicted with the powerful economic interests of proslavery forces. To Washington as to many Americans, even some whose opinions on slavery were far more radical than his own, the institution had become a subject so divisive that public comments were best left unsaid.

Washington himself was far from being an egalitarian. In spite of the Revolution's rhetoric, the United States was still a society of deference and Washington never seriously questioned the political and social validity of the prevailing ideas of rule by an elite any more than he questioned his own position in such a society. Publicly no comments came from him on slavery. For Washington, as for most of the other founders, when the fate of the new republic was balanced against his own essentially conservative opposition to slavery, there was really no contest. And there was a widely held, if convenient, feeling among many opponents of slavery that if left alone, the institution would wither by itself. Ironically, the clause of the Constitution barring the importation of slaves after 1808 fostered this salve to the antislavery conscience by imparting the feeling that at least some progress had been made.

A major factor in Washington's failure to put his growing opposition to slavery into practice in the 1790s was certainly his own conception of his presidential role. He assumed the office on a wave of bipartisan support and reverence.... But he went into office with scarcely a specific blueprint for his presidency. At the convention none of the delegates except possibly Hamilton, James Wilson, and Gouverneur Morris had clearly formulated ideas as to the kind of executive that would emerge.... To many of the delegates at the convention in Philadelphia, the provisions of Article II [of the Constitution, which outlines the duties of the president] were based on the assumption that Washington would accept the office of president. Pierce Butler noted the presidential powers were "full great and greater than I was disposed to make them," and that members would not have expanded Article II had they not "cast their eyes toward General Washington as President, and shaped their Ideas of the Powers to be given to a President, by their opinions of his virtue."

Washington was well aware of the general public uneasiness concerning executive power and other aspects of the new government. He had carefully created his role of a national icon—John Adams called him "the best actor of the presidency that we have ever had"—and he had an extraordinary grasp of the symbolic function of his office as a unifying force for the new nation. Even the most cursory examination of the political correspondence of the period indicates how important Washington was in holding the fabric of the new nation together.... He was not about to risk this role in ... [an] attempt to challenge the South's peculiar institution.

As president, Washington proceeded tentatively and with his customary caution. "To form a new government," he had written John Washington in 1776, "requires infinite care & unbounded attention; for if the foundation is badly laid the superstructure must be bad.... A matter of such moment cannot be the Work of a day." He believed, as he wrote [in a letter to the French General, who had fought with the Americans in the Revolutionary War, the compte de] Rochambeau in the summer of 1790, that "in a government which depends so much in its first stages on public opinion, much circumspection is still necessary for those who are engaged in its administration." He cherished the approval of his peers and of the public; he had worked hard to deserve it. But probably more than any other of the Founders, he was acutely aware how fragile it all was and how easily the slavery controversy could destroy it. Through both of his administrations he feared [that] the new Republic was still on experimental ground.

WASHINGTON'S VIEWS ON SLAVERY

Washington's few private comments during the presidential years regarding slavery have been widely quoted. Clearly his own economic necessities seconded his political caution. He wrote [to his secretary] Tobias Lear in 1794 giving elaborate instructions on the sale of land to put his financial affairs in order. "I have no scruple to disclose to you, that my motives to these sales . . . are to reduce my income, be it more or less, to specialties, that the remainder of my days may, thereby, be more tranquil & freer from cares; and that I may be enabled . . . to do as much good with it as the resource will admit; for although, in the estimation of the world I possess a good, & clear estate, yet, so unproductive is it, that I am oftentimes ashamed to refuse aids which I cannot afford unless I was to sell part of it to answer the purpose." Washington added a coda to the letter, which, ever cautious, he marked "Private": "Besides these, I have another motive which makes me earnestly wish for the accomplishment of these things, it is indeed more powerful than all the rest: namely to liberate a certain species of property—which I possess, very repugnantly to my own feelings; but which imperious necessity compels . . . until I can substitute some other expedient, by which expences not in my power to avoid (however well disposed I may be to do it) can be defrayed."

In the same year he told Alexander Spotswood: "With respect to the other species of property, concerning which you ask my opinion, I shall frankly declare to you that I do not like even to think much less talk of it. However, as you have put the question, I shall, in a few words, give you my ideas of it. Were it not then, that I am principled [against] selling Negroes, as you would Cattle in the market, I would not, in twelve months from this date, be possessed of one as a slave." Most frequently quoted is his remark to [his friend Dr.] David Stuart after the failure of one of the myriad Quaker petitions to Congress: "The memorial of the Quakers (& a very mal-apropos [ill-suited] one it was) has at length been put to sleep, from which it is not <illegible> it will awake before the year 1808." Stuart had reported to Washington the growing feeling in Virginia that a "Northern phalanx" was bearing down on the state and that it was said that "many who were warm Supporters of the government, are changing their sentiments, from a conviction of the impracticability of Union with States, whose interests are so dissimilar with those of Virginia." The Quaker petitions to Congress, Stuart contended had given "particular umbrage" in Virginia as had the fact that the "Quakers should be so busy in this business. That they will raise up a storm against themselves, appears to me very certain."

On a personal level, Washington, with his passion for order, feared the element of anarchism in the antislavery movement. In general he did not give a warm reception to gadflys [critics], especially Quaker-gadflys—and the tone of many of the antislavery appeals with which he was deluged in the 1780s and 1790s, combining imperious demands with evangelical piety, were not likely to incline him in their favor. Edward Rushton's was not the only castigation [reproof] that he received in these years from antislavery sources. One of Washington's weaknesses as a politician was the fact that he was extraordinarily thin-skinned and criticism of either his personal or political behavior often troubled him far out of proportion to the event. The copy of Edward Rushton's polemic bears a notation in a contemporary hand, dated Liverpool [England], 20 Feb. 1797, that the letter was transmitted to Washington in July 1796 and "a few weeks ago it was returned under cover, without a syllable in reply."

Even in a private capacity Washington's achievements in regard to slavery during the presidency were not impressive. In April 1791, fearing the impact of a Pennsylvania law freeing slaves after six months' residence in that state, he instructed his secretary Tobias Lear to ascertain what effect the law would have on the status of the slaves who served the presidential household in Philadelphia. In case Lear believed that any of the slaves were likely to seek their freedom under Pennsylvania law, Washington wished them sent home to Mount Vernon. "If upon taking good advise it is found expedient to send them back to Virginia, I wish to have it accomplished under pretext that may decieve both them and the Public." When one of his slaves ran away in 1795 Washington told his overseer to take measures to apprehend the slave "but I would not have my name appear in any advertisement, or other measure, leading to it."

AVOIDING FACTIONS AND DIVISIVENESS

To Washington, factions were the death knell of republics, introducing party squabbles and leading to the divisiveness that would destroy his dream of creating a republic with a responsible citizenry, free of political strife. He exhibited great skill in defusing potential domestic crises during his first administration, and ... he hoped to remain above the fray. When party faction and internal strife developed during the second administration ... Washington took it as a personal defeat of his view of the Republic. And the slavery question, he well knew, dwarfed the other controversies that troubled his administraton. Many southerners had already come to regard opposition to slavery as a symbol for the mistrust and disillusion with which they regarded the new government. And there are strong indications in the correspondence of many that they still considered Washington as their only bulwark against the ravishment by northern politicians.

WASHINGTON REACTS TO A SLAVE REVOLT

If Washington still had any doubts concerning reaction in the United States to the specter raised by the question of emancipation, public reaction toward the slave revolt in the French colony of Saint Domingue in 1791 would have confirmed his determination to avoid pursuing the issue at all costs. The horrors of the revolt of the slaves on Saint Domingue against their French masters were immediately apparent although less understood in the United States were the appalling conditions that had inspired the revolt. Daily reports appeared in American newspapers on the insurrection.

The revolution struck Americans on two fronts. It played to their views of the sanctity of property, which to most Americans was part of the basic natural rights for which they had fought Britain for eight and a half long years, and it fed the fear in the Deep South of slave insurrections. Southern slaveholders were understandably most vocal in support of their Saint-Domingan counterparts. But nationwide sympathy, even among antislavery supporters, swung immediately to the planters, many of whom were important, both financially and politically, and many of whom had major economic connections in the United States. Washington wrote Jean Baptiste de Ternant, the French minister, in September 1791, promising to lose no time in dispatching orders to furnish money and arms requested by the French government to quell the revolt. "I am happy in the opportunity of testifying how well disposed the United states are to render every aid in their power to our good friends and Allies the French to quell 'the alarming insurrection of the Negros in Hispanola' and of the ready disposition to effect it, of the Executive authority thereof." The administration bowed immediately to French requests that portions of the Revolutionary War debt still owed to France by the United States be used to aid French efforts to put down the revolt and provision the colony. Strongly supported by the Washington administration with money and arms and by public opinion in the United States, thousands of refugees fled to America, settling in seaboard cities, where their tales of the death and destruction left in the path of the rebelling slaves appalled Americans in the North and fed southern paranoia.

No one was more aware than Washington of the potential the slavery issue had for the destruction of the Republic. As he had written to Alexander Spotswood in 1794, "I shall be happily mistaken if [slaves] are not found to be a very troublesome species of property ere many years pass over our heads." From Washington's occasional comments on slavery expressing his desire to see it disappear from the new American nation it is difficult to decipher how deep his sentiments ran. It is likely that he had come to disapprove of the institution on moral grounds and that he considered it a serious impediment to economic development. Although he did not make sufficient comments on the institution of slavery for us to be certain, it appears that his opposition dealt more with the immorality of one man holding ownership over another than with the cruelty and abuse to individuals that slavery might engender. But there is no indication in his correspondence that he advocated any immediate policy of abolition. Obsessed with order both in his personal life and in politics, he would hardly have contemplated saddling the fragile new nation with the enormous problems resulting from immediate abolition—the disruption in the labor market, the care of blacks too old or too sick to work. In the eighteenth century immediate abolition found few supporters except among antislavery radicals. Many of the founding generation feared the idle poor of whatever color, and the anticipation that emancipation would contribute to a vast idle population made, even for such statesmen as Jefferson, foreign settlement of freed slaves a corollary to emancipation. "Justice is in one scale," Jefferson observed, "and self preservation is in the other." Such apprehensions were not confined to the South. A New York law of the colonial period contended that "it is found by Experience, that the free Negroes of this colony are an Idle slothful people and prove very often a charge on the place where they be."

When Washington freed his own slaves at his death, he made relatively elaborate arrangements to prevent them from becoming a liability to the community. Washington specified that those of his slaves who were too old, too young, or too infirm to support themselves should be "comfortably cloathed & fed by my heirs while they live." Young slaves were to be taught to read and write. Like most of his peers Washington regarded stability and the sanctity of property as basic tenets of the new Republic.

It is likely, also, that Washington subscribed to the widely held belief that slavery would die a natural death, bolstered by the prohibition of importation of slaves after 1808, although that argument was weakened by the extensive natural increase among the slave population along the Chesapeake after 1730. To his credit Washington, unlike most of his peers, did free his slaves in his will, and during much of his public life he gave at least private support to the idea of emancipation. But, given his accurate conception of his own great and pivotal role in the infant country and his fears for the survival of the Republic itself, it is far from likely that he was ever sorely tempted to open as a national issue the Pandora's box that the Constitutional Convention appeared to contemporaries to have closed for the next twenty years.

Understanding Washington's Retirement

Bruce G. Peabody

In this selection, Bruce G. Peabody, assistant professor of political science at Fairleigh Dickinson University, explains why Washington decided to retire after serving two terms as president. He refutes the claim that Washington chose that time to retire because he wished to set a precedent for future presidents. Instead, he asserts that Washington's desire to retire to a more serene life at Mount Vernon, away from the emerging political partisanship, was the reason for his retirement. He further states that besides the desire to return to private life, Washington was disturbed by the American public's distrust of the executive office, and that his stepping down was his way of demonstrating that the president could be trusted because he was willing to give up his power. Another reason Washington retired when he did, Peabody contends, is to maintain his reputation. By stepping down, he became a model of selflessness to be admired and copied.

Perhaps the most celebrated aspect of Washington's legacy arises not from his considerable accomplishments as a general and statesman but from his refusal to accumulate further political honors. After reluctantly agreeing to serve as commander of the Continental Army and as president for two terms, Washington refused to run for a third term despite the widely held view of contemporary scholars that he would have been victorious. Instead, Washington returned to his beloved Mount Vernon estate and to what he described as the contentment of retired life. In the process, Washington quelled fears about the executive office and facilitated a

Bruce G. Peabody, "George Washington, Presidential Term Limits, and the Problem of Reluctant Political Leadership," *Presidential Studies Quarterly*, September 2001. Copyright © 2001 by *Presidential Studies Quarterly*. Reproduced by permission.

peaceful transition to the next administration.

Numerous political commentators and analysts have advanced several questionable claims about Washington and the tradition of limited presidential service believed to have emerged from his example. To begin with, they have insufficiently accounted for the origins of the two-term tradition. A common account suggests that Washington, concerned that open-ended presidential service would lead to abuses of executive power and threaten individual liberties, retired to set an example for his successors. As the House of Representatives summarized in a resolution passed in 1875,

> the precedent established by Washington and other presidents of the United States in retiring from the presidential office after their second term has become, by universal concurrence, a part of our republican system of government . . . [and] any departure from this time-honored custom would be unwise, unpatriotic, and fraught with peril to our free institutions.

Rejecting a Third Term

But while Washington's retirement in 1796 surely had some impact on the practice of presidents refusing to seek more than two terms, portraying him as the willful founder of this custom is misleading. Washington was personally resistant to serving as president at all, and he originally indicated he would retire after his first term; he reversed himself only after Hamilton, Thomas Jefferson, and James Madison all pleaded with him to run for a second term and as his own fears about the increasingly partisan air of national politics coalesced. But Washington's reluctance does not seem to have been a principled commitment against continued service per se. After all, Washington presided over the constitutional proceedings that endorsed a perpetually reeligible president: "The matter was fairly discussed in the Convention," Washington wrote to the Marquis de Lafayette in 1788, "and to my full convictions . . . I can see no propriety in precluding ourselves from the services of any man, who on some great emergency shall be deemed universally, most capable of serving the Public" even after serving two terms. The Constitution, Washington explained, retained sufficient checks against political corruption and stagnant leadership without a presidential term limits provision.

Other evidence suggesting that Washington did not consider a third term as inherently conflicting with constitutional or republican principles includes his 1796 Farewell Address, in which he somewhat apologetically explained that his retirement was consistent with the good of the nation and that he had carefully weighed the benefits of retirement versus continued service. Three years after this farewell address (in the last year of the president's life), Washington's reply to a letter sent by Jonathan Trumbull, the governor of Connecticut, is similarly revealing. Trumbull, along with other federalists, correctly anticipated that incumbent president John Adams would lose to Jefferson in the election of 1800, and they urged Washington to come out of retirement to run for a third term.

Washington's 1799 response, while rejecting the draft effort, reflected his personal distaste with the emergent partisanship at the turn of the century and his doubts about his continuing viability as a candidate, rather than a belief that a third term would itself be harmful to the polity. The "well meant, but mistaken views of my friends, to introduce me again into the chair of Government" were "impracticable in the present order of things" and unappealing to someone who hoped to "pass through the vale of life in retirement, undisturbed in the remnant of the days I have to sojourn here. . . ." In short, whatever misgivings Washington had about his own continued service as president, there is little evidence that he opposed reeligibility or saw himself as establishing a precedent of limited presidential tenure.

If not motivated by wanting to set an example of limited presidential service (and thereby check overweening executive and federal power), what did prompt Washington to retire? Washington's decision to leave office seems to have been inspired by three intertwined factors: a desire to strengthen the institution of the presidency, his longstanding interest in securing personal honor and reputation, and a deepening weariness with public service (and a corresponding wish to return to his private affairs in Virginia).

STRENGTHEN THE PRESIDENCY

Washington's refusal to seek a third presidential term in 1796 seems to have been partly brought about by his awareness of pervasive domestic distrust of federal executive power, which he sought to assuage. While commander of the Continental Army, Washington developed a firsthand sense of the necessity of strong centralized leadership—and particularly the need for energetic, independent executive action—views that did not change after ratification of the Articles of Confederation or after establishing peace with Britain in 1783. Writing to Hamilton in the midst of the constitutional ratification process in 1788, Washington chastised those "who oppose a strong & energetic government" as either "narrow minded politicians, or under the influence of local views." But while Washington supported the Constitution's powerful executive office, a number of his contemporaries fiercely opposed the institution, viewing it as the "fetus of monarchy" and a likely seat of despotic rule.

Thus, Washington perceived the utility of stepping down from office as a means of alleviating lingering concerns about the nascent presidential office. Washington's example suggested that a strong chief executive need not come at the expense of the citizenry's liberties. As [political science professor and author] Glenn Phelps explained [in his book *George Washington and American Constitutionalism*], Washington retired "believ[ing] that the public and the Congress needed to be shown that the president could be trusted." In this way, Washington's personal abnegation of presidential power helped secure the long-term strength of the institution.

In addition to stepping away from public life as a way of diffusing misgivings about the new presidency, Washington retired to burnish his personal reputation. In the eighteenth-century Virginian society with which Washington was most familiar, the public exhibition of distinguished service and virtuous political behavior, especially disinterested commitment to the public good, secured an individual's social standing. Throughout his years of public service, Washington expressed a recurring desire to "obtain the applause of deserving men." As [historian] Paul Longmore argued [in his book *The Invention of George Washington*],

> throughout his life, Washington marshaled his prodigious energies in a continuous quest for honor, for validation by his society of his personal and public character. . . . Back of George Washington's extraordinary exertions stirred a desire for distinction, a yearning for public esteem that ultimately became a quest for historical immortality.

Washington's accumulation of national honors and the esteem of his country culminated with his refusal to assume a third term. In turning away from further service, Washington established himself as a model of selfless leadership.

A Desire for Domestic Comfort

In addition to these considerations, Washington's retirement from the presidency was influenced by his enthusiasm for private life as well as his increasing fatigue and vexation with political attacks on his administration and person (criticism that he believed threatened the reputation and honor so carefully cultivated in the course of his lengthy public career). During both his military and political service, Washington constantly expressed his longing for the comfort (and labor) he associated with domestic life in Virginia, a view that seems to have colored not only his decision to retire in 1796 but his reluctant attitude toward public leadership generally.

For example, in his June 1783 "Circular to State Governments" (in which Washington surrendered his military commission following the Revolutionary War), the departing general expressed his fervent desire "to return to that domestic retirement, which, it is well known, I left with the greatest reluctance, a Retirement, for which I have never ceased to sigh through a long and painful absence." He hoped to enjoy quietly "in private life . . . the benefits of [the] wise and liberal Government" he had helped to establish. Five years later, in 1788, Washington tried to discourage speculation about his potential candidacy as the nation's first president, indicating to Hamilton that "it is my great and sole desire to live and die, in peace and retirement, on my own farm." As [University of Virginia professor S.M.] Milkis and [Rhodes College professor M.] Nelson concluded [in *The American Presidency*], Washington "stepped down voluntarily from the presidency after two terms . . . not as a matter of principle but because he longed for 'the shade of retirement.'"

Washington's decision to retire was influenced not only by the attraction of his abandoned life in Mount Vernon but by his growing aversion to (and exhaustion with) late-eighteenth-century politics. Even before entering office, Washington expressed profound doubts about public leadership. He noted in 1788 that becoming the chief executive "would be the greatest sacrifice of my personal feelings & wishes that ever I have been called upon to make. It would be to forego repose and domestic enjoyment; for trouble, perhaps; for public obloquy."

As president, Washington chafed against criticisms of his policies. In his second term, for example, he was angered when both the Neutrality Proclamation and Jay's Treaty attracted vehement opposition. Washington seemed particularly perturbed by partisan attacks in the press—which included personal denunciations of the president as a "supercilious tyrant" who had "debauched" the nation in pursuing his federalist agenda—as well as by charges that he and his administration were assuming a monarchical air. As Woodrow Wilson suggested (in somewhat exaggerated fashion), "harder things had never been said of king and parliament than were now said of Washington and his advisers." In any event, the nation's first president expressed great relief upon permanently leaving political life and returning to Mount Vernon.

CHAPTER 5

THE IMPORTANCE OF GEORGE WASHINGTON

PEOPLE WHO MADE HISTORY

GEORGE WASHINGTON

The Enlightened American Hero

Gordon S. Wood

In the following selection, university professor and Pulitzer Prize–winning historian Gordon S. Wood explains why people should remember George Washington and continue to celebrate him as an American hero. He notes that Washington was "a child of the eighteenth-century Enlightenment." The Enlightenment was an intellectual movement that began in Europe and was based on the idea that human reason could triumph over ignorance. The movement was led by writers and philosophers who worked to turn people away from superstition, including most forms of religion, and toward reason. Ideas that are considered truly American, such as freedom and democracy, are tenets of this movement. Wood contends that Washington was a man "willing to sacrifice his personal desires for the greater good of his community or his country." Washington, he says, based his life on the adherence to enlightened conventions such as virtue and stoicism. Finally, Wood agrees with the legion of historians who believe that Washington's most important asset was his strong moral character, and that it is Washington's character that leaders today should attempt to emulate.

George Washington may still be first in war and first in peace, but he no longer seems to be first in the hearts of his countrymen. Or at least in the hearts of American historians. A recent poll of 900 American historians shows that Washington has dropped to third place in presidential greatness behind Lincoln and FDR. Which only goes to show how little American historians know about American history.

Polls of historians about presidential greatness are proba-

Gordon S. Wood, "The Greatness of George Washington," *George Washington Reconsidered*, edited by Don Higginbotham. Charlottesville: University Press of Virginia, 2001. Copyright © 2001 by The Rector and Visitors of the University of Virginia. Reprinted by permission of the publisher.

bly silly things, but, if they are to be taken seriously, then Washington fully deserved the first place he has traditionally held. He certainly deserved the accolades his contemporaries gave him. And as long as this republic endures he ought to be first in the hearts of his countrymen. Washington was truly a great man and the greatest president we have ever had.

But he was a great man who is not easy to understand. He became very quickly, as has often been pointed out, more a monument than a man, statuesque and impenetrable. Even his contemporaries realized that he was not an ordinary accessible human being. He was deified in his own lifetime. "O Washington," declared Ezra Stiles, president of Yale, in 1783. "How I do love thy name! How have I often adored and blessed thy God, for creating and forming thee, the great ornament of human kind! . . . Thy fame is of sweeter perfume than Arabian spices. Listening angels shall catch the odor, waft it to heaven and perfume the universe!"

One scholar has said that Washington has been "the object of the most intense display of hero worship this nation has ever seen." Which helps explain the continuing efforts to humanize him—even at the beginning of our history. Parson Mason Weems, his most famous biographer, was less of a churchman than he was a hustling entrepreneur. He was ready when Washington died in 1799: "I've something to whisper in your lug [ear]," Weems wrote to his publisher Matthew Carey a month after the great man's death. "Washington you know, is gone! Millions are gaping to read something about him. I am very nearly primed and cocked for 'em." Weems had his book out within the year.

From Another World

The most famous anecdotes about Washington's early life come from Weems. He wanted to capture the inner private man—to show the early events that shaped Washington's character, even if he had to make them up. Weems presumed that the source of Washington's reputation for truthfulness lay in his youth. He tells a story that he said he had heard from Washington's nurse. It was, he says, "too valuable to be lost, too true to be doubted." This was, of course, the story of the cherry tree about whose chopping down Washington could not tell a lie.

Despite the continued popularity of Parson Weems' attempt to humanize him, Washington remained distant and unapproachable, almost unreal and unhuman. There have been periodic efforts to bring him down to earth, to expose his foibles, to debunk his fame, but he remained, and remains, massively monumental. By our time in the late 20th century he seems so far removed from us as to be virtually incomprehensible. He seems to come from another time and another place—from another world.

And that's the whole point about him: he does come from another world. And his countrymen realized it even before he died in 1799. He is the only truly classical hero we have ever had. He acquired at once a worldwide reputation as a great patriot-hero.

And he knew it. He was well aware of his reputation and his fame earned as the commander-in-chief of the American revolutionary forces. That awareness of his heroic stature and his character as a republican leader was crucial to Washington. It affected nearly everything he did for the rest of his life.

Washington was a thoroughly 18th-century figure. So much so, that he quickly became an anachronism. He belonged to the pre-democratic and pre-egalitarian world of the 18th century, to a world very different from the world that would follow. No wonder then that he seems to us so remote and so distant. He really is. He belonged to a world we have lost and we were losing even as Washington lived.

An Unlikely Hero

In many respects Washington was a very unlikely hero. To be sure, he had all the physical attributes of a classical hero. He was very tall by contemporary standards, and was heavily built and a superb athlete. Physically he had what both men and women admired. He was both a splendid horseman at a time when that skill really counted and an extraordinarily graceful dancer. And naturally he loved both riding and dancing. He always moved with dignity and looked the leader.

Yet those who knew him well and talked with him were often disappointed. He never seemed to have very much to say. He was most certainly *not* what we would today call an "intellectual." We cannot imagine him, say, expressing his views on Plato in the way [Thomas] Jefferson and John Adams did in their old age. Adams was especially contemptuous of Washington's intellectual abilities. It was certain, said Adams, that Washington was not a scholar. "That he was too illiterate, unlearned, unread for his station and reputation is equally past dispute."

Adam's judgment is surely too harsh. Great men in the 18th century did not have to be scholars or intellectuals. But there is no doubt that Washington was not a learned man, especially in comparison with the other Founding Fathers. He was very ill at ease in abstract discussions. Even Jefferson, who was usually generous in his estimates of his friends, said that Washington's "colloquial talents were not above mediocrity." He had " neither copiousness of ideas nor fluency of words."

Washington was not an intellectual, but he was a man of affairs. He knew how to run his plantation and make it pay. He certainly ran Mount Vernon better than Jefferson ran Monticello [his estate]. Washington's heart was always at Mount Vernon. He thought about it all the time. Even when he was president he devoted a great amount of his energy worrying about the fence posts of his plantation, and his letters dealing with the details of running Mount Vernon were longer than those dealing with the running of the federal government.

But being a man of affairs and running his plantation or even the federal government efficiently were not what made him a world-renowned hero. What was it that lay behind his extraordinary reputation, his greatness?

His military exploits were of course crucial. But Washington was not really a traditional military hero. He did not resemble Alexander, Caesar, Cromwell, or Marlborough; his military achievements were nothing compared to those Napoleon would soon have. Washington had no smashing, stunning victories. He was not a military genius, and his tactical and strategic maneuvers were not the sort that awed men. Military glory was *not* the source of his reputation. Something else was involved.

Washington's genius, his greatness, lay in his character. He was, as [French writer] Chateaubriand said, a "hero of an unprecedented kind." There had never been a great man quite like Washington before. Washington became a great man and was acclaimed as a classical hero because of the way he conducted himself during times of temptation. It was his moral character that set him off from other men.

A Man of the Enlightenment

Washington fit the 18th-century image of a great man, of a man of virtue. This virtue was not given to him by nature. He had to work for it, to cultivate it, and everyone sensed that. Washington was a self-made hero, and this impressed an 18th-century enlightened world that put great stock in men controlling both their passions and their destinies. Washington seemed to possess a self-cultivated nobility.

He was in fact a child of the 18th-century Enlightenment. He was very much a man of his age, and he took its moral standards more seriously than most of his contemporaries. Washington's Enlightenment, however, was not quite that of Jefferson or [Benjamin] Franklin. . . .

Washington's Enlightenment was a much more down-to-earth affair, concerned with behavior and with living in the everyday-world of people. His Enlightenment involved what eventually came to be called cultivation and civilization. He lived his life by the book—not the book of military rules but the book of gentility. He was as keenly aware as any of his fellow Americans of the 18th-century conventions that defined what a proper gentleman was. . . .

An enlightened, civilized man was disinterested and impartial, not swayed by self-interest and self-profit. He was cosmopolitan; he stood above all local and parochial considerations and was willing to sacrifice his personal desires for the greater good of his community or his country. He was a man of reason who resisted the passions most likely to afflict great men, that is, ambition and avarice. Such a liberal, enlightened gentleman avoided enthusiasms and fanaticisms of all sorts, especially those of religion. Tolerance and liberality were his watchwords. Politeness and compassion toward his fellow man were his manners. Behaving in this way was what constituted being civilized.

Washington was thoroughly caught up in this enlightened promotion of gentility and civility, this rational rolling back of parochialism, fanaticism, and barbarism. He may have gone to church regularly, but he was not an emotionally religious person. In all of his writings there is no mention of Christ, and God is generally referred to as "the great disposer of human events." Washington loved [English playwright Joseph] Addison's play *Cato* and saw it over and over and incorporated its lines into his correspondence. The play, very much an Enlightenment tract, helped to teach him what it meant to be liberal and virtuous, what it meant to be a stoical classical hero. He had the play put on for his troops during the terrible winter at Valley Forge in 1778.

One of the key documents of Washington's life is his "Rules of Civility and Decent Behaviour in Company and Conversation," a collection of 110 maxims that Washington wrote down sometime before his 16th birthday. The maxims were originally drawn from a 17th-century etiquette book and were copied by the young autodidact. They dealt with everything from how to treat one's betters ("In speaking to men of Quality do not lean nor Look them full in the Face") to how to present one's countenance ("Do not Puff up the Cheeks, Do not Loll out the tongue, rub the Hands, or beard, thrust out the lips, or bite them or keep the Lips too open or too Close").

All the Founding Fathers were aware of these enlightened conventions, and all in varying degrees tried to live up to them. But no one was more serious in following them than Washington. It is this purposefulness that gave his behavior such a copybook character. He was obsessed with having things in fashion and was fastidious about his appearance to the world. It was as if he were always on stage, acting a part. He was very desirous not to offend, and he exquisitely shaped his remarks to fit the person to whom he was writing—so much so that some historians have accused him of deceit. "So anxious was he to appear neat and correct in his letters," recalled Benjamin Rush [colonial doctor and patriot] that he was known to "copy over a letter of 2 or 3 sheets of paper because there were a few erasures on it." He wanted desperately to know what were the proper rules of behavior for a liberal gentleman, and when he discovered those rules he stuck by them with an earnestness that awed his contemporaries. His remarkable formality and stiffness in company came from his very self-conscious cultivation of what he considered proper, genteel, classical behavior. . . .

THE WORLD OF POLITICS

Yet it was in the political world that Washington made his most theatrical gesture, his most moral mark, and there the results were monumental. The greatest act of his life, the one that made him famous, was his resignation as commander-in-chief of the American forces. This act, together with his 1783 circular letter to the states in which he promised to retire from public life, was his "legacy" to his countrymen. No American leader has ever left a more important legacy.

Following the signing of the peace treaty and British recognition of American independence, Washington stunned

> ### Washington as a Modern Hero
> *While Washington was venerated as a great hero during and after his lifetime, in modern times he is sometimes portrayed in a light harsh enough to reveal and magnify his flaws. He was a quiet, even reticent hero, unlike the bold, outgoing type of hero that has become more popular in recent years. But as acclaimed historian and biographer Richard Norton Smith explains, Washington, while he may have been remote and stoic, is still deserving of lasting respect.*
>
> Nearly two centuries after his death George Washington is out of fashion, too remote in time and temperament, too encased in marbled veneration, to engage our emotions. Even among contemporaries his physical and moral courage, his endless capacity for self-sacrifice, and his patience in adversity may have sparked more awe than affection. This, too, he would have understood, for he grasped the limitations of his fellows even as he refused to see them through the tinted glass of ideology. When [writer Ralph Waldo] Emerson declared, "Every hero at last becomes a bore," he was thinking of America's first president. Modern scholars delight in finding flaws in the marble, arraigning Washington for his treatment of Native Americans, for example, or denouncing his part in an economic system that wrung luxury for a privileged few from the sweat of slave labor.
>
> Moreover, Washington does not conveniently fit the mold of executive greatness as defined by twentieth-century standards. He was no Rooseveltian swashbuckler, wielding the personal pronoun like a deadly weapon while placing his personal stamp upon every program of his age. He did not martyr himself for a great cause, like Lincoln, or thrill the multitudes with Wilsonian eloquence; indeed, by all contemporary evidence he was something less than a Great Communicator. Even [early Washington biographer John] Marshall [who was the first Supreme Court Chief Justice and knew Washington] called Washington "more solid than brilliant." For him silence, backed by deeds and buttressed by character, was the most eloquent language of all.
>
> Richard Norton Smith, *Patriarch: George Washington and the New American Nation.* New York: Houghton Mifflin, 1993.

the world when he surrendered his sword to the Congress on Dec. 23, 1783 and retired to his farm at Mount Vernon. This was a highly symbolic act, a very self-conscious and unconditional withdrawal from the world of polities. Here was the commander in chief of the victorious army putting down his sword and promising not to take "any share in public business hereafter." Washington even resigned from his local vestry in Virginia in order to make his separation from the political world complete.

His retirement from power had a profound effect everywhere in the Western world. It was extraordinary, it was unprecedented in modern times—a victorious general surrendering his arms and returning to his farm. [English rulers] Cromwell, William of Orange, Marlborough—all had sought political rewards commensurate with their military achievements. Though it was widely thought that Washington could have become king or dictator, he wanted nothing of the kind. He was sincere in his desire for all the soldiers "to return to our Private Stations in the bosom of a free, peaceful and happy Country," and everyone recognized his sincerity. It filled them with awe. Washington's retirement, said the painter John Trumbull writing from London in 1784, "excites the astonishment and admiration of this part of the world. 'Tis a Conduct so novel, so unconceivable to People, who, far from giving up powers they possess, are willing to convulse the empire to acquire more.". . .

Washington was not naïve. He was well aware of the effect his resignation would have. He was trying to live up to the age's image of a classical disinterested patriot who devotes his life to his country, and he knew at once that he had acquired instant fame as a modern Cincinnatus [a fifth-century Roman dictator]. His reputation in the 1780's as a great classical hero was international, and it was virtually unrivaled. Franklin was his only competitor, but Franklin's greatness still lay in his being a scientist, not a man of public affairs. Washington was a living embodiment of all that classical republican virtue the age was eagerly striving to recover. . . .

GUARDING HIS REPUTATION

Washington had earned his reputation, his "character," as a moral hero, and he did not want to dissipate it. He spent the rest of his life guarding and protecting his reputation, and worrying about it. He believed Franklin made a mistake going back into public life in Pennsylvania in the 1780's. Such involvement in politics, he thought, could only endanger Franklin's already achieved international standing. In modern eyes Washington's concern for his reputation is embarrassing; it seems obsessive and egotistical. But his contemporaries understood. All gentlemen tried scrupulously to guard their reputations, which is what they meant by their honor. Honor was the esteem in which they were held, and they prized it. To have honor across space and time was to have fame, and fame, "the ruling passion of the noblest minds," was what the Founding Fathers were after, Washington above all. And he got it, sooner and in greater degree than any other of his contemporaries. And naturally, having achieved what all his fellow Revolutionaries still anxiously sought, he was reluctant to risk it.

Many of his actions after 1783 can be understood only in terms of this deep concern for his reputation as a virtuous leader. He was constantly on guard and very sensitive to any criticism. Jefferson said no one was more sensitive. He judged all his actions by what people might think of them. This sometimes makes him seem silly to modern minds, but not to those of the 18th century. In that very suspicious age where people were acutely "jealous" of what great men were up to, Washington thought it important that people understand his motives. The reality was not enough; he had to *appear* virtuous. He was obsessed that he not seem base, mean, avaricious, or unduly ambitious. No one, said Jefferson, worked harder than Washington in keeping "motives of interest or consanguinity, of friendship or hatred" from influencing him. He had a lifelong preoccupation with his reputation for "disinterestedness" and how best to use that reputation for the good of his country. This preoccupation explains the seemingly odd fastidiousness and the caution of his behavior in the 1780's. . . .

A Leadership Role

After the Constitution was established, Washington still thought he could retire to the domestic tranquillity of Mount Vernon. But everyone else expected that he would become president of the new national government. He was already identified with the country. People said he was denied children in his private life so he could be the father of his country. He had to be the president. Indeed, the Convention had made the new chief executive so strong, so kinglike, precisely because the delegates expected Washington to be the first president.

Once again this widespread expectation aroused all his old anxieties about his reputation for disinterestedness and the proper role for a former military leader. Had he not promised the country that he would permanently retire from public life? How could he then now assume the presidency without being "chargeable with levity and inconsistency; if not with rashness and ambition?" His protests were sincere. He had so much to lose, yet he did not want to appear "too solicitous for my reputation."

Washington's apparent egotism and his excessive coyness, his extreme reluctance to get involved in public affairs and endanger his reputation, have not usually been well received by historians. Douglas Southall Freeman, his great biographer, thought that Washington in the late 1780's was "too zealously attentive to his prestige, his reputation and his popularity—too much the self-conscious national hero and too little the daring patriot." Historians might not understand his behavior, but his contemporaries certainly did. They rarely doubted that Washington was trying *always* to act in a disinterested and patriotic way. His anxious queries about how this or that would look to the world, his hesitations about serving or not serving, his expressions of scruples and qualms—all were part of his strenuous effort to live up to the classical idea of a virtuous leader.

He seemed to epitomize public virtue and the proper character of a republican ruler. Even if John Adams was not all that impressed with George Washington, Adams' wife Abigail was certainly taken with him. She admired his restraint and trusted him. "If he was not really one of the best-intentioned men in the world," she wrote, "he might be a very dangerous one." As [twentieth-century American writer] Garry Wills has so nicely put it, Washington gained his power by his readiness to give it up.

As president he continued to try to play the role he thought circumstances demanded. He knew that the new government was fragile and needed dignity. People found that dignity in his person. [James] Madison believed that Washington was the only part of the new government that captured the minds of the people. He fleshed out the executive, established its independence, and gave the new government the pomp and ceremony many thought it needed. . . .

As president he tried to refuse accepting any salary just as he had as commander-in-chief. Still, he wanted to make the presidency "respectable," and he spared few expenses in doing so; he spent 7 percent of his $25,000 salary on liquor and wine for entertaining. He was especially interested in the size and character of the White House and of the capital city that was named after him. The scale and grandeur of Washington, D.C., owe much to his vision and his backing of Pierre L'Enfant as architect. If Secretary of State Thomas Jefferson had had his way, L'Enfant would never have kept his job as long as he did, and the capital would have been smaller and less magnificent—perhaps something on the order of a college campus, like Jefferson's University of Virginia.

Washington was keenly aware that everything he did would set precedents for the future. "We are a young nation," he said, "and have a character to establish. It behoves us therefore to set out right, for first impressions will be lasting." It was an awesome responsibility. More than any of his contemporaries, he thought constantly of future generations, of "millions unborn," as he called them.

He created an independent role for the president and made the chief executive the dominant figure in the government. . . .

The presidency is the powerful office it is in large part because of Washington's initial behavior. He understood power and how to use it. But as in the case of his career as commander-in-chief, his most important act as president was his giving up of the office.

The significance of his retirement from the presidency is easy for us to overlook, but his contemporaries knew what it meant. Most people assumed that Washington might be president as long as he lived, that he would be a kind of elective monarch—something not out of the question in the 18th century. Some people even expressed relief that he had no heirs. Thus his persistent efforts to retire from the presidency enhanced his moral authority and helped fix the republican character of the Constitution.

He very much wanted to retire in 1792, but his advisors and friends talked him into staying on for a second term. Madison admitted that when he had first urged Washington to accept the presidency he had told him that he could protect himself from accusations of overweening ambition by "a voluntary return to public life as soon as the state of the Government would permit." But the state of the government, said Madison, was not yet secure. So Washington reluctantly stayed on.

But in 1796 he was so determined to retire that no one could dissuade him, and his voluntary leaving of the office set a precedent that was not broken until FDR secured a third term in 1940. So strong was the sentiment for a two-term limit, however, that the tradition was written into the Constitution in the 22nd amendment in 1951. Washington's action in 1796 was of great significance. That the chief executive of a state should willingly relinquish his office was an object lesson in republicanism at a time when the republican experiment throughout the Atlantic world was very much in doubt. . . .

The Changing Times

In July 1799 Governor Jonathan Trumbull of Connecticut with the backing of many Federalists urged Washington once again to stand for the presidency in 1800. Only Washington, Trumbull said, could unite the Federalists and save the country from "a French President." Finally Washington had had enough. In his reply he no longer bothered with references to his reputation for disinterestedness and his desire to play the role of Cincinnatus. Instead he talked about the new political conditions that made his candidacy irrelevant. In this new democratic era of party politics, he said, "personal influence," distinctions of character, no longer mattered. If the members of the Jeffersonian Republican party "set up a broomstick" as candidate and called it "a true son of Liberty" or "a Democrat" or "any other epithet that will suit their purpose," it still would "command their votes in toto!" But, even worse, he said, the same was true of the Federalists. Party spirit now ruled all, and people voted only for their party candidate. Even if he were the Federalist candidate, Washington was "thoroughly convinced I should not draw a *single* vote from the anti-Federal side." Therefore his standing for election made no sense; he would "stand upon no stronger ground than any other Federal character well supported."

Washington wrote all this in anger and despair, but, though he exaggerated, he was essentially right. The political world was changing, becoming democratic, and parties, not great men, would soon become the objects of contention. To be sure, the American people continued to long for great heroes as leaders, and from Jackson through Eisenhower they have periodically elected Washington-*manqués* to the presidency.

But democracy made such great heroes no longer essential to the workings of American government. And Washington, more than any other single individual, was the one who made that democracy possible. . . .

Washington was an extraordinary heroic man who made rule by more ordinary mortals possible. He virtually created the presidency, and gave it a dignity that through the years it has never lost. But, more important, he established the standard by which all subsequent presidents have been ultimately measured—not by the size of their electoral victories, not by their legislative programs, and not by the number of their vetoes, but by their moral character. Although we live in another world than his, his great legacy is still with us.

Above All, the Man Had Character

Hugh Sidey

In this selection from 1983, *Time* magazine editor Hugh Sidey marvels on how the character of George Washington has survived nearly intact to this day and reflects on how George Washington might be treated if he were president in modern times. Sidey satirizes the modern media by predicting the kinds of questions Washington would be asked and the kinds of criticism he would receive. He ultimately concludes that Washington was a man for his time, a man who imposed upon himself a strict code of conduct and who has been a role model for every president who followed him.

Each year George Washington gains more luster in our reveries on how we got where we are. Our sophisticated scholarship and painstaking restoration, which so often dismantle heroes, have revealed the human dimensions of the father of the country but have failed to dim the aura of greatness that clings to Washington. . . .

His contemporaries felt the same awe and wonder. In Washington's last years, Mount Vernon became a mecca for the great and the grateful, for the curious and the ambitious. So many people arrived at the doorstep that Washington, who would turn none away, finally engaged a social secretary to handle the flow. Sometimes he did not attend the dinners he gave because the company was so numerous and foreign to him. One night when he dined alone with Mrs. Washington, the event was so unusual he made a note of it in his diary.

The legend of the man is safely sheltered these days behind high fences of respect. Were the real Washington on hand today, that might not be the case, and therein may lie

Hugh Sidey, "Above All, the Man Had Character," *Time*, vol. 121, February 21, 1983. Copyright © 1983 by Time, Inc. Reproduced by permission.

a lesson. We have in this nation erected standards for our public people that dim anyone's glow if he or she falls short of perfection. It is reasonable, then, to wonder if people can enter public life and make a difference as they did in the first years of the Republic. Even as our expectations have grown, our respect for and sympathy with Presidents have diminished.

A Modern View of George Washington

By our modern measures, George Washington did not read the right books. He relished how-to-do-it texts, with their new ideas on the use of manure, turning soil, and animal husbandry. But he did not delve very far into art, philosophy, or science. When John Kennedy was coaxed into supplying a list of his ten favorite books, the collection was heavy with history, biography and geopolitics, the kind of reading that he knew critical journalists would admire. Twenty years ago, we took Presidents at their word. The suspicion now is that the list was a bit fraudulent.

Washington knew no foreign languages (Thomas Jefferson spoke or read five). Washington never traveled to Europe, while Benjamin Franklin, John Adams, and Jefferson all spent years there. He was not an accomplished public speaker. His military achievements were judged for their perseverance rather than their brilliance. Yet the battle of Trenton might have been as important a battle as this nation ever won. The Trenton victory brought the Revolution back to life. The colonies dared hope again for independence. France began to look with more favor on the American struggle, and Britain began to lose heart. But the battle was technically a shambles.

Three columns were to have crossed the Delaware River. Only Washington's made it across. The powder of his troops was soaked by a freezing rain, so they could not fire their arms. They had to depend on bayonets several times during the night. Washington's officers pleaded with him to call off the attack. The story goes that he stood on an old beehive in a muddy New Jersey field and turned aside entreaty. The battle of Trenton was won by the determination of one man, but certainly not by his military expertise. Would he have done what he did on that miserable night if the failing campaign had been on the evening news with closeup shots of the ragged men?

How Modern Critics Would Treat Washington

Washington sometimes looked on his twenty-two years of public service as a kind of prison sentence that took him away from his land. Washington was not one of the boys. The thought of him in blue jeans around the graceful drives of Mount Vernon is, thank goodness, still shattering. Once, when Gouverneur Morris, a friend and supporter, put his hand on Washington's shoulder to show doubters how close he was to the chief, Washington coldly took Morris' hand and removed it. Nobody in Washington's inner circle tried that again. Sometimes, the stories go, when Washington was with his old Army friends and had a few glasses of wine, he became what they called "merry," and he would talk and reminisce into the night. But that was rather rare, according to the scholars. With his kind of record, one wonders how George Washington might have fared in the style of the *Washington Post* under the arch questioning of [journalist] Sally Quinn: "Mr. President, do you and Mrs. Washington have separate bedrooms?"

George Washington accumulated nearly 100,000 acres of land in his last years and was judged one of the wealthiest men in the nation. He would have been suspected of conflict of interest at every turn. Investigative reporters would have been in clover—literally, perhaps, because Washington might have cornered the clover-seed market and been nabbed for restraint of trade.

Washington was meticulous about dress, selecting with care his shoes and their buckles, the cloth for his suits and shirts. In our time we are a little uneasy with Presidents who pay too much attention (or too little) to their dress. That may be changing. Grubbiness has proved less of a political asset than some thought a few years back. Still, any hint of vanity is deplored. John Kennedy became angry when the fashion magazine *Gentlemen's Quarterly* put him on its cover and announced that he had posed for the magazine in his new two-button suit. Kennedy told an astonished group around his desk that he would now be remembered as the President who posed in his new suit, just as Calvin Coolidge was most renowned for having been pictured in an Indian war bonnet.

Mount Vernon was almost totally George Washington's creation, another dimension of the man that would have been of dubious value in this age. Correspondents would have reported during the war that after a battle (with the fortunes of

America ebbing, soldiers hungry and sick) the Commander in Chief sometimes penned many pages of instructions to his plantation manager, telling him what to build and plant and harvest. Neglect of duty? Washington designed his home, laid out the drives, selected the colors (green was his favorite), chose the trees, plants and flowers. The only decorating that Martha did was to choose some curtains. Surely today's social analysts would have been delighted at such domestic concern by Washington, but just as surely there would have been criticism of such dominance by the general of his wife.

Washington's favorite recreation was fox hunting. Consider

George Washington

that now: a President pounding over the hills on horseback, his hounds in full cry after a scraggly fox. Environmentalists would have jumped out at him from behind every hedge, waving placards. A "save the foxes" society would have been organized. Columnist Ellen Goodman would have rushed to detail the plight of the ill-fed, ill-housed, ill-treated foxes of Fairfax County. News magazines might have noted that photographs of Washington mounting his horse revealed he had wide hips. The temptation would have been too much: "President Washington, displaying a broad beam and a narrow mind, last week chased a 10-lb. fox to an unseemly death in the lovely hills of Virginia."

A Man for His Time

Washington cannot be reconstituted and placed in our century, of course, nor would he want to be. His time and his land were not necessarily more simple, but they certainly were different. The nation had 4 million people and only six cities of more than 8,000 souls each. The Federal Government, when Washington ran it, had 350 civil employees. If numbers and complexity were not the adversaries, then distance, time, disease, weather, Indians and ignorance were. It took a week to get to New York City. Early death stalked almost everyone. Washington was remarkably durable for his time—and lucky. His horses and uniforms were riddled with bullets at Braddock's defeat in the French and Indian War. He was untouched. But even his luck ran out finally. He died at 67 of a throat inflammation. A young physician in attendance wanted to open the trachea but was overruled by his seniors, still fearful of the new technique. A sturdy figure like Washington might have been around many more years with only a little bit of today's medical knowledge.

Writers who journey through the accounts of his life almost always confess some bafflement about why he was such a great figure in his time and remains so in ours. British Historian Marcus Cunliffe points out that Washington was a good man but not a saint, a competent soldier but not great, thoughtful but not brilliant like Alexander Hamilton. He was a respectable administrator but certainly not a genius. All this and more his biographers have put down. Washington was a prudent conserver but not a brilliant reformer. He was sober unto dullness. He lacked the common touch so much that not even his British enemies had a derogatory nickname for him during the war. He could strip off his coat and help the field hands, but he had no very close friends. The Marquis de Lafayette, his French ally, was as close as anyone. To humanize Washington, suggests Cunliffe, would be to falsify him, though of course many have tried to do that in the past two centuries.

Why Honor George Washington?

We would do well in this age of total and instant analysis to ponder why it is we honor George Washington as we do, why the legend goes on in the face of the reservations and doubts that scholars keep raising. It is true that simply being an American and being around for the start of the United States would have assured Washington some place in history. There was more.

The sum of his rather normal parts added up to an exceptional figure. George Washington had character. That is easily said but not easily defined. Writers have been trying to do it since time began, but character defies scientific analysis. Duke University's James David Barber based an entire book about Presidents on the analysis of character. It was fascinating. But Barber raised as many questions as he answered. Nobody is quite certain what character is, but everybody captures a piece of the truth. Here are a few thoughts from Washington's contemporaries and his later biographers about the qualities that lifted him above others.

One writer noted Washington's "cool dignity." Washington's aloofness and reserve made him stand out from other men, several authors insisted. Washington understood power, wrote one. Another claimed simply: "Washington had quality." From there the scholars get more subjective. Washington merged his honor with that of America, recounted a writer, not to mention his fortune and everything he planned and built. During the Revolution, a British raiding party sailed up the Potomac and at Mount Vernon received some provisions from the farm manager. When Washington heard about it (he was off leading the Army), he was disturbed. He wrote that his people should have let the raiders burn down the place before they aided the enemy. Biographers have written that "Washington proved the soundness of America" and that he "had a true American vision." By that they meant that he, almost alone among those great men, understood in totally the wealth and strength of the land that lay before him and how it formed and held a society together. "The man is the monument; the monument is America," wrote Cunliffe with a poetic touch. Those nine words may say as much as anything about the source of our reverence.

George Washington was sensible and wise. He was not the most informed or imaginative of men. But he understood himself and this nation-to-be. That understanding came from the many elements that make up any person. His heart and mind were shaped by his family, his land, his community and the small events that touched him every day. Those were the normal experiences. They were added to his natural endowments. Only one power can fully fathom such a formula—God. Washington had the tolerance of a landsman, the faith that comes with witnessing the changing seasons year in and year out, the sensitivity that accumulates from watching buds burst and colts grow. Optimism, perseverance, patience and an eager view of the distant horizon have always been a gift of the earth to those who stayed close to it.

Why He Succeeded

We pay too much attention these days to college degrees, to public displays of so-called brilliance. We are overawed by the listings in Who's Who, by prizes and travels and speeches.

We pay too much heed to organizational charts, office tension, human friction, and how paper flows or does not. We busy ourselves too much in searching for minor flaws in our Presidents, finding petty shortfalls and mistakes, relishing pratfalls and humiliations.

The presidency to this day still rests more on the character of the person who inhabits the office than on anything else, try as we may in our books and papers to develop formulas and charts that explain success and failure. The founding fathers designed it that way. It was their idea to find a man in America with a great character and let him invest a tradition and shape a national character. They found George Washington. He did his job splendidly. He might even have known what he was doing. When he took the presidency he wrote, "I walk on untrodden ground. There is scarcely any part of my conduct which may not hereafter be drawn into precedent." That is at once beautiful and profound. It is no wonder he succeeded, entering office with such a code of conduct.

Our task is to rekindle the tradition, to search in our system for people of great character and then bring them to power and rally behind them; not blindly, to be sure, but with understanding and even sympathy and tolerance. Character like Washington's is not a blend of everything that is perfect. In fact, we have not done too badly through [more than forty] men who became President. Even today, in the midst of great national worry, the quality in the presidency that helps keep a beleaguered nation together is the character of the man we glimpse in the White House. Over these past decades some of our Presidents have had more than others. We have not always been alert to those who have had outstanding characters, and sometimes we have been fooled by those who did not have the depths of character we thought they had. Character has come in different sizes and shapes, and some Presidents seemed to have enlarged it as time went on, while others have appeared to lose character under stress.

More than all the other Presidents, George Washington has marched through our centuries untouched by critics, growing larger under the baleful eye of history. An uncommon man made from common parts remains our grand legacy and our hope in this moment of bewilderment in our third century.

Appendix of Documents

Document 1: The Stamp Act
In 1765, Britain's Parliament imposed a Stamp Act on the American colonies. The Act required that a special stamp, which purchasers had to pay for, be put on many everyday paper products, such as newspapers and playing cards. In this excerpt from a letter to Francis Dandridge (Martha's English relative), Washington expresses his views on the Stamp Act and what its enforcement may mean to England and the colonies. The letter was written on September 20, 1765.

At present few things are under notice of my observation that can afford you any amusement in the recital. The Stamp Act Imposed on the Colonies by the Parliament of Great Britain engrosses the conversation of the Speculative part of the Colonists, who look upon this unconstitutional method of Taxation as a direful attack upon their Liberties, and loudly exclaim against the Violation; what may be the result of this and some other (I think I may add) ill judgd Measures, I will not undertake to determine; but this I may venture to affirm, that the advantage accrueing to the Mother Country will fall greatly short of the expectations of the Ministry; for certain it is, our whole Substance does already in a manner flow to Great Britain and that whatsoever contributes to lessen our Importation's must be hurtful to their Manufacturers. And the Eyes of our People, already beginning to open, will perceive, that many Luxuries which we lavish our substance to Great Britain for, can well be dispensd with whilst the necessaries of Life are (mostly) to be had within ourselves. This consequently will introduce frugality, and be a necessary stimulation to Industry. If Great Britain therefore Loads her Manufactures with heavy Taxes, will it not facilitate these Measures? they will not compel us I think to give our Money for their exports, whether we will or no, and certain I am none of their Traders will part from them without a valuable consideration. Where then is the Utility of these Restrictions?

George Washington, Letter to Francis Dandridge, September 20, 1765.

Document 2: A Series of Questions
One of Washington's closest friends, particularly in his youth, was Bryan Fairfax. The Fairfax family's estate, Belvoir, was close to

Mount Vernon, and Washington spent many happy hours there. Because they were Loyalists, however, most members of the Fairfax family returned to England when the Revolution began. Although Washington obviously had political differences with them, it is a testimony to his loyalty to his friends that he continued his correspondence with them. In this letter to Bryan Fairfax, written on July 4, 1774, Washington presents Fairfax with a series of questions that reveal the grievances he and his fellow Patriots had against the English government.

As to your political sentiments, I would heartily join you in them, so far as relates to a humble and dutiful petition to the throne, provided there was the most distant hope of success. But have we not tried this already? Have we not addressed the Lords, and remonstrated to the Commons? And to what end? Did they deign to look at our petitions? Does it not appear, as clear as the sun in its meridian brightness, that there is a regular, systematic plan formed to fix the right and practice of taxation upon us? Does not the uniform conduct of Parliament for some years past confirm this? Do not all the debates, especially those just brought to us, in the House of Commons on the side of government, expressly declare that America must be taxed in aid of the British funds, and that she has no longer resources with in herself? Is there any thing to be expected from petitioning after this? Is not the attack upon the liberty and property of the people of Boston, before restitution of the loss to the India Company was demanded, a plain and self-evident proof of what they are aiming at? Do not the subsequent bills (now I dare say acts), for depriving the Massachusetts Bay of its charter, and for transporting offenders into other colonies or to Great Britain for trial, where it is impossible from the nature of the thing that justice can be obtained, convince us that the administration is determined to stick at nothing to carry its point? Ought we not, then, to put our virtue and fortitude to the severest test?

George Washington, Letter to Bryan Fairfax, July 4, 1774.

DOCUMENT 3: WASHINGTON ACCEPTS HIS APPOINTMENT AS COMMANDER IN CHIEF

The Continental Congress named Washington to lead the Continental army in 1775. On June 16 he stood before Congress and made the following acceptance speech. In it, Washington shows his usual modesty as well as his never-ending concern for his reputation. He surprised several members of Congress and impressed the American public when he declared that he desired no pay for doing the job.

Mr. President,
    Though I am truly sensible of the high honor done me in this appointment, yet I feel great distress from a consciousness that my abilities and military experience may not be equal to the extensive and

important trust. However, as the Congress desire it, I will enter upon the momentous duty and exert every power I possess in the service and for support of the glorious cause. I beg they will accept my most cordial thanks for this distinguished testimony of their approbation. But lest some unlucky event should happen unfavourable to my reputation, I beg it may be remembered by every gentleman in the room, that I this day declare with the utmost sincerity I do not think myself equal to the command I am honored with.

As to pay, Sir, I beg leave to assure the Congress, that as no pecuniary consideration could have tempted me to accept this arduous employment at the expense of my domestic ease and happiness, I do not wish to make any profit from it. I will keep an exact account of my expenses. Those I doubt not they will discharge, and that is all I desire.

George Washington, Speech to Congress, June 16, 1775.

DOCUMENT 4: FAREWELL TO MARTHA

After his appointment as commander in chief of the Continental army at the Continental Congress in Philadelphia in 1775, Washington did not have time to return to Mount Vernon to say good-bye to his wife, Martha, and to the rest of his family and friends. In this letter, written on June 18, 1775, two days after he accepted the appointment, Washington tells his wife—whom he called "Patsy"—that he must serve his country. He also reveals his reluctance to undertake the responsibility he has been given and his feeling of powerlessness to do anything but accept it.

My Dearest: I am now set down to write to you on a subject, which fills me with inexpressible concern, and this concern is greatly aggravated and increased, when I reflect upon the uneasiness I know it will give you. It has been determined in Congress, that the whole army raised for the defence of the American cause shall be put under my care, and that it is necessary for me to proceed immediately to Boston to take upon me the command of it.

You may believe me, my dear Patsy, when I assure you, in the most solemn manner that, so far from seeking this appointment, I have used every endeavor in my power to avoid it, not only from my unwillingness to part with you and the family, but from a consciousness of its being a trust too great for my capacity, and that I should enjoy more real happiness in one month with you at home, than I have the most distant prospect of finding abroad, if my stay were to be seven times seven years. But as it has been a kind of destiny, that has thrown me upon this service, I shall hope that my undertaking it is designed to answer some good purpose. You might, and I suppose did perceive, from the tenor of my letters, that I was apprehensive I could not avoid this appointment, as I did not pretend to intimate when I should return. That was the case. It was utterly out of my power to refuse this appointment, without exposing my character to such censures, as would have reflected dishonor upon myself, and given pain to my friends. This, I am sure, could not, and ought not, to be pleasing to you, and must have lessened me considerably in my own esteem. I shall rely, therefore, confidently on that Providence, which has heretofore preserved and been bountiful to me, not doubting but that I shall return safe to you in the fall. I shall feel no pain from the toil or the danger of the campaign: my unhappiness will flow from the uneasiness I know you will feel from being left alone. I therefore beg, that you will summon your whole fortitude, and pass your time as agreeably as possible. Nothing will give me so much sincere satisfaction as to hear this, and to hear it from your own pen. My earnest and ardent desire is, that you would pursue any plan that is most likely to produce content, and a tolerable degree of tranquillity; as it must add greatly to my uneasy feelings to hear, that you are dissatisfied or complaining at what I really could not avoid.

As life is always uncertain, and common prudence dictates to every man the necessity of settling his temporal concerns, while it is in his power, and while the mind is calm and undisturbed, I have, since I came to this place (for I had not time to do it before I left home) got Colonel Pendleton to draft a will for me, by the directions I gave him, which will I now enclose. The provision made for you in case of my death will, I hope, be agreeable.

I shall add nothing more, as I have several letters to write, but to desire that you will remember me to your friends, and to assure you that I am, with the most unfeigned regard, my dear Patsy, your affectionate, &c.

George Washington, Letter to Martha, June 18, 1775.

DOCUMENT 5: A DISTRESSING SHORTAGE OF SUPPLIES

In the fall of 1777, Washington's troops set up camp at Valley Forge, Pennsylvania. The winter of 1777–1778 was extremely harsh, and all necessities were in short supply. Washington had petitioned Congress for more money to buy supplies, to little avail. In this letter to Lt. Col. Alexander Hamilton—later Washington's treasury secretary—Washington authorizes him and other officers to go to nearby Philadelphia and demand blankets and clothing from its residences. The letter was written on September 22, even before the severe winter began.

The distressed situation of the army for want of blankets, and many necessary articles of cloathing, is truly deplorable; and must inevitably be destructive to it, unless a speedy remedy be applied. Without a better supply than they at present have, it will be impossible for the men to support the fatigues of the campaign in the further progress of the approaching inclement season. This you well know to be a melancholy truth. It is equally the dictate of common sense and the opinion of the Physicians of the army, as well as of every officer in it. No supply can be drawn from the public magazines. We have therefore no resource but from the private stock of individuals. I feel, and I lament, the absolute necessity of requiring the inhabitants to contribute to those wants, which we have no other means of satisfying, and which if unremoved would involve the ruin of the army, and perhaps the ruin of America. Painful as it is to me to order and as it will be to you to execute the measure, I am compelled to desire you immediately to proceed to Philadelphia, and there procure from the inhabitants contributions of blankets and cloathing, and materials to answer the purposes of both, in proportion to the ability of each. This you will do with as much delicacy and discretion, as the nature of the business demands; and I trust the necessity will justify the proceeding in the eyes of every person well affected to the American cause, and that all good citizens will chearfully afford their assistance to soldiers, whose sufferings they are bound to commiserate, and who are eminently exposed to danger and distress, in defence of every thing they ought to hold dear.

As there are also a number of horses in Philadelphia both of public and private property, which would be a valuable acquisition to the enemy, should the city by any accident fall into their hands, you are hereby authorized and commanded to remove them thence into the Country to some place of greater security, and more remote from the operations of the enemy. You will stand in need of assistance from others to execute this commission with despatch and propriety, and you are therefore empowered to employ such persons as you shall think proper to aid you therein.

George Washington, Letter to Alexander Hamilton, September 22, 1777.

DOCUMENT 6: WASHINGTON'S POSITION ON INDEPENDENCE

On April 21, 1778, at the end of the long, hard winter at Valley Forge, Washington wrote the following letter to John Banister, a Congressional delegate from Virginia. The letter reveals Washington's feelings about the revolution and the colonies' separation from Great Britain.

It really seems to me, from a comprehensive view of things, that a period is fast approaching, big with events of the most interesting importance; when the counsels we pursue, and the part we act, may lead decisively to liberty or to slavery. Under this idea, I cannot but regret that inactivity, that inattention, that want of something, which unhappily I have but too often experienced in our public affairs. I wish that our representation in Congress was complete and full from every State, and that it was formed of the first abilities among us. Whether we continue to war or proceed to negotiate, the wisdom of America in council cannot be too great. Our situation will be truly delicate. To enter into a negotiation too hastily, or to reject it altogether, may be attended with consequences equally fatal. The wishes of the people, seldom founded in deep disquisitions, or resulting from other reasonings than their present feelings, may not entirely accord with our true policy and interest. If they do not, to observe a proper line of conduct for promoting the one, and avoiding offence to the other, will be a work of great difficulty. Nothing short of independence, it appears to me, can possibly do. A peace on other terms would, if I may be allowed the expression, be a peace of war. The injuries we have received from the British nation were so unprovoked, and have been so great and so many, that they can never be forgotten. Besides the feuds, the jealousies, the animosities, that would ever attend a union with them; besides the importance, the advantages, we should derive from an unrestricted commerce; our fidelity as a people, our gratitude, our character as men, are opposed to a coalition with them as subjects, but in case of the last extremity. Were we easily to accede to terms of dependence, no nation, upon future occasions, let the oppressions of Britain be never so flagrant and unjust, would interpose for our relief; or, at most, they would do it with a cautious reluctance, and upon conditions most probably that would be hard, if not dishonorable to us. France, by her supplies, has saved us from the yoke thus far; and a wise and virtuous perseverance would, and I trust will, free us entirely.

George Washington, Letter to John Banister, April 21, 1778.

DOCUMENT 7: WASHINGTON'S FRIENDSHIP WITH LAFAYETTE

During the Revolutionary War, troops from France helped Americans fight the British. The Marquis de Lafayette purchased a ship in 1777 and, with a group of adventurers, sailed to America. He worked directly with Washington and had the title of major general. The two became close friends. Washington was twenty-five years older than Lafayette and grew to love him as a son. The below letter, written on September 30, 1779, to Lafayette at West Point, New York, reveals the extent of their friendship.

Your forward zeal in the cause of liberty; Your singular attachment to this infant world; your ardent and persevering efforts, not only in America, but since your return to France, to serve the United States; your polite attention to Americans, and your strict and uniform friendship for *me*, has ripened the first impressions of esteem and attachment, which I imbibed for you, into such perfect love and gratitude, that neither time nor absence can impair. Which will warrant my assuring you, that, whether in the character of an officer at the head of a corps of gallant French (if circumstances should require this), whether as a major-genl. commanding a division of the American army, or whether, after our Swords and spears have given place to the ploughshare and pruning-Hook, I see you as a private gentleman, a friend and companion, I shall welcome you in all the warmth of friendship to Columbia's shores; and, in the latter case, to my rural cottage, where homely fare and a cordial reception shall be substituted for delicacies of costly living. This, from past experience, I know *you* can submit to; and if the lovely partner of your happiness will consent to participate with *us* in such rural entertainment and amusemem'ts, I can undertake, in behalf of Mrs. Washington, that she will do every thing in her power to make Virginia agreeable to the Marchioness. . . . I assure you, that I love every body that is dear to you . . .

You are pleased, my dear Marquis, to express an earnest desire of seeing me in France (after the establishment of our independency) . . . Let me entreat you to be persuaded, that to meet you any where . . . would contribute to my happiness; and that to visit a country, to whose generous aid we stand so much indebted, would be an additional pleasure; but remember, my good friend, that I am unacquainted with your language, that I am too far advanced in years to acquire a knowledge of it, and that, to converse through the medium of an interpreter upon common occasions, especially with the Ladies, must appear so extremely awkward, insipid, and uncouth, that I can scarce bear it in idea. I will, therefore, hold myself disengaged for the present; but when I see you in Virginia, we will talk of this matter and fix our plans.

George Washington, Letter to the Marquis de Lafayette, September 30, 1779.

DOCUMENT 8: INSTRUCTIONS TO A YOUNG MAN

George Washington had no children of his own, but he took great interest in his stepchildren and in his nieces and nephews, urging them to study hard and become respectable, productive citizens. These instructions are from a letter Washington wrote to his nephew, Bushrod, on January 15, 1783, as Bushrod was about to go to Philadelphia to study law. It is not clear whether he adhered to his uncle's advice, but Bushrod Washington did go on to have a distinguished law career and even became an associate justice of the Supreme Court, appointed by then President John Adams.

Let the object, which carried you to Philadelphia, be always before your Eyes; remember, that it is not the mere study of the Law, but to become eminent in the Profession of it which is to yield honor and profit; the first was your choice, let the second be your ambition, and that dissipation is incompatible with both.

That the Company in which you will improve most, will be least expensive to you; and yet I am not such a Stoic as to suppose you will, or to think it right that you ought, always to be in Company with Senators and Philosophers; but, of the young and juvenile kind let me advise you to be choice. It is easy to make acquaintances, but very difficult to shake them off, however irksome and unprofitable they are found after we have once committed ourselves to them; the indiscretions, and scrapes which very often they involuntarily lead one into, proves equally distressing and disgraceful.

Be courteous to all, but intimate with few, and let those few be well tried before you give them your confidence; true friendship is a plant of slow growth, and must undergo and withstand the shocks of adversity before it is entitled to the appellation.

Let your *heart* feel for the affliction, and distresses of everyone, and let your *hand* give in proportion to your purse; remembering always, the estimation of the Widows mite. But, that it is not every one who asketh, that deserveth charity; all however are worthy of the enquiry, or the deserving may suffer.

Do not conceive that fine Clothes make fine Men, any more than fine feathers make fine Birds. A plain genteel dress is more admired and obtains more credit than lace and embroidery in the Eyes of the judicious and sensible.

The last thing I shall mention, is first of importance, and that is, to avoid Gaming. This is a vice which is productive of every possible evil, equally injurious to the morals and health of its votaries. It is the child of Avarice, the brother of inequity, and father of Mischief. It has been the ruin of many worthy familys; the loss of many a man's honor; and the cause of Suicide. To all those who enter the list, it is equally fascinating; the Successful gamester pushes his good fortune till it is over taken by a reverse; the loosing gamester, in hopes of retrieving past misfortunes, goes on from bad to worse; till grown desperate, he pushes at every thing; and looses his all. In a word, few gain by this abominable practice (the profit, if any, being diffused) while thousands are injured.

Perhaps you will say my conduct has anticipated the advice, and that "not one of these cases apply to me." I shall be heartily glad of it. It will add not a little to my happiness, to find those, to whom I am so nearly connected, pursuing the right walk of life; it will be the sure road to my favor, and to those honors, and places of profit, which their Country can bestow, as merit rarely goes unrewarded. I am, etc.

George Washington, Letter to Bushrod Washington, January 15, 1783.

DOCUMENT 9: WASHINGTON'S CONCERNS FOR HIS COUNTRY

Once the war was over, Washington became concerned about how the new nation would be governed. At the time, the United States was operating under the Articles of Confederation, but as a federalist Washington hoped for a stronger national government built upon a constitution. The following is from a letter written to Lafayette on April 5, 1783. At the end of this excerpt, Washington speaks of his longed-for retirement and his withdrawal to private life. That "glide down the stream of life" did not last long, though; Washington became president in 1789, with all the duties and trials that accompany that office.

We now stand an Independent People, and have yet to learn political Tactics. We are placed among the Nations of the Earth, and have a character to establish; but how we shall acquit ourselves time must discover; the probability, at least I fear it is, that local, or state Politics will interfere too much with that more liberal and extensive plan of government which wisdom and foresight, freed from the mist of prejudice, would dictate; and that we shall be guilty of many blunders in treading this boundless theatre before we shall have arrived at any perfection in this Art. In a word that the experience which is purchased at the price of difficulties and distress, will alone convince us that the honor, power, and true Interest of this Country must be measured by a Continental scale; and that every departure therefrom weakens the Union, and may ultimately break the band, which holds us together. To avert these evils, to form a Constitution that will give consistency, stability and dignity to the Union; and sufficient powers to the great Council of the Nation for general purposes is a duty which is incumbent upon every Man who wishes well to his Country, and will meet with my aid as far as it can be rendered in the private walks of life; for henceforward my Mind shall be unbent; and I will endeavor to glide down the stream of life 'till I come to that abyss, from whence no traveller is permitted to return.

George Washington, Letter to the Marquis de Lafayette, April 5, 1783.

DOCUMENT 10: TOO GOOD AN OPINION OF HUMAN NATURE

Before the Constitution was written in 1787, the United States was governed by the Articles of Confederation and was more a confederation of separate states than a unified nation. In this August 1, 1786, letter to John Jay, who later became the first Supreme Court justice, Washington expresses his doubts about the longevity of the confederation. His words echo of the feelings of all federalists, who believed that a strong central government was necessary for the survival of the country.

Your sentiments, that our affairs are drawing rapidly to a crisis, accord with my own. What the event will be is beyond the reach of my foresight. We have errors to correct; we have probably had too good an opinion of human nature, in forming our confederation. Experience has taught us that men will not adopt and carry into execution, measures the best calculated for their own good, without the intervention of coercive power. I do not conceive, we can exist long as a nation, without lodging, somewhere, a power which will pervade the whole Union in as energetic a manner, as the authority of the state governments extends over the several states.

To be fearful of investing Congress, constituted as that body is, with ample authorities for national purposes, appears to me the very climax of popular absurdity and madness. Could Congress exert them for the detriment of the people, without injuring themselves in an equal or greater proportion? Are not their interests inseparably connected with those of their constituents? By the rotation of appointments, must they not mingle frequently with the mass of citizens? Is it not rather to be apprehended, if they were not possessed of the powers before described, that the individual members would be induced to use them, on many occasions, very timidly and inefficaciously, for fear of losing their popularity and future election? We must take human nature as we find it; perfection falls not to the share of mortals.

What then is to be done? Things cannot go on in the same strain forever. It is much to be feared, as you observe, that the better kind of people, being disgusted with these circumstances, will have their minds prepared for any revolution whatever. We are apt to run from one extreme to another. To anticipate and prevent disastrous contingencies, would be the part of wisdom and patriotism.

What astonishing changes a few years are capable of producing! I am told that even respectable characters speak of a monarchical form of government without horror. From thinking proceeds speaking: thence to acting is often but a single step. But how irrevocable and tremendous! What a triumph for our enemies, to verify their predictions! What a triumph for the advocates of despotism, to find that we are incapable of governing ourselves, and that systems, founded on the basis of equal liberty, are merely ideal and fallacious. Would to God that wise measures may be taken in time to avert the consequences we have but too much reason to apprehend.

Retired as I am from the world, I frankly acknowledge I cannot feel myself an unconcerned spectator. Yet having happily assisted in bringing the ship into port, and having been fairly discharged, it is not my business to embark again on the sea of troubles. Nor could it be expected that my sentiments and opinions would have much weight on the minds of my countrymen.

George Washington, Letter to John Jay, August 1, 1786.

DOCUMENT 11: WASHINGTON'S FIRST INAUGURAL ADDRESS

Washington gave the first-ever U.S. presidential inaugural address on April 30, 1789. The address was presented to Congress in its chambers in New York. For his inauguration, Washington maintained a solemn demeanor. In his address, he refers to his pleasurable retirement being interrupted by the call to lead his country. The language used in this speech is formal but typical for Washington's time.

Washington spends about a quarter of the speech talking about the "Almighty Being" and "Great Author of every public and private good." Washington was not an extremely religious man; like several other of the nation's founders, he was a deist. As such he rarely, if ever, spoke of "God." Instead, he believed that there was a benevolent, providential force that wished only good on the human race.

Fellow Citizens of the Senate and of the House of Representatives

Among the vicissitudes incident to life, no event could have filled me with greater anxieties than that of which the notification was transmitted by your order, and received on the fourteenth day of the present month. On the one hand, I was summoned by my Country, whose voice I can never hear but with veneration and love, from a retreat which I had chosen with the fondest predilection, and, in my flattering hopes, with an immutable decision, as the asylum of my declining years: a retreat which was rendered every day more necessary as well as more dear to me, by the addition of habit to inclination, and of frequent interruptions in my health to the gradual waste committed on it by time. On the other hand, the magnitude and difficulty of the trust to which the voice of my Country called me, being sufficient to awaken in the wisest and most experienced of her citizens, a distrustful scrutiny into his qualifications, could not but overwhelm with despondence, one, who, inheriting inferior endowments from nature and unpractised in the duties of civil administration, ought to be peculiarly conscious of his own deficiencies. In this conflict of emotions, all I dare aver, is, that it has been my faithful study to collect my duty from a just appreciation of every circumstance, by which it might be affected. All I dare hope, is, that, if in executing this task I have been too much swayed by a grateful remembrance of former instances, or by an affectionate sensibility to this transcendent proof, of the confidence of my fellow-citizens; and have thence too little consulted my incapacity as well as disinclination for the weighty and untried cares before me; my error will be palliated by the motives which misled me, and its consequences be judged by my Country, with some share of the partiality in which they originated.

Such being the impressions under which I have, in obedience to the public summons, repaired to the present station; it would be peculiarly improper to omit in this first official Act, my fervent supplications to that Almighty Being who rules over the Universe, who presides in the Councils of Nations, and whose providential aids can supply every human defect, that his benediction may consecrate to the liberties and happiness of the People of the United States, a Government instituted by themselves for these essential purposes: and may enable every instrument employed in its administration, to execute with success, the functions allotted to his charge. In tendering this homage to the Great Author of every public and private good, I assure myself that it expresses your sentiments not less than my own; nor those of my fellow-citizens at large, less than either: No People can be bound to acknowledge and adore the invisible hand, which conducts the Affairs of men more than the People of the United States. Every step, by which they have advanced to the character of an independent nation, seems to have been distinguished by some token of providential agency. And in the important revolution just accomplished in the system of their United Government, the tranquil deliberations, and voluntary consent of so many distinct communities, from which the event has resulted, cannot be compared with the means by which most Governments have been established, without some return of pious gratitude along with an humble anticipation of the future blessings which the past seem to presage. These reflections, arising out of the present crisis, have forced themselves too strongly on my mind to be suppressed. You will join me I trust in thinking, that there are none under the influence of which, the proceedings of a new and free Government can more auspiciously commence.

By the article establishing the Executive Department, it is made the duty of the President "to recommend to your consideration, such measures as he shall judge necessary and expedient." The circumstances under which I now meet you, will acquit me from entering into that subject, farther than to refer to the Great Constitutional Charter under which you are assembled; and which, in defining your powers, designates the objects to which your attention is to be given. It will be more consistent with those circumstances, and far more congenial with the feelings which actuate me, to substitute, in place of a recommendation of particular measures, the tribute that is due to the talents, the rectitude, and the patriotism which adorn the characters selected to devise and adopt them. In these honorable qualifications, I behold the surest pledges, that as on one side, no local prejudices, or attachments; no seperate views, nor party animosities, will misdirect the comprehensive and equal eye which ought to watch over this great Assemblage of communities and interests: so, on another, that the foundations of our national policy, will be laid in the pure and immutable principles of private morality; and the pre-eminence of free Government, be exemplified by all the attributes which can win the affections of its Citizens, and command the respect of the world. I dwell on this prospect with every satisfaction which an ardent love for my Country can inspire: since there is no truth more thoroughly established, than that there exists in the œconomy and course of nature, an indissoluble union between virtue and happiness, between duty and advantage, between the genuine maxims of an honest and magnanimous policy, and the solid rewards of public prosperity and felicity: Since we ought to be no less persuaded that the propitious smiles of Heaven, can never be expected on a nation that disregards the eternal rules of order and right, which Heaven itself has ordained: And since the preservation of the sacred fire of liberty, and the destiny of the Republican model of Government, are justly considered as deeply, perhaps as finally staked, on the experiment entrusted to the hands of the American people.

Besides the ordinary objects submitted to your care, it will remain with your judgment to decide, how far an exercise of the occasional power delegated by the Fifth article of the Constitution is rendered expedient at the present juncture by the nature of objections which have been urged against the System, or by the degree of inquietude which has given birth to them. Instead of undertaking particular recommendations on this subject, in which I could be guided by no lights derived from official opportunites, I shall again give way to my entire confidence in your discernment and pursuit of the public good: For I assure myself that whilst you carefully avoid every alteration which might endanger the benefits of an United and effective Government, or which ought to await the future lessons of experience; a reverence for the characteristic rights of freemen, and a regard for the public harmony, will sufficiently influence your deliberations on the question how far the former can be more impregnably fortified, or the latter be safely and advantageously promoted.

To the preceding observations I have one to add, which will be most properly addressed to the House of Representatives. It concerns myself; and will therefore be as brief as possible. When I was first honoured with a call into the service of my Country, then on the eve of an arduous struggle for its liberties, the light in which I contemplated my duty required that I should renounce every pecuniary compensation. From this resolution I have in no instance departed—And being still under the impressions which produced it, I must decline as inapplicable to myself, any share in the personal emoluments, which may be indispensably included in a permanent provision for the Executive Department; and must accordingly pray that the pecuniary estimates for the Station in which I am placed, may, during my continuance in it, be limited to such actual expenditures as the public good may be thought to require.

Having thus imparted to you my sentiments, as they have been awakened by the occasion which brings us together, I shall take my present leave; but not without resorting once more to the benign Parent of the human race, in humble supplication that since he has been pleased to favour the American people, with opportunities for deliberating in perfect tranquility, and dispositions for deciding with unparellelled unanimity on a form of Government, for the security of their Union, and the advancement of their happiness; so this divine blessing may be equally conspicuous in the enlarged views—the temperate consultations, and the wise measures on which the success of this Government must depend.

George Washington, First Inaugural Address—Final Version, April 30, 1789.

DOCUMENT 12: PERSUADING JEFFERSON TO BE SECRETARY OF STATE

From 1784 to 1790, Thomas Jefferson was U.S. ambassador to France and lived in Paris. When Washington became president, he asked Jefferson to be his secretary of state. At first, Jefferson did not want the job. He had grown to love the sophistication and excitement of Paris and had hoped to continue his ambassadorship. In a letter to Washington regarding the offer, he said he had "gloomy forebodings" and fears of criticism if he became secretary of state. In this excerpt from a letter written by Washington to Jefferson in Jan-

uary 1790, Washington responds to Jefferson's misgivings. *The letter shows Washington's persuasive and leadership abilities.*

I consider the successful Administration of the general Government as an object of almost infinite consequence to the present and future happiness of the Citizens of the United States. I consider the Office of Secretary for the Department of State as *very* important on many accts: and I know of no person, who, in my judgment, could better execute the Duties of it than yourself. Its duties will probably be not quite so arduous & complicated in their execution, as you might have been led at the first moment to imagine. At least, it was the opinion of Congress, that, after the division of all the business of a domestic nature between the Department of the Treasury, War and State, that those wch would be comprehended in the latter might be performed by the same Person, who should have the charge of conducting the Department of Foreign Affairs. The experiment was to be made; and if it shall be found that the fact is different, I have little doubt that a farther arrangement or division of the business in the Office of the Department of State will be made, in such manner as to enable it to be performed, under the superintendance of one man, with facility to himself, as well as with advantage & satisfaction to the Public. These observations, however, you will be pleased to remark are merely matters of opinion. But, in order that you may be the better prepared to make your ultimate decision on good grounds, I think it necessary to add one fact, which is this, so far as I have been able to obtain information from all quarters, your late appointment has given very extensive and very great satisfaction to the Public. My original opinion & wish may be collected from my nomination.

George Washington, Letter to Thomas Jefferson, January 1790.

DOCUMENT 13: ADVICE ON MARRIAGE

The following is from a letter to Elizabeth Park Custis, Martha Washington's granddaughter. Written on September 14, 1794, the letter shows George Washington's ideas on love and marriage.

Do not then in your contemplation of the marriage state, look for perfect felicity before you consent to wed. Nor conceive, from the fine tales of Poets and lovers of old have told us, of the transports of mutual love, that heaven has taken its abode on earth: Nor do not deceive yourself in supposing, that the only mean by which these are to be obtained, is to drink deep of the cup, and revel in an ocean of love. Love is a mighty pretty thing; but like all other delicious things, it is cloying; and when the first transports of the passion begins to subside, which it assuredly will do, and yield, oftentimes too late, to more sober reflections, it serves to evince, that love is too dainty a food to live upon *alone,* and ought not to be considered farther than as a necessary ingredient for that matrimonial happiness which results from a combination of causes; none of which are of greater importance, than that the object on whom it is placed, should possess good sense, good dispositions, and the means of supporting you in the way you have been brought up. Such qualifications cannot fail to attract (after marriage) your esteem and regard, into wch. or into disgust, sooner or later, love naturally resolves itself; and who at the same time, has a claim to the respect, and esteem of the circle he moves in. Without these, whatever may be your first impressions of the man, they will end in disappointment; for be assured, and experience will convince you, that there is no truth more certain, than that all our enjoyments fall short of our expectations; and to none does it apply with more force, than to the gratification of the passions.

George Washington, Letter to Elizabeth Park Custis, September 14, 1794.

DOCUMENT 14: WASHINGTON'S FAREWELL ADDRESS

In 1796, Washington decided to retire from the presidency in March 1797. When he first thought of retiring in 1792, Washington had asked James Madison to write a farewell speech for him. He used this as a basis of the first draft of his 1796 speech, then asked Alexander Hamilton to read the draft and comment on it. Using Hamilton's notes, Washington revised the draft. The speech is long—below is only an excerpt. In it, Washington explains why he is retiring, then exhorts Americans to remain unified against future challenges.

The acceptance of, & continuance hitherto in, the Office to which your Suffrages [votes] have twice called me, have been a uniform sacrifice of inclination to the opinion of duty, and to a deference for what appeared to be your desire. I constantly hoped, that it would have been much earlier in my power, consistently with motives, which I was not at liberty to disregard, to return to that retirement, from which I had been reluctantly drawn. The strength of my inclination to do this, previous to the last Election, had even led to the preparation of an address to declare it to you; but mature reflection on the then perplexed & critical posture of our Affairs with foreign nations, and the unanimous advice of persons entitled to my confidence, impelled me to abandon the idea.

I rejoice, that the state of your concerns, external as well as internal, no longer renders the pursuit of inclination incompatible with the sentiment of duty, or propriety; & am persuaded whatever partiality may be retained for my services, that in the present circumstances of our country, you will not disapprove my determination to retire. The impressions, with which, I first undertook the arduous trust, were explained on the proper occasion. In the discharge of this trust, I will only say, that I have, with good intentions, contributed towards the Organization and Administration of the government, the best exertions of which a very fallible judgment was capable. Not unconscious, in the outset, of the inferiority of my qualifications, experience in my own eyes, perhaps still more in the eyes of others, has strengthened the motives to diffidence of myself; and every day the encreasing weight of years admonishes me more and more, that the shade of retirement is as necessary to me as it will be welcome. Satisfied that if any circumstances have given peculiar value to my services, they were temporary, I have the consolation to believe, that while choice and prudence invite me to quit the political scene, patriotizm does not forbid it.

In looking forward to the moment, which is intended to terminate the career of my public life, my feelings do not permit me to suspend the deep acknowledgment of that debt of gratitude wch I owe to my beloved country, for the many honors it has conferred upon me; still more for the steadfast confidence with which it has supported me; and for the opportunities I have thence enjoyed of manifesting my inviolable attachment, by services faithful & persevering, though in usefulness unequal to my zeal. If benefits have resulted to our country from these services, let it always be remembered to your praise, and as an instructive example in our annals, that, under circumstances in which the Passions agitated in every direction were liable to mislead, amidst appearances sometimes dubious, viscissitudes of fortune often discouraging, in situations in which not unfrequently want of Success has countenanced the spirit of criticism, the constancy of your support was the essential prop of the efforts, and a guarantee of the plans by which they were effected. Profoundly penetrated with this idea, I shall carry it with me to my grave, as a strong incitement to unceasing vows that Heaven may continue to you the choicest tokens of its beneficence—that your Union & brotherly affection may be perpetual—that the free constitution, which is the work of your hands, may be sacredly maintained—that its Administration in every department may be stamped with wisdom and Virtue—that, in fine, the happiness of the people of these States, under the auspices of liberty, may be made complete, by so careful a preservation and so prudent a use of this blessing as will acquire to them the glory of recommending it to the applause, the affection—and adoption of every nation which is yet a stranger to it.

Here, perhaps, I ought to stop. But a solicitude for your welfare, which cannot end but with my life, and the apprehension of danger, natural to that solicitude, urge me on an occasion like the present, to offer to your solemn contemplation, and to recommend to your frequent review, some sentiments; which are the result of much reflection, of no inconsiderable observation, and which appear to me all important to the permanency of your felicity as a People. These will be offered to you with the more freedom as you can only see in them the disinterested warnings of a parting friend, who can possibly have no personal motive to bias his counsel. Nor can I forget, as an encouragement to it, your endulgent reception of my sentiments on a former and not dissimilar occasion.

Interwoven as is the love of liberty with every ligament of your hearts, no recommendation of mine is necessary to fortify or confirm the Attachment. The Unity of Government which constitutes you one people is also now dear to you. It is justly so; for it is a main Pillar in the Edifice of your real independence, the support of your tranquility at home; your peace abroad; of your safety; of your prosperity; of that very Liberty which you so highly prize. But as it is easy to foresee, that from different causes & from different quarters, much pains will be taken, many artifices employed, to weaken in your minds the conviction of this truth; as this is the point in your political fortress against which the batteries of internal & external enemies will be most constantly and actively (though often covertly & insidiously) directed, it is of infinite moment, that you should properly estimate the immense value of your national Union to your collective & individual happiness; that you should cherish a cordial, habitual & immoveable attachment to it; accustoming yourselves to think and speak of it as of the Palladium of your political safety and prosperity; watching for its preservation with jealous anxiety; discountenancing whatever may suggest even a suspicion that it can in any event be abandoned, and indignantly frowning upon the first dawning of every attempt to alienate any portion of our Country from the rest, or to enfeeble the sacred ties which now link together the various parts.

For this you have every inducement of sympathy and interest. Citizens by birth or choice, of a common country, that country has a right to concentrate your affections. The name of American, which belongs to you, in your national capacity, must always exalt the just pride of Patriotism, more than any appellation derived from local discriminations. With slight shades of difference, you have the same Religeon, Manners, Habits & political Principles. You have in a common cause fought & triumphed together—The independence & liberty you possess are the work of joint councils, and joint efforts—of common dangers, sufferings and successes.

But these considerations, however powerfully they address themselves to your sensibility are greatly outweighed by those which apply more immediately to your Interest. Here every portion of our country finds the most commanding motives for carefully guarding & preserving the Union of the whole.

The North, in an unrestrained intercourse with the South, protected by the equal Laws of a common government, finds in the productions of the latter, great additional resources of maritime & commercial enterprise and—precious materials of manufacturing industry. The South in the same Intercourse, benefitting by the Agency of the North, sees its agriculture grow & its commerce expand. Turning partly into its own channels the seamen of the North, it finds its particular navigation envigorated; and while it contributes, in different ways, to nourish & increase the general mass of the National navigation, it looks forward to the protection of a maritime strength, to which itself is unequally adapted. The East, in a like intercourse with the West, already finds, and in the progressive improvement of interior communications, by land & water, will more & more find a valuable vent for the commodities which it brings from abroad, or manufactures at home. The West derives from the East supplies requisite to its growth & comfort—and what is perhaps of still greater consequence, it must of necessity owe the Secure enjoyment of indispensable outlets for its own productions to the weight, influence, and the future maritime strength of the Atlantic side of the Union, directed by an indissoluble community of Interest as one Nation. Any other tenure by which the West can hold this essential advantage, whether derived from its own seperate strength, or from an apostate & unnatural connection with any foreign Power, must be intrinsically precarious.

While then every part of our country thus feels an immediate & particular Interest in Union, all the parts combined cannot fail to find in the united mass of means & efforts greater strength, greater resource, proportionably greater security from external danger, a less frequent interruption of their Peace by foreign Nations; and, what is of inestimable value! they must derive from Union an exemption from those broils and Wars between themselves, which so frequently afflict neighbouring countries, not tied together by the same government; which their own rivalships alone would be sufficient to produce, but which opposite foreign alliances, attachments & intrigues would stimulate & imbitter. Hence likewise they will avoid the necessity of those overgrown Military establishments, which under any form of Government are inauspicious to liberty, and which are to be regarded as particularly hostile to Republican Liberty: In this sense it is, that your union ought to be considered as a main prop of your liberty, and that the love of the one ought to endear to you the preservation of the other.

George Washington, Farewell Address, September 19, 1796.

DISCUSSION QUESTIONS

CHAPTER 1

1. In the selection by Paul K. Longmore, the author points out that Washington was concerned about his reputation and carefully guarded it. According to Longmore, what aspects of Washington's early education provided good training for a young man who intended to rise to a station of distinction?
2. Willard Sterne Randall describes Washington's first career as a surveyor. How do you think Washington's experiences as a surveyor helped him in his future careers as plantation owner and military commander?
3. A.J. Langguth relates Washington's early experiences in the military. According to Langguth, what military blunders did Washington make in 1754? Which of these blunders does Langguth say resulted in many of the Iroquois withdrawing their support of the British and giving it to the French?

CHAPTER 2

1. In their article, Robert F. Dalzell Jr. and Lee Baldwin Dalzell describe George Washington's life at home at Mount Vernon. The Dalzells state that Washington lived much of his life as a performance. How did he achieve this? Did this performance extend to his private life? Do you believe that this way of living contributed to Washington's success? What sacrifices, if any, did he have to make to ensure that people viewed him the way he wished?
2. Using entries from Washington's personal diary, Ralph K. Andrist depicts Washington's life at Mount Vernon and his involvement in its management. What kind of man do the diary entries reveal Washington to be?
3. In his selection, Paul Leicester Ford implies that Washington was a reluctant slave owner and a kind master. Does he present solid evidence for this assertion? Do you believe Washington's statement that he was "well dis-

posed" to a "gradual abolition," or even to an entire emancipation of that description of people (if the latter was in itself practicable)? Why did Washington think emancipation was not "practicable"?

Chapter 3

1. Douglas Southall Freeman demonstrates in his article that Washington was reluctant to accept the position of commander in chief of the Continental army. Do you agree that, based on the evidence Freeman provides, Washington's action revealed a lack of enthusiasm for the office? Why, then, do you think Washington accepted the position?
2. In his assessment of Washington as a military leader, John E. Ferling states that Washington was driven by an "inescapable quest for esteem." Do you think Ferling's statement is a fair one? What kind of evidence does Ferling go on to provide to back up his statement?
3. According to the article by Thomas Fleming, what techniques did Washington use to overcome the British? How did espionage fit in to his plan? What tactics of spying did Washington employ to gain the upper hand?
4. Mackubin Owens claims that Washington's strategies on the battlefield were crucial to American success in the Revolutionary War. What strategies does he say were employed by Washington during the war? Do you agree that his military leadership was indispensable to American victory?

Chapter 4

1. In his article, Forrest McDonald describes Washington as being reluctant to serve as president. Do you think Washington's reluctance was genuine? After accepting the office, Washington concerned himself with the protocol and procedure of every detail of his new position. Do you think that Washington was correct in paying so much attention to the ritual and ceremony that went with the job? Washington proclaimed the United States neutral on the issue of the French Revolution. Why was this a difficult and, for some, an unpopular decision?
2. David E. Maas provides a list of precedents George Washington set as the first president. Do you believe that the items Maas has selected are important ones? Based on the information provided in this article, what do you think were Washington's goals with regard to the office of the president?
3. Dorothy Twohig maintains that, during his presidency, Washington never considered doing away with slavery,

even though he claimed to be personally against it. What reasons does Twohig give for Washington's inaction on this issue? Do you agree that Washington had no choice but to avoid dealing with the slavery problem while president?

4. What are the three reasons Bruce G. Peabody gives for Washington's decision to retire from the office of president? How did his decision affect his contemporaries? How has it affected presidents since Washington?

Chapter 5

1. Gordon S. Wood claims that Washington was a great American hero. What does Wood say was the greatest act of Washington's life? Why does he consider this act to be so significant? Does Wood's assertion that Washington spent his life protecting and guarding his reputation make him more or less of an admirable character?

2. What reasons does Hugh Sidey give for his assertion that Washington's legend might not hold up under today's scrutiny? Does he make a convincing argument? What in Washington's character does Sidey find admirable?

Chronology

1732

On February 22, George Washington is born in a small house on the banks of Popes Creek, Virginia. He is the first child of Mary Ball Washington, Augustine (Gus) Washington's second wife. By his first wife, Gus had three other children.

1735

Gus Washington moves his family to another of his properties on Little Hunting Creek in Virginia. The farm, on a bluff above the Potomac River, is called Epsewasson.

1738

Gus Washington buys another farm on the banks of the Rappahannock River near Fredericksburg, Virginia, called Ferry Farm and moves his family there. When he is not attending school in Fredericksburg, young George spends a great deal of time outside hunting, fishing, swimming, and sailing.

1743

Gus Washington dies, leaving George several plots of the land he had accumulated.

1746

Colonel William Fairfax, a neighbor of George's older half-brother Lawrence and Lawrence's brother-in-law, obtains a commission in Britain's Royal Navy for George as a midshipman. However, George's mother and uncle refuse to allow him to go.

1748

Thomas Lord Fairfax, William's cousin, decides to survey the millions of acres he owns in the frontier. He invites sixteen-year-old George to go along on the surveying trip.

1749

In July, George Washington becomes a county surveyor in Culpepper County, Virginia, earning fifteen pounds a year. For the next three years, he leads surveying teams into the western frontier, and his income rises to 125 pounds a year. Sometimes he is paid in land.

1751

George accompanies Lawrence Washington to Barbados, where Lawrence seeks a cure for his tuberculosis. While in Barbados, George contracts smallpox but survives. He returns to Virginia in December, while Lawrence sails on to Bermuda, hoping its climate will restore his health.

1752

George resumes surveying. In the summer, his beloved half-brother Lawrence dies. Later that year, Washington receives the post of adjutant general that was vacated by Lawrence's death.

1753

The Ohio Valley becomes an area of dispute between the British and the French. France sends fifteen hundred troops into the area to claim it. Virginia's royal governor, Robert Dinwiddie, acts for Britain by calling for a messenger to go to the French and inform them that Britain has claimed the area. If France will not leave, he declares, there will be a battle between the countries over the land. Washington volunteers to be the messenger. The mission takes six weeks. Governor Dinwiddie asks Washington upon his return to write down a narrative of his time in the frontier, then has it printed. It sells so well that it is reprinted several times.

1754

In May, Washington leads 134 men into the frontier as a sign to the Indians that Virginians are serious about claiming the Ohio Valley. Washington acts rather harshly and attacks a small band of French soldiers as they camp in the woods. Ten French soldiers and their commander die. One Virginian dies. This marked the first battle in the French and Indian War, which was to last seven years. The French retaliate with an army of about 900 men against Washington's newly reinforced army of 284. One-third of Washington's men are killed or wounded. Washington returns to Williamsburg having made military blunders, but receives little blame for the incidents. In December, he leases Epsewasson, now called Mount Vernon, from Lawrence's widow, who has remarried.

1755

Washington joins General Edward Braddock in May to help him push French troops out of the Ohio Valley. On July 9, their army meets with nine hundred French soldiers. Braddock is killed, along with hundreds of British and Virginian soldiers. Later in the year, Washington is named commander of Virginia's army.

1758

Washington becomes engaged to Martha Dandridge Custis, the wealthiest widow in Virginia and mother of two young children. Washington is elected to the Virginia House of Burgesses, representing Frederick County. In December, he resigns from the army.

1759

On January 6 Washington marries Martha. A few weeks later, he brings her and her children to Mount Vernon, where he turns to the life of plantation manager.

1770

Washington goes to the Ohio River valley, near Pittsburgh, to survey tracts of land that were to be granted to officers who had fought in the French and Indian War.

1773

On December 16, the Boston Tea Party is held in reaction to British taxation on tea and other products. When the news reaches Virginia, the House of Burgesses proclaims June 7, 1774, as a day of sympathy to show support for the protest.

1774

Britain continues to tax the colonies. The House of Burgesses, now called the Virginia Convention, meets in August and makes plans for the Continental Congress in Philadelphia in September. Washington is chosen as one of seven Virginia delegates to go to Philadelphia. At the Congress, delegates vote to boycott British goods until taxes on them are repealed.

1775

In April, British troops destroy a weapons storehouse in Concord, Massachusetts, and Massachusetts militiamen strike back. Seventy-three British soldiers are killed, and forty-nine colonists are killed. War against the British appears to be inevitable. Washington is named as a delegate for the Second Continental Congress, which is held in May in Philadelphia. At the Congress, Washington is selected to be commander in chief of the Continental army.

1776

On March 17, the British leave Boston after being forced out by the Continental army. On July 4, the Declaration of Independence is adopted. That same month, more than ten thousand British troops land in New York City with the intention of occupying. On August 27, the British defeat the Continentals on Long Island, New York, forcing the Americans to retreat. In November, the British take Fort Lee, New Jersey. On December 25, Washington and his army cross the Delaware and launch a surprise attack on Hessian troops at Trenton, New Jersey.

1777

In January, the Continental army forces the British out of New Jersey. In September the two forces meet in Brandywine, Pennsylvania, and the British are victorious. They then take over Philadelphia. On October 17, the Continentals capture five thousand British in New York and force the British to surrender at Saratoga. In November, Congress presents a draft of the Articles of Confederation, which is a basis for federal government. At the end of the year, Washington's troops make camp at Valley Forge, Pennsylvania. Washington pleads with Congress to provide money for supplies, food, and wages for the army. Thousands of cold and starving soldiers desert.

1778

In Valley Forge, the Continental army continues to suffer during a particularly cold winter. In May, Congress creates an alliance with France, which joins the colonies in fighting the British. Later in the year, the British take Savannah, Georgia, and plan to continue invading the South.

1780

In July and August, five thousand French troops under General Comte de Rochambeau arrive in Rhode Island to assist the Continental army.

1781

In August, British general Charles Cornwallis leads his troops to Yorktown, Virginia. Washington asks Rochambeau to send troops into the bay alongside Yorktown. American and French troops surround the British. On October 19, the British surrender. A few weeks later, Washington rushes to Mount Vernon to be with his stepson, Jackie Custis, who is dying. After Jackie's death, Washington goes to Philadelphia to meet with Congress and plan what to do next if British troops continue to occupy the colonies.

1783

In early November, a peace treaty is negotiated between Britain and the colonies, now the United States, in Paris. On

November 25 the last British soldiers sail from New York. By Christmas, Washington is back at Mount Vernon.

1784

Washington, along with other investors, revives the Dismal Swamp Company with the hopes of linking western Virginia and North Carolina to the Atlantic Ocean by canal. He also presents plans for extending the Potomac River into western Virginia, to be joined with the Ohio River.

1787

The Constitutional Convention is held in Philadelphia in May and goes on for four months. In Philadelphia, Washington is greeted by cheering crowds, and at the convention he is elected presiding officer. Delegates originally plan to revise the Articles of Confederation but soon decide instead to write a new constitution.

1789

At the meeting of the electoral college in January, Washington is nominated for president. He accepts in April; his inauguration is held on April 30 in the federal capital, New York City. Late in the year, Washington departs for a trip through New England.

1790

Washington makes the first State of the Union address on January 7. The site for a new federal district, later to be called Washington, D.C., is selected near the Potomac River in Virginia.

1791

Washington takes a trip through the southern states. Later, he tackles the problem of Native Americans and western expansion, attempting to create policies for dealing peacefully with the Indians.

1793

Washington is reelected. The French Revolution has begun and much of Europe is at war. Washington is determined that the United States remain neutral in the conflict. He issues a Proclamation of Neutrality that puts the United States in jeopardy with Great Britain. There is some controversy in the United States about whether the president has the authority to issue such a foreign policy statement.

1794

Washington sends John Jay, chief justice of the Supreme Court, to England to work out a treaty to resolve its difference with the United States. In the summer, farmers in western Pennsylvania rebel against federal taxes on whiskey. Washington approves the use of force against them and calls on local militias to enforce the peace. More than twelve thousand volunteers offer to help, but the Whiskey Rebellion, as it is called, quickly dies down.

1795

The Jay Treaty is ratified by Congress and signed by Washington in August, although many Americans are outraged by some of its provisions. For example, southern states are incensed that the treaty does not provide compensation for the slaves that were carried away by the British army during the Revolutionary War.

1796

On September 19, Washington's Farewell Address is published in several newspapers, the first public notice that he does not intend to run for president again.

1797

In March, Washington's term ends and he returns to Mount Vernon, where he lives in retirement.

1799

After a long ride around Mount Vernon during a snowstorm, Washington gets a sore throat that grows worse. On December 14, he dies at age sixty-seven.

FOR FURTHER RESEARCH

COLLECTIONS OF ORIGINAL DOCUMENTS PERTAINING TO GEORGE WASHINGTON

W.W. Abbot and Dorothy Twohig, eds., *The Papers of George Washington: Confederate Series 1, January–July 1784.* Charlottesville: University of Virginia Press, 1992.

Ralph K. Andrist, *The Founding Fathers: George Washington: A Biography in His Own Words.* New York: Newsweek, 1972.

Thomas J. Fleming, ed., *Affectionately Yours, George Washington: A Self-Portrait in Letters of Friendship.* New York: W.W. Norton, 1967.

Saul K. Padover, ed., *The Washington Papers: Basic Selections from the Public and Private Writings of George Washington.* New York: Harper & Brothers, 1955.

Dorothy Twohig, Mark A. Mastromarino, and Jack D. Warren, eds., *The Papers of George Washington: Presidential Series 5, January–June 1790.* Charlottesville: University of Virginia Press, 1996.

BIOGRAPHIES AND STUDIES OF GEORGE WASHINGTON

Morton Borden, ed., *Great Lives Observed: George Washington.* Englewood Cliffs, NJ: Prentice-Hall, 1969.

Kevin L. Cope, *George Washington in and as Culture.* New York: AMS Press, 2001.

Robert F. Dalzell Jr. and Lee Baldwin Dalzell, *George Washington's Mount Vernon: At Home in Revolutionary America.* New York: Oxford University Press, 1998.

John E. Ferling, *The First of Men: A Life of George Washington.* Knoxville: University of Tennessee Press, 1988.

Thomas Fleming, "George Washington, Spymaster," *American Heritage*, February/March 2000.

James Thomas Flexner, *George Washington in the American Revolution: 1775–1783*. Boston: Little, Brown, 1968.

Paul Leicester Ford, *The True George Washington*. Philadelphia: J.B. Lippincott, 1896.

Douglas Southall Freeman, *George Washington: A Biography. Vol. 3: Planter and Patriot*. New York: Charles Scribner's Sons, 1951.

Gary L. Gregg II and Matthew Spalding, eds., *Patriot Sage: George Washington and the American Political Tradition*. Wilmington, DE: ISI Books, 1999.

Mac Griswold, *Washington's Gardens at Mount Vernon: Landscape of the Inner Man*. New York: Houghton Mifflin, 1999.

Don Higginbotham, ed., *George Washington Reconsidered*. Charlottesville: University Press of Virginia, 2001.

Fritz Hirschfeld, *George Washington and Slavery: A Documentary Portrayal*. Columbia: University of Missouri Press, 1997.

Paul K. Longmore, *The Invention of George Washington*. Berkeley and Los Angeles: University of California Press, 1988.

Forrest McDonald, *The American Presidency: An Intellectual History*. Lawrence: University Press of Kansas, 1994.

———, "Presidential Character: The Example of George Washington," *Perspectives on Political Science*, Summer 1997.

Blair Niles, *Martha's Husband: An Informal Portrait of George Washington*. New York: McGraw-Hill, 1951.

Bruce G. Peabody, "George Washington, Presidential Term Limits, and the Problem of Reluctant Political Leadership," *Presidential Studies Quarterly*, September 2001.

Willard Sterne Randall, *George Washington: A Life*. New York: Henry Holt, 1997.

William Guthrie Sayen, "George Washington's 'Unmannerly' Behavior," *Virginia Magazine of History and Biography*, Winter 1999.

Hugh Sidey, "Above All, the Man Had Character," *Time,* February 21, 1983.

Richard Norton Smith, *Patriarch: George Washington and the New American Nation.* New York: Houghton Mifflin, 1993.

Elswyth Thane, *Potomac Squire.* New York: Duell, Sloan, and Pearce, 1963.

RELEVANT HISTORIES OF EARLY AMERICA

Joseph J. Ellis, *Founding Brothers: The Revolutionary Generation.* New York: Alfred A. Knopf, 2000.

Steven M. Gillon and Cathy D. Matson, *The American Experiment: A History of the United States.* New York: Houghton Mifflin, 2002.

A.J. Langguth, *Patriots: The Men Who Started the Revolution.* New York: Simon and Schuster, 1988.

David McCullough, *John Adams.* New York: Simon and Schuster, 2001.

Roger Wilkins, *Jefferson's Pillow: The Founding Fathers and the Dilemma of Black Patriotism.* Boston: Beacon Press, 2001.

WEBSITE

The Papers of George Washington, www.virginia.edu/gwpapers. Maintained by the University of Virginia, this is the official website for the Washington Papers Project. The goal of the project is to publish all of Washington's correspondence. The website includes several articles about Washington, a list of frequently asked questions about him, maps and images, and an index of names mentioned in Washington's correspondence.

Index

Abbot, William W., 11, 12, 143
Abercrombie, James, 147
Adams, Abigail, 56, 178
Adams, John
   on causes of British defeat in Revolutionary War, 97
   form of address for president and, 130, 148
   on George Washington
      cultivation of public image by, 156
      inaugural address of, 145, 146
      intellectual abilities of, 171–72
      position of commander of Continental army and, 81, 83
      reputation of, 82–83
Adams, Samuel, 83
African Americans
   Continental army and, 94–95
   Revolutionary War and, 94–95
   see also slaves/slavery
Alton, John, 78
American Presidency, The (Milkis and Nelson), 166
Andre, John, 104–105, 107–108
Andrist, Ralph K., 59
Arnold, Benedict, 107–109, 123–24
Articles of Confederation, 17, 115–16, 152

Barber, James David, 186
Bates, Ann, 105
Billias, George Athan, 112
Bishop, Thomas, 78
Boston, 80–81, 116–17
Braddock, Edward, 11–12, 47–48
Brookes, Joshua, 55
Butler, Pierce, 17–18, 153, 156

Carleton, Sir Guy, 109
Cary, Robert, 13, 65
Church, Benjamin, 99
Clark, John, 103–104
Clinton, Sir Henry, 106

clothing, 28–29
Compleat Surveyor (Leybourn), 34–35
Confederation Congress, 130
Constitutional Convention
   George Washington at, 17–18
   presidency and
      expectation of George Washington's acceptance and powers of, 17–18, 141, 156, 177–78
   term limits and, 163
   slavery and, 152–54
Continental army
   African Americans in, 94–95
   Continental Congress and control of, 114
   orders from, 87, 89, 92, 115, 120
   George Washington as commander of
      acceptance of position as, 13–14, 82, 85–86
      concerns about public image as, 84, 89–90
      conflict between desire for private life and, 13–14, 20
      Continental Congress and, 13, 81, 83–84
      criticism as, 149
      disinformation campaigns as, 99, 103–10
      leadership style as, 89, 90, 94, 95, 112, 117
      military ability as, 172
      opinion of others as, 88, 90
      powers and duties of, 86–87
      previous military experience and, 92–93
      reimbursements requested while, 144
      resignation as, 174–76
      salary of, 85, 92, 96, 144
      strategy as
         avoidance of engagements, 93,

98-99, 121-22
  criteria for judging, 112-13
  factors in developing, 114-15
  modern opinions of, 111-12
  offensive, 89, 116-18, 120, 123, 124-26
  symbolic value as, 91-92, 97
  soldiers in
    desertion by, 105
    morale of, 124
    number of, 120
    patriotism and, 119
    short enlistment terms for, 118
  see also espionage
Continental Congress
  First, 13
  Second
    British spies and, 105
    orders to Continental army by, 87, 89, 92, 115, 120
    political factions and, 123
    power of, 115-16
Cornell, Ezekiel, 18
Cunliffe, Marcus, 29, 186, 187
Custis, Eleanor Parke (stepgranddaughter "Nelly"), 54, 147
Custis, George Washington Parke (step-grandson "Wash"), 54
Custis, Jackie (stepson), 54, 60, 66-67
Custis, Martha. *See* Washington, Martha Custis
Custis, Martha Parke (stepdaughter "Patsy"), 54, 60

Dalzell, Lee Baldwin, 50
Dalzell, Robert F., Jr., 50
Darragh, Lydia, 104
decorum, models of, 8-9, 26-27, 133-34
Democratic Republicans
  criticism of George Washington by, 149
  development of, 137, 180
  election of 1800 and, 180
Dinwiddie, Robert
  behavior of George Washington and, 29
  commission from, 11, 42, 43
  Fort Necessity and, 46
disinformation campaigns, 99, 103-10
Dubourg, Baron Cromot, 9-10

Ellsworth, Oliver, 131
Emerson, Ralph Waldo, 175
espionage
  by Americans, 100-104, 107-109
  by British, 99, 104-105, 107-108

  techniques used in, 102

Fairfax, Anne, 9, 25
Fairfax, George William, 35, 39, 40
Fairfax, Sally, 41, 47
Fairfax, Thomas
  influence of, 9
  surveying and, 10-11, 34
Fairfax, William
  influence of, 9, 25, 28
  Virginia militia appointment and, 11
farming, 12, 15, 61-65, 67
Federalists
  election of 1800 and, 180
  philosophy of, 17
Ferling, John E., 88
Fleming, Thomas, 98
Flexner, James Thomas, 117
Ford, Paul Leicester, 68
Fort Necessity, 11, 45-46
France
  Citizen Genet and, 138-39
  debt to, 160
  possible war with, 20
  Revolutionary War alliance with, 122-23, 124-25
  revolution in, 138
  see also French and Indian War
Franklin, Benjamin, 154, 176-77
Freeman, Douglas Southall, 80, 178
French and Indian War
  beginning of, 42-44
  behavior during, 29
  Braddock expedition and, 11-12, 47-48
  Fort Necessity and, 11, 45-46
  Ohio River Valley and, 11, 42-44, 47-48
  public image and, 46, 48

Genet, Edmond, 138-39
Genn, James, 34, 39
gentry
  dancing and, 31
  emulation of English culture by, 30
  end of era of, 171
  horses and, 30-31
  public duty and, 165
  public image and, 24-25, 133-34, 177, 178
  values of, 9, 28, 173
George Washington and American Constitutionalism (Phelps), 165
Great Britain
  culture of, 30
  slavery and, 155
  see also French and Indian War;

Index 221

Revolutionary War
Greene, Nathanael, 120–21, 124
Griswold, Mac, 63

Hale, Nathan, 100–101
Half-King (Iroquois chief), 44, 45, 46
Hamilton, Alexander
  George Washington's presidency and, 129, 163
  neutrality and, 138–39
  as secretary of treasury, 20
  slavery and, 154
  Whiskey Rebellion and, 140
Hancock, John
  federal-state relations and, 132–33
  George Washington and, 83, 85
Hedges, Solomon, 38
Henry, Patrick, 154
Hirschfeld, Fritz, 94–95
Hite, Jost, 36
Honeyman, John, 101–102
Humphreys, David, 145

Indians, 38, 44–46
Invention of George Washington, The (Longmore), 165
Iroquois Confederation, 44–46

Jay, John, 137, 154
Jefferson, Thomas
  formation of Democratic Republican Party and, 137
  George Washington's presidencey and, 163, 177
  neutrality and, 138–39
  presidential veto and, 137
  slavery and, 154
  Washington, D.C., and, 179
  Whiskey Rebellion and, 140
Jumonville, Coulon de, 44

Ketchum, Richard, 112
Knox, Henry
  neutrality and, 138
  treaties and, 136
  Whiskey Rebellion and, 139

Lafayette, Marquis de, 90
Langguth, A.J., 41
Latrobe, Benjamin, 55
Laurens, Henry, 91
Lear, Tobias, 145
Lee, Charles, 81, 88, 90
Lee, Henry "Light-Horse Harry," 139–40
Leybourn, William, 34–35
Liston, Henrietta, 10, 142

Livingston, Robert, 145
Longmore, Paul K., 24, 165

Maas, David E., 141
Maclay, William
  executive departments and, 135
  on George Washington's inaugural address, 145, 146
  presidential protocols and, 131
  treaties and, 136
  White House social events and, 148–49
Madison, James
  executive powers of Senate and, 135
  formation of Democratic Republican Party and, 137
  on George Washington's presidency, 163, 178–80
  presidential veto and, 136–37
  slavery and, 154
Marshall, John, 175
McDonald, Forrest, 128
Mercer, George, 143
Militia Act (1792), 139
Morris, Gouverneur
  on George Washington, 10, 152
  slavery and, 153
Morris, Robert, 101
Mount Vernon
  additions to, 66
  agents and, 65–66
  duties of Martha at, 55, 61
  as English estate, 30
  gardens of, 63
  importance of, to George Washington, 172, 184–85
  inheritance of, 42
  as national symbol, 14–15
  as private refuge, 14–17, 52–53
  as public place, 15–16, 50–52, 53, 182
  retirement to, 20
  slaves of
    concern for well-being of, 74–75, 76
    emancipation in Washington's will of, 76–78, 161
    number of, 68, 69
    punishment of, 72–73
    purchase of, 66, 68, 74–75
    runaway, 69–70
    sickness and, 70–72
  as working farm, 12, 15, 61–65, 67

New York City, 100, 106–107, 109, 120–21, 122, 125, 126
New York Royal Gazette (newspaper), 103

Niemcewicz, Julian, 55
Niles, Blair, 9

Ohio River Valley, 11, 42–44
Owens, Mackubin, 111

Paine, Thomas, 149
Peabody, Bruce G., 162
Pendleton, Edmund, 82, 84
Phelps, Glenn, 165
Philadelphia, 122, 123
Pinckney, Charles C., 153
political factions
  criticism of George Washington and, 149
  development of, 123, 137–38, 180–81
  election of 1800 and, 180
  George Washington's distaste for, 164, 166, 167
  slavery and, 156, 158
  strength of Union and, 19
  two-term limit to presidency and, 163–64
presidency
  acceptance of
    reluctance about, 13–14, 19–20, 128–29
    sense of public duty and, 19
  accomplishments of, 20, 129
  defining executive powers of, 134, 150
    choice of advisers, 137, 144–45, 150
    departments and, 134–35
    foreign policy and, 138–39, 150
    rebellion and, 139–40
    treaties and, 136
    veto and, 136–37
  establishment of protocols during
    awareness of precedent-setting nature of actions and, 179, 188
    federal-state relations and, 132–33
    form of address and, 130–31, 147–48
    inauguration and, 132, 145–46
    social events and, 131, 148–49
  expectation of Washington's acceptance and powers of, 17–19, 141, 156, 177–78
  historians' view of, 169–70, 175
  nature of
    character of incumbent and, 188
    duality of, 133
  privacy and, 142–43
  religion and, 147
  retirement from, 179–80
  as role model for, 181, 183

  salary of, 132, 144, 179
  second term of
    reluctance to accept, 19, 163
    vilification during, 130, 149, 166–67
  two-term limit to
    Constitution and, 162–63
    desire for private life and, 166
    general distrust of executive power and, 164–65
    precedent of, 149–50
    public image and, 165
public duty
  acceptance of presidency and, 129
  gentry and, 165
  importance of, to George Washington, 19, 175
  nature of, 8
  as republican virtue, 97
public image
  appearance of George Washington and, 174
  concerns about
    Constitutional Convention and, 17
    Continental army and, 87
    as commander of, 14, 84, 89–90
    refusal of salary and, 92, 96
    resignation as commander of, 176
    presidency and
      reluctance to accept, 129, 151–52
      second term of, 130
      while in office, 149
    at conclusion of Revolutionary War, 152, 171
  demands on George Washington because of, 16, 53, 125, 131
  French and Indian War and, 46, 48
  military glory and, 172
  mythic aspects of, 18, 91, 142, 170–71, 187
  protection of, 176–77, 178
  as young man, 32

Rail, Johann, 101, 102
Randall, Willard Sterne, 33
Randolph, Edmund, 139
religion
  lack of importance of, to George Washington, 173
  presidency and, 147
  slavery and, 155
Republicans (Jeffersonian)
  criticism of George Washington by, 149
  development of, 137, 180

Index 223

election of 1800 and, 180
Revolutionary War
 African Americans during, 94–95
 American goals during
  early, 116–17, 118
  ultimate, 113, 114, 118–19
 American morale during, 105
 American victories during, 97
 Boston during, 80–81, 116–17
 Continental currency during, 101, 104–105
 France and, 122–23, 124–25, 160
 George Washington as symbol of, 91–92, 97
 Great Britain and
  causes of defeat of, 97
  goals and strategies of, 113–14, 118, 120, 121–22
  resources of, 114, 119
  victories of, 97, 98–99
 Mount Vernon during, 184–85
 New York City during, 100, 106–107, 109, 120–21, 122, 125, 126
 Philadelphia during, 122, 123
 Princeton during, 121–22
 sanctity of property and, 159
 sea power and, 119, 122
 South during, 106, 123
 stages of
  defense of independence, 118–22
  revolutionary period, 116–18
  winning peace, 125–26
  as world war, 122–25
 Trenton and, 101–102, 121–22, 183
 Yorktown and, 125
 see also Continental army; espionage
Rivington, James, 109–10
role model(s)
 for George Washington, 9, 25, 28
 George Washington as
  classical, 115, 172, 173–74, 176
  modern, 169–70, 175, 181, 183
Rules of Civility and Decent Behaviour in Company and Conversation, 8–9, 26–27, 133–34, 174
Rush, Benjamin
 on George Washington, 10, 87, 174
 on public duty, 8
Rutledge, James, 38

Saint Domingue, 159–60
Sayen, William Guthrie, 9, 29
Seven Years' War. See French and Indian War

Sidey, Hugh, 182
Six Nations, 44–46
slaves/slavery
 belief in withering away of institution of, 156, 161
 British emancipation of, 95
 concern for well-being of, 74–75, 76
 Constitutional Convention and, 152–54
 critics of owning, 68, 154–55
 economics of, 154, 155, 157–59
 emancipation of
  fear of indigent ex-slaves and, 160–61
  by George Washington in will, 76–78, 161
 excess of, 69
 inheritance of, 68
 opinion of behavior of, 73–74
 political factions and, 156, 158
 punishment of, 72–73
 purchase of, 66, 68, 74–75
 revolt in Saint Domingue of, 159–60
 Revolutionary War debt to France and, 160
 runaway, 69–70, 154
 sanctity of property and, 159
 sickness and, 70–72
 tightened legislation regarding owning, 154
 trade in, 77
  Constitution and, 153–54
  opposition to, 155
 views of George Washington on institution of, 157–59, 160
Smith, Richard Norton, 175
Smith, William Loughton, 134–35
spies. See espionage
stain, the, 102
Stamp Act (1765), 13
surveying
 early efforts at, 34, 35
 of Fairfax frontier land, 10–11, 34, 35–40
 as profession, 41

Tallmadge, Benjamin, 100–101, 102, 107, 108, 109
Tanacharison. See Half-King
Thane, Elswyth, 9, 10, 12, 16–17
Townsend, Robert (Culper Jr.), 102–103, 106–107, 108
Trenton, New Jersey, 101–102, 121–22, 183
Trumbull, John, 176
Trumbull, Jonathan, 179–80
Twohig, Dorothy, 151

U.S. Congress
  defining of constitutional government by executive departments and, 134–35
  foreign policy and, 138–39, 150
  treaties and, 136
  inauguration and, 145–46
U.S. Constitution
  ratification of, 18–19
  two-term limit of presidency and, 162–63
  see also Constitutional Convention

van Braam, Jacob, 43–44, 45–46
Virginia
  British emancipation of slaves in, 95
  colonial society of, 30
  House of Burgesses and, 12–13, 60
  militia of
    commission in, 11, 42, 47
    French and Indian War and, 44–46
    Lawrence Washington and, 42
    leadership style in, 43
    Ohio River expeditions and, 11, 42–44
  Yorktown, 125

Washington, Augustine (father), 9, 25
Washington, D.C., 179
Washington, George
  administrative abilities of, 172
  appearance of, 143–44, 171, 184
  clothing and, 28–29
  cultivation of public image and, 174
  deportment and, 10, 31
  characteristics of
    aloofness and reserve, 184, 187
    arrogance, 29
    brash behavior, 29, 93–94, 97
    bravery, 47–48, 95
    conservatism, 156–57, 186
    fastidiousness, 174
    gentry values and, 19, 24–25
    ingratitude, 29
    need for admiration, 91
    need to be in control, 90
    optimism, 187
    perseverance, 34, 95, 112, 175, 187
    politeness, 8–9
    quick temper, 10, 29, 136
    self-control, 8–9, 10, 91, 92, 133–34, 142, 143
    self-enhancement. See public image
    suspiciousness, 95
  death of, 20, 186
  early influences on, 8–9, 25, 26–27, 28, 29
  education of, 27–28
  funeral of, 150
  health of, 42, 47
  intellectual abilities of, 171–72, 175
  lack of close friends and, 186
  landholdings of, 11, 12
  leadership style of, 43, 89, 90, 94, 95, 112, 117
  marriage of, 12, 59
  racism of, 94–95
  religion and, 147
  romantic pursuits of, 41, 47
  as stepparent and step-grandparent, 54
  wealth of, 66–67, 184
Washington, Lawrence (half-brother)
  death of, 42
  importance of, 9
  as role model, 25, 28
Washington, Martha Custis (wife)
  appearance of, 56, 60
  characteristics of, 55–56, 59–60
  children of, 54, 57–58, 60
  with Continental army, 14
  correspondence of, with George, 57, 143
  duties of, at Mount Vernon, 55, 61
  marriage of, 12, 59
  relationship with George, 56–57
  wealth of, 60
  White House social events and, 148
Washington, Mary (mother)
  military service of George and, 42–43
  relationship to children of, 54–55
Way of the Fox, The (Palmer), 99
Weems, Mason (Parson), 142, 170–71
Whiskey Rebellion, 139–40
William (slave), 75–76
Wills, Garry, 178
Wilson, Woodward, 167
Wood, Gordon S., 169
Woodhull, Abraham (Culper Sr.), 102–103

Yorktown, Virginia, 125